BEST

GAY

ROMANCE

2013

BEST
GAY
ROMANCE
2013

EDITED BY

RICHARD LABONTÉ

CLEIS
PRESS

Published in the United States by Cleis Press Inc., 2246 Sixth Street, Berkeley, California 94710.

Printed in the United States.
Cover design: Scott Idleman/Blink
Cover photograph: Dimitri Vervitsiotis/Getty Images
Text design: Frank Wiedemann
First Edition.
10 9 8 7 6 5 4 3 2 1

Trade paper ISBN: 978-1-57344-902-1
E-book ISBN: 978-1-57344-919-9

For Asa. Who else?
Love you.

CONTENTS

INTRODUCTION:
LOVE UNDER "A DIFFERENT LIGHT"

As a new employee at Cleis Press in 2008, I could hardly believe that I would get to work directly with Richard Labonté. "Are you sure?" I had asked timidly at an editorial meeting. It just didn't seem right. After all, he was a revered literary lion and one of the founders of A Different Light Bookstore, which I trawled every weekend after matinees at the Castro Theater with my dear friend Duncan back in the day. Dunkie was fresh out of the closet and, subsequently, out of his house when his mother 86ed him after he came out to her. He ended up couchsurfing with me in the Lower Haight and we explored the beauty of San Francisco on foot together every weekend. Since we were both new to the city, it was simply electrifying to wake up in a place that enfolded us in her Golden Gate wings and accepted us, flaws and all.

Duncan gave me a crash course in cool culture, badly needed by this Appalachian transplant. I had met him at a séance on Steiner Street, and I thought he was possibly the most advanced person on planet Earth with his "fauntleroons," cut-off blue jeans trimmed in white lace. Duncan had an eidetic memory, and very long, very black hair that featured an under-layer of cobalt blue. Even better, he was a barback at The Stud.

On Saturday mornings, we would gather his tip money and head over to Castro Street, planting ourselves for hours at A Different Light and reading everything we could get our hands on. I still have a prized remainder copy of Gertrude Stein's collected plays, as well as several Oscar Wilde tomes, a handsome coffee table book of Aubrey Beardsley's art, and a battered copy of Louise Hay's *You Can Heal Your Life*. I remember Duncan patiently explaining that gay men had made cassette tapes of Louise's book and passed them around, sort of like bootlegged Grateful Dead tapes, and that those had launched Hay's career. I remember thinking I would also like to pen something bootleg-worthy one day.

As it turns out, gay men did make my career as well. When I returned to the Lower Haight as Associate Publisher at Cleis Press, I was agog at the very idea of contacting the legendary editor that is Richard Labonté. I worked up my nerve, picked up the phone, and introduced myself. He was unimaginably kind and seemed to know and understand everything

I did not know until my second year at Cleis that for a story to be classified as "romance," it has to have a happy ending. While Richard is a writer and editor with an incredibly sophisticated sensibility who curates what he calls "literary porn" of the highest order, Richard is also a great romantic.

How do I know?

His own story reads like a fairy tale, complete with a handsome prince and a mystical bonny isle. From my seat in Berkeley, it looks like Richard and Asa live quite happily ever after on Bowen Island, the result of a chance meeting at A Different

Light. I have learned much about love from poring over Labonté's volumes, following his first crushes, first real heartbreak, and the lasting satisfaction of married love. Richard once said "Romance. It's the emotional component of the erotic... However romance happens, however long love lasts—a heartbeat to a lifetime—it's a wondrous thing." And so it is with great pride that I present to you this latest labor of love from Cleis Press. Selected and collected by the inimitable Richard Labonté, *Best Gay Romance 2013* offers at least seventeen happy endings. Use these stories to inspire a few of your own.

And to Richard, thank you for the sanctuary within your bookstore and within the pages of your many marvelous anthologies.

Brenda Knight
Berkeley, California
2013

THE BAKER

Neil Plakcy

Monday morning, on my way to the unemployment office on Miami Beach to register, I decided to treat myself to a chocolate croissant from the little French bakery around the corner from my apartment. I was about to start tightening my belt, finances-wise, but I figured I could afford one last small indulgence.

I entered the bakery, my senses immediately assaulted by the smell of fresh bread, the rows of beautifully decorated pastries, and the French reggae music playing softly in the background. The bell over the door tinkled as I entered, but the heavyset Frenchwoman who normally waited on customers didn't appear.

I scanned the bakery case in front of me. What, no chocolate croissants? Oh, man. What a disappointment.

Then the baker himself appeared from the kitchen, carrying a tray of mixed breakfast pastries, including the *pain au chocolat* I was jonesing for. "Sorry," he said. "My clerk, she has left me. I am all alone here."

He was about my age, late twenties, and about my height as

well, just over six feet. But there the similarities stopped. He was broad-shouldered and beefy, with big hands and a broad smile. He wore a white chef's coat with the collar turned down, already spotted with what looked like raspberry jelly, and a white toque.

"Are you hiring?" I asked. "I haven't worked a register in a couple of years, but I spent four years while I was in college working at fast-food places."

He quizzed me for a few minutes about my skills, and then said, "You are a gift from God. How soon can you start?"

"Now?"

I stepped behind the counter and he grabbed me in a big bear hug, kissing me on each cheek. My body tingled, and my cock stiffened almost immediately. Embarrassed, I backed away, as the bell over the door rang and a customer entered.

My shift was seven to three. The other clerk, who came in at one, spent her first two hours in the tiny office next to the kitchen, ordering supplies and paying bills. By the time she relieved me, my feet hurt, my shoulders ached, and I wanted to luxuriate in a hot bath for hours. But it all went away when the baker, whose name was Jean-Pierre, hugged me again and kissed both my cheeks.

"How can I thank you," he said, his French accent making each word as sexy as a proposition. "I know! I will cook for you. Dinner, tomorrow night."

"Okay," I said, as he released me. My dick had popped back up and I tried to turn away as fast as possible so he wouldn't notice.

Back home, naked in a tub of hot, lavender-scented bubbles, I had only to remember the baker's embrace and I was instantly hard again. I closed my eyes and jerked myself to orgasm, remembering the scent of flour and lemon that surrounded him, the touch of his lips against my cheek. In my head I heard him murmuring soft French words as my body shook and milky white cum spurted out of my dick.

The next morning I wore sneakers with thick white socks to cushion my feet. Jean-Pierre unlocked the door for me, greeting me once again with a big bear hug and a kiss on both cheeks. I felt my whole body glowing with his touch—and the memory of my bathtub adventure the afternoon before.

We chatted off and on as he baked. He was excited about the meal he was preparing for me that evening, and he kept popping out of the kitchen to ask if I liked oysters, spinach, chicken, mushrooms, garlic. With each new ingredient, with each time I saw his shining eyes and the sexy triangle of flesh where his collar folded over, I came closer to orgasm.

He lived in an apartment above the bakery, he said. Very convenient when it was time to start baking, at four in the morning. No commute.

I left at three, promising to return that evening at seven. I lounged in another hot, lavender-scented bath, but this time I wouldn't touch myself at all. I didn't think Jean-Pierre was gay, and didn't expect anything to happen—but I wanted to leave myself in a heightened state of expectation anyway.

After my bath, I stood in front of the mirror examining myself. I hadn't had a serious boyfriend for a year or more; I'd worked too hard at my last job, and all I had the energy for was the occasional bar pickup. But I'd kept going to the gym, and my body was toned and sexy: muscular calves and thighs, slim waist, seven-inch cock nestled in a patch of wiry, black pubic hair, six-pack abs, nicely defined pecs and biceps. If nothing happened with Jean-Pierre, I might head over to one of the gay bars on Lincoln Road and see if any of the available hunks floated my boat.

I pulled on a pair of Ginch Gonch briefs decorated with fruits and vegetables, a form-fitting black T-shirt, and a pair of khaki pants that accentuated my butt. Promptly at seven, I was ringing the bell at the back of the bakery.

Jean-Pierre was delighted to see me. He engulfed me in another of his big bear hugs. He took my face in both hands, kissing me on each cheek, and then, unexpectedly, on the mouth. Though the kiss was brief, his full, moist lips sent a jolt of electricity through me. Then he turned and bounded up the stairs to his second-floor apartment, leaving me to wonder if his ebullience was simply French, or something more.

I also got a great view of his ass as I followed him up the stairs. Without the white chef's coat to cover it, I saw two round globes gripped by a pair of form-fitting jeans. I liked what I saw.

"You must sit here," Jean-Pierre said, when I entered his apartment. He stood by an oak table, pointing at an armchair covered in a colorful Provencal fabric. "You like white wine, yes?"

I said yes, and he filled a stemmed glass for me. "Appetizers in one minute, please," he said, and disappeared into the kitchen.

I looked around. The impression was of a French country farmhouse: an oak armoire opposite a black metal baker's rack; curtains and cushions in the same blue, white, and green floral fabric as my chair. The air smelled wonderful: roast chicken, lemon, and a host of other fragrant aromas. Jean-Pierre reappeared, carrying a tray of oysters Rockefeller, which he placed before me with a small bow.

"Smells heavenly," I said, as he sat down opposite me.

He wore a blue-and-white-striped shirt, the kind French sailors wear, short-sleeved and open at the neck. I eyed his muscular arms and large hands as he dished out the oysters. But when I tasted the first one, I forgot everything but their orgasmic taste. "Mmm," I said, and sighed happily.

They were silky smooth, accentuated by the spinach and the seasonings. I'd never tasted anything so good. "You like?" Jean-Pierre said.

"I like," I said.

We chatted as we ate, moving from the oysters to a roast chicken accompanied by a dish of creamy scalloped potatoes and a tray of warm asparagus dusted with olive oil and sea salt. I didn't think I'd ever eaten such a delicious meal, but Jean-Pierre dismissed my compliments. "Is a simple meal," he said. "Because I must bake all day. When I have the day off, then you will see, I make something good."

"I can't imagine anything better," I said, and when Jean-Pierre caught my eye and smiled a shiver ran through my body and my dick jumped to attention. Damn, I thought, this guy was a flirt. But again, I wasn't sure if it was his native Gallic charm or something more.

When he cleared the dishes, I said, "I can only imagine what kind of pastry you've made for dessert."

"No pastry," he said. "I cannot bake one more thing when I come home. For you, I have the chocolate mousse."

I sighed once again with pleasure. How could he have known that I considered chocolate mousse the perfect dessert? And Jean-Pierre's did not disappoint. He brought out two elegant parfait glasses, each filled with mousse and topped with home-made whipped cream.

From the first bite, I was hooked. The texture was thick and silky, rolling across my tongue, and there were hints of vanilla and another fragrance I couldn't identify. "Is my secret," he said. He smiled. "But I tell you. Essence of violets. Just a drop, but the perfume..." He ended the sentence by bringing his fingers to his lips and kissing them.

I remembered the touch of those lips against my cheek, and

against my own lips, and I experienced another of those electric jolts. I couldn't spend another minute in suspense; I had to know if Jean-Pierre was anything more than a flirt. I leaned back in my chair and stretched my legs, and with just the slightest pressure, my foot grazed his leg, and I smiled.

Jean-Pierre smiled back and I saw his shoulders relax. "You would like to move to the sofa?" he asked. "I make cappuccino?"

"Yes to the sofa," I said, standing, and making no effort to hide my boner. "The cappuccino, maybe later."

I sat on the sofa and looked at him. He sat next to me, and I snaked my right hand behind his head and pulled him close. Our lips met, and I tasted the chocolate, vanilla, and violets on his. Our tongues dueled together, and my dick throbbed. I wanted to eat him up, my second dessert.

He pulled me around so that I straddled him, my legs wrapped around his torso, our dicks pulsing against each other through the fabric of our pants. He gripped me in one of his bear hugs, and I luxuriated in the feel of his strong arms wrapped around me, his chest against mine, our bodies merging into one incredibly sexy organism.

I reached my hand under his blue-and-white-striped shirt and started caressing him gently, as he nibbled on my ear and whispered those same French words I'd imagined him saying the day before. "*Quel beau*," he said. "*Quel homme.*"

I thought he was handsome, too, and certainly a hell of a man. I kissed his neck, and he ran his hands under my T-shirt, up my back, and then down under the waistband of my khakis. I don't know how long we sat, making out. The rest of the world disappeared. I was just a mass of sensations.

"Come with me," he said finally, picking me up as easily as he hefted a tray of bread loaves in the bakery. Damn, I love a man who can do that! He carried me into his bedroom, a big oak bed with a spread in another bright Provencal pattern, and he settled me onto it with great delicacy. Then he lay down next to me and we curled together, fully clothed, kissing and fondling each other.

His shirt and my tee came off, and he ran his slightly rough hands over my chest as gently as a butterfly's wing, each touch sending another electric jolt directly to my cock. I thought I might explode.

Then I was unzipping his jeans. His cock was fat and stiff, and I leaned down to take him in my mouth. He stroked my hair as I sucked, and then pulled me off to kiss him again. I couldn't bear the sensation of my cock remaining trapped for a moment longer, so I scooted out of my jeans. I was about to pull off my briefs when Jean-Pierre gripped my hands.

"Good enough to eat," he said, pointing at the fruits and vegetables.

"You have no idea," I said, kissing him again.

He reached over to the table by the bed and fumbled in the drawer, pulling out a condom, which he unwrapped and slid onto his dick. I found a bottle of lube there and squirted some onto his stiff dick, massaging it, then took a dollop on my index finger and began to grease the way for him.

"I will do that," he said, and as he kissed me again, his lubed finger found my asshole and began to work it. I was panting with longing by the time he lifted me up and, with a little guidance from me, slid himself into me.

All that work on my thighs and calves at the gym paid off. I leveraged myself up and down on his stiff dick, as he lubed his hand and began jerking me off. I couldn't hold out for long, and neither could he. I began panting and whimpering just as I saw his body stiffen, and we ejaculated at nearly the same time, him first, and then me just a few seconds later.

I collapsed onto his nearly hairless but very muscular chest, kissing his neck; he nestled his head against mine. At some point we separated, and then I fell into a deep, dreamless sleep, my body totally satiated.

It was close to six A.M. when I woke, alone in Jean-Pierre's big bed. For a moment or two I was disoriented, trying to figure out exactly where I was. Then I looked at his bedside table and saw a note that read *Come downstairs for breakfast,* and I remembered all that had happened the night before.

I rescued my clothes from the floor and shrugged into them, then climbed down the stairs, stepping out into the South Florida dawn for a moment as I moved from the door to his apartment to the door to the bakery. The back door led directly into the kitchen, and I saw Jean-Pierre bent over a tray of croissants, sliding them into one of his big ovens.

My body sighed with the joy of seeing him. He looked up at the sound of the door; his smile was as broad as the ocean. In a moment we were locked in an embrace, kissing and hugging as if it had been years since we'd seen each other, instead of just minutes.

"*Pain au chocolat* for you," he said, finally pulling back. "And the cappuccino I promised you last night."

We ate together, sitting at a small table in the kitchen. I'd never been one for morning-afters, preferring to get out while the sexual glow was still hot, but I couldn't imagine getting up from that table and walking away from Jean-Pierre. In the space of forty-eight hours he had become as essential to me as breathing.

At seven o'clock I moved to the front of the bakery and opened for business. When I was ready to leave at three, Jean-

Pierre said, "You will come for dinner again tonight?"

"Are you kidding? You won't be able to get rid of me."

A month later I gave up my apartment, and moved in with Jean-Pierre above the bakery. If you visit South Beach, you are welcome to come by and sample the wares—but the baker is all mine.

CLOSER TO THE SKY

Georgina Li

It was different here at night, tall grass shifting in the shadows
and the river rushing in, black and wild before it picked up the
glow of the fire. Weekdays hardly anyone else bothered, and Jake
liked to ride out with his paints and his brushes, his easel on his
back. He'd set up about half a mile down river, usually, but he
liked to come up this way sometimes, too. It felt more like home
than his apartment, one room over the hardware store in town,
dusty books and old photographs, a kitchenette, notes stuck in
random places. Out here there was honeysuckle and clover and
flat gray stones in the riverbed, cold beneath his feet. Out here
Jake could forget about all the things he couldn't remember.

He hadn't planned on being out here tonight, but someone
had pressed a hand-drawn card into his hands at Finn's night
before last, and right after that Tommy had followed him
through the parking lot, sliding into his truck and jerking him
off slow and dirty, murmuring about flyboys and fallen angels
and the fiery taste of Mary Lou Miller's pussy, back in the day.

He didn't much care about Mary Lou Miller one way or the other, but he was going to come anyway, Tommy's voice in his ear and Tommy's hand on his cock, his thumb sliding over the slit just right, making his hips buck up hard. He was still trying to catch his breath when Tommy ran his fingers through the spunk on his belly, gathered up as much as he could and used it to jerk himself off, too, his mouth open and his legs spread wide. Moonlight was shining through the windshield, turning Tommy's skin pale blue, and Jake wouldn't have looked away right then for all the memories in the world.

It seemed fitting that Mary Lou Miller was here tonight, too, smiling and laughing, dark curls loose around her face, dancing up against some boy at the edge of the bonfire's glow. Jake didn't recognize him right off, the slope of his bare shoulders and his khakis hanging low, but he sure looked pretty enough from here. Everyone looked pretty from here, Jake thought. It was the firelight, and the smoke shine, too; hazy and sweet, sparks in the air and crushed grass underfoot, Tommy singing softly, strumming his guitar.

Jake made his way toward Tommy roundabout, Sadie Harris's warm hand in his for a while, twirling away and spinning back again, her body soft against his, her earrings sparkling in the night. Jake took a joint from Billy Zee's thick fingers as he passed them by, and Sadie kissed his cheek and danced away, taking Billy with her. Tommy caught his eye and licked his lips, and Jake smiled, looked up at the sky.

Anything was possible on a night like tonight, with the river and the fire, home brew in dark bottles, the stars shining bright. Tommy said, "Sit for a minute," and even now Jake knew how Tommy's minutes turned into hours and he sat anyway, close enough to feel the heat of Tommy's skin, different from the heat of the fire. Tommy's heat was like the air and his voice like the smoke, raspy and sweet, curling into Jake when he breathed.

Tommy leaned close and Jake blinked real slow, smiling as Tommy *tsk, tsked* and lifted Billy Zee's joint from his fingers. Jake had turquoise-blue paint caked into his cuticles, yellow ochre smudged across his wrist. He had scars he couldn't explain yet, smooth skin that tingled and itched across the front of his shoulder, the back of his thigh, his hip. "These are our friends," Jake said and Tommy nodded, picked out a new rhythm on his guitar.

"You remember this one?" Tommy asked, and Jake hummed a little, shook his head. He did and he didn't.

Tommy's eyes were green and gold and he had freckles all over, the same color as his hair; he liked strawberry ice cream, and mayonnaise on his fries, and he could fix anything with a motor, anything at all. An unconquered wolf was tattooed on his bicep, a burst of red, white and blue inside his elbow from when he first joined the Guard, a trail of shamrocks on his side that twisted way down low.

Jake had a trail of shamrocks, too. He didn't remember getting them, but he knew they were there, could imagine him and Tommy driving into the city back before Jake took off for flight school, Tommy's fingers in his hair, his lips kissed dark and swollen, both of them reeking of beer and whiskey and laughing their asses off, toasting the luck of the Irish. Jake imagined that a lot, especially in the shower, his fingers tracing over the shamrocks, thinking about Tommy, the way he'd taste, the way he'd feel, wet and slippery, the way he'd sound with Jake's dick buried deep inside him and his breath caught up in his throat.

Fuck, Jake thought, shifting uncomfortably, his dick hard, trapped between his belly and his briefs. Tommy strummed his guitar and his voice sang out, and Jake tried to think about something else.

"It wasn't like this before," Tommy said softly, setting his guitar aside to run his thumb over Jake's bottom lip and kiss him slow, one hand on the back of Jake's neck holding him close. "With us, I mean. I didn't know if you knew."

Jake closed his eyes, leaned into Tommy's touch. He didn't know what they'd been like before, but from the way his brain filled in the missing pieces he thought he must have wanted Tommy even then, couldn't imagine ever wanting anything else. He remembered Tommy in ways he couldn't explain, details and dreams and fleeting faded images. He felt safer around Tommy than around anyone else, like he was okay again, like Tommy was cool with him even if he wasn't the same guy he'd been before the war. "Does that matter?"

"Not to me," Tommy said, and just then someone threw a log on the fire and the embers popped, sparks flying in the air. One of the girls squealed and out of the corner of his eye Jake could see Billy Zee wrap his big arms around her, could hear her laugh, sweet and high, could hear him laugh, too.

Jake's hands were sweaty, hot on his thighs, and Tommy's eyes were on his, leaning in to kiss him, his fingers spread on Jake's jaw, his throat. Jake's body knew how to do things that Jake didn't remember learning—he could tie a knot in a fishing line without thinking about it, cast out over the water and make the fly dance just so; he could drive his old truck no problem; hell, he could climb into the cockpit of a fighter and fly her just fine, not that anyone would let him. Not anymore.

Tommy bit at Jake's lip, sharp and teasing, soothing the bite with his tongue before licking his way back into the kiss. Jake heard himself moan and it sounded sexy even to his own ears, and he knew his body remembered fucking, remembered it well.

His hips pressed closer, Tommy's mouth on his, his hands, the heat in the air and the river rushing by, the scrape of stubble against his throat.

He pulled away just enough to see Tommy's eyes, his flushed cheeks, and his smile as he picked up his guitar. It was easy, being here like this, and Jake leaned back and closed his eyes, listened to the night close in around them. Sadie Harris sat down beside him for a while, ran her fingers through his hair. She stood up to leave, kissed Tommy's cheek and climbed into Billy Zee's arms, and when Jake looked around again it was just him and Tommy, the fire burning low.

"I want you," Jake said, and it was simple enough, Tommy's smile against his, the way his eyes crinkled up at the corners. He liked to think he'd been smoother before, had known the right thing to say, to do, but Tommy was smooth enough for the both of them, Jake thought, because Tommy's fingers were curled under the hem of Jake's shirt, dragging over his stomach, his ribs, Tommy's mouth following close behind, hot lick of his tongue, scrape of his teeth, and Jake had meant to be self-conscious about this, about his scars, about his body, about the way the dark head of his dick was already poking out of his jeans, but he couldn't be, not now, not with Tommy leaning right up against him, spreading their shirts out on the grass behind them.

Tommy's dick was hard against Jake's hip, soft denim right there, slick skin everywhere else, his voice raspy in Jake's ear, "So fuckin' hot, you have no idea," and with the way he looked, Jake's back on the grass and Tommy above him, the last of the firelight in his eyes, in his hair, Jake thought he might be right.

"Tommy," Jake breathed, and Tommy kissed his way down Jake's body, his palm pressed over Jake's fly, tongue darting out to taste the slick trail of precome on his belly before he wrapped his lips around the head of Jake's dick, hot and wet and Jake couldn't help rocking his hips a little, couldn't help the flex of his fingers on the back of Tommy's neck. "Fuck, Tommy."

"Yeah, later," Tommy said, grinning a wicked grin, popping open the buttons of Jake's jeans and tugging them off his hips, knuckles sliding over the scars on the back of his thigh, making Jake shiver. Tommy kept one of his hands right there, palm open, fingers splayed wide, and Jake tried not to squirm. Tommy shifted lower, rubbed his cheek on Jake's belly, in the crease of his thigh, stubble scraping over the shamrocks, his mouth pressed to the lowest one. "You remember these?"

"Luck of the Irish," Jake whispered, and Tommy bit his lip and swallowed hard.

Jake tensed, wondering, but Tommy just shook his head and laughed real low, his eyes flashing bright as he licked up the length of Jake's dick and sucked it back down. Jake wanted to flip them over, feel the weight of Tommy's cock in his mouth, nudging at the back of his throat, wanted to taste him there, lower, everywhere, and then Tommy's calloused fingers were in his mouth, earthy and smoke-sweet, then gone way too soon, and Jake could hear himself moaning way up high, needy sounds he couldn't stop, Tommy's fingers circling his hole and pressing in, spit-slick and rough, so different from his own.

Jake leaned up on his elbows, scrubbed his hand through Tommy's hair. "Tommy, fuck, c'mon," and Tommy let Jake's dick slip out his mouth and slap wetly against his belly. Jake was breathing hard and Tommy was, too, his skin flushed and his lips swollen, his fingers in Jake's ass twisting slow. "Christ, were you always this much a tease?"

"Yup," Tommy said, grinning. He still had his jeans on, and that was wrong in ways Jake was too dazed to really think about, but Jake could see how hard he was at least, could see where the head of his cock pressed against the faded denim, leaking. "Been teasin' you for years."

"Yeah?" He wasn't sure if that was true or not, but it didn't matter. This was what mattered, what he had now, what he could touch, taste, remember. "Huh."

"Sure took you long enough to notice."

"Hard not to, now," Jake said. He pulled at Tommy's jeans, buttons popping open and Tommy's dick jutting out, shiny at the tip, red-gold curls dark around the base. Tommy shifted to his knees, mumbling "Sorry, sorry," as he wiped his fingers on their shirts, dug a rubber out his pocket and tore the packet open with his teeth.

Jake reached for it, but Tommy shook his head, rolled it on himself. "Too close," he whispered, leaning in to brush a kiss across Jake's lips, his hips pressing Jake's thighs open, his cock sliding in the hot crease of Jake's ass. "Tell me you're ready."

Jake wrapped his hands around his thighs and hitched them higher, the blunt head of Tommy's dick against his hole, rub of Tommy's hand against his skin guiding it in, thick and hot and bigger than his fingers, better, Tommy's mouth on his, sweat dripping from his forehead, pressing in slow, slow, Tommy's hips twisting, both of them moaning low.

Jake swallowed hard, wished he could see Tommy's cock fucking in and out of him, wished he could see his body stretch to take it, and then Tommy shifted, kneeled up and angled Jake's hips high, and fuck, it was so good like this, the slow burn and the impossible heat, his hips rocking up and up, Tommy's hand wrapped around his dick just right. Jake knew he wasn't going to last, was going to come just like this, too soon, his shoulders pressed into the ground and Tommy's cock in his ass, thrusting deep.

He bit down hard on his lip, on his fingers, but he couldn't stop it, hot splash of come on his belly, his chest, Tommy cursing low and breathless, his voice hoarse and his hips losing their rhythm. "Fuck, Jake, fuck." It still felt so goddamn good, so right, fireflies in the tall grass and the stars overhead, slow buzz in his blood and Tommy fucking him hard, leaning over, "Gonna make me come," his mouth pressed against Jake's throat and Jake's fingers twisted in his hair, in the hot well at the base of his spine.

"I missed this, last tour over there," Tommy said later, his dick soft and sticky on Jake's stomach, his knees tucked up against Jake's ribs. Jake nodded, imagined he probably missed this, too. "We learned to fish right here, back when we were kids," he said, smiling, his fingers tracing the scars on Jake's shoulder, certain, like he was playing his guitar. "You remember?"

Jake shook his head, ran his thumb over Tommy's bottom lip, and Tommy laughed, licked at rough edges of Jake's nail, the soft pad of his skin. "I just remember you," Jake said, watching Tommy's eyes light up, listening to the river. It was different here at night, Jake thought, but not so different. It still felt more like home than anywhere else.

YOU'RE A DOG

Edward Moreno

The Big Fella

They say a man's heart is as big as his fist. I have no reason to dispute that, but in Ben's case it begs the question. His heart must be the size of a bucket; I accept that.

I met him on the almost-leafy banks of the Yarra, on that almost-green promenade in Melbourne's liquid heart. There's something about Melbourne I've never liked—something hard. I feel most times like I've been bent by the wind, hung out to dry by the drought, leveled by the tough, flat surface of the city. Every leaf on every tree is edged in brown, every footpath a display of dust. It's not pretty, but it's home.

I've never been one for pretty anyway.

"You're a dog," he said—the first thing he said to me. "You're an ugly motherfucker."

He came right up to me—his enormous feet practically trod on mine—and his eyes widened. He brought his face close, getting an eyeful, then pulled back to look me up and down, head to toe, and cracked a smile.

"I can't even stand to look at you," he said and turned away, looked up the river to Prince's Bridge, then twisted his torso back toward me and said it again. *You're a dog.*

I didn't take it badly. I've been broken, bent and trod on over the years—my face and body are crisscrossed with scars, I'm not pretty—but I was taken aback. I hadn't met anyone this forward in years. I couldn't help but stare after catching sight of him sprawled across the bluestone pillars on the water's edge—his long legs stretched out across the promenade, the river at his back—and the next thing I knew he was in front of me, telling me what a dog I was and asking for my number.

His hair was shaggy, a lion's mane, but his twentysomething face was keen edged, fine and dark. Whenever he spoke, he'd open his eyes wide and run them over the whole of my face, my body, nodding to confirm the truth of whatever he'd just said—but when he talked about what a dog I was he'd shake that shaggy head and turn away, look up or down the river and then look back at me, dark eyes ablaze. We exchanged the basics as he moved in and out of my space—coming in close, inspecting me, stepping back.

Buskers spruiked their shows in his shadow on the promenade, families with prams rolled past; the brown leaves of the plane trees crackled in the dry wind, and Ben circled me like a boxer in the ring.

He had my attention. He sized me up, He stepped back and balled his bucket-sized hands into fists. He landed two quick jabs on my chest. He came in close again, looking down at our toes, drawing my eyes down, his enormous toes and my trembling toes almost touching. He said, "Man, I'd love to go toe-to-toe with you."

He gave me an eyes-wide nod and then turned on his heel,

looming as he sauntered away on his chunky legs; shaggy headed, yes, but clean and crisp in his preppy jumper and his A&F shorts, walking light in his loafers, a pretty but gigantic young man who'd just called me a dog.

At home five minutes later, I mentioned nothing to Ivan, just double-checked my face in the mirror, to make sure I wasn't that much of a dog. I couldn't decide either way—I'd had a bottle broken in my face in a bar fight, and one of the scars from that night rambles right across my uneven nose. I inspected it and wondered about the meaning of toe-to-toe. In the bed or in the ring? It didn't matter. I smiled at my image before—absently, distractedly—joining Ivan on the couch.

We fumbled around in front of the TV, and I squeezed a few big-hearted cuddles out of my Ivan, and he laid a strip of kisses across my chest, while the TV couples and comedy families squabbled and one-lined each other. We fell asleep at some point, intertwined and sweating wherever our skin touched, behind my knees and on my chest where his head rested. I woke up a little later, untwined myself and went for a swim.

In the Pool

When I'm in the pool everything liquefies, myself included. On solid ground I feel fairly square with the boundaries between myself and other objects in the world, but in the pool those straight lines fall away and everything collapses and I whirl through the water, digging the sound it makes as it percolates through my head. I take pleasure in stretching time and space: I'm infinite when I extend my arm again and again—I'm the universe.

That night I swam for over an hour in my endless bubble state, watching the navy-blue tile floor revolve below me and around me like a marble globe, while outside the sky darkened above the city and the orange clouds moved through me, inside and outside the building. It was good to be in the water then, with everything mixing together, with all the lines blurred, with the tiles and the city undulating past, rolling past without end, and me thinking of the giant boy with his giant hands, his heart the size of a bucket, his wide-eyed gaze.

My body was rubber when I pulled myself out of the water, into the dark.

Ivan was doing push-ups at the foot of the bed when I walked back into the apartment. He finished and looked at me, his chest and face galah-pink from pumping out a set. I smiled. "Have you always been such an ugly fucker, or is this something new?"

I didn't ruffle his feathers—no one could, he was unruffleable. He just laughed. "Don't tell me you're only just working that out."

There's something that separates Ivan and me, and it's not just the quiet space between us, or the length of the hall, or even where I end and he begins. Sometimes we're so close—I'll be inside him, or he'll be inside me—and I'll be free-falling without a net.

Right Fist

I sat on the sofa in front of the TV with the sound turned down. I looked at my hands: one held the TV remote; the other cupped my balls through my tracksuit pants. Ivan was in bed. Watching porn in semidarkness is like moving through water: time stretches out and nearly slows to a stop; my right fist becomes the universe; lines and boundaries blur when I'm bathing in the blue TV light.

I'm only interested in the beginning—the very beginning—of the encounter: the first flicker of possibility, the first glance, the first moment one man begins to lean his head toward the other's, the unbuttoning of the top button. I shoved my hand into the waistband of my tracksuit, watching the men on the screen as they caught each other's eyes, gave each other a second glance. I rocked my cock in my right fist while the other fist rocked the remote, pausing, replaying in slow motion, pausing, replaying, pausing, replaying; recalling the exact moment earlier in the day when I first caught sight of Ben, with his long legs like tree trunks, his arms like tree branches: that exact moment when one guy first moves toward the other.

In the morning, Ivan woke me with his regular routine. He grinned over the ironing board, nodding toward my right arm, immobilized by my waistband, and asked, "How you going there, champ?"

"I could use a hand," I said.

"Looks like you're doing all right there by yourself."

I watched him from the black hole of the sofa that had swallowed me overnight. The rain that morning was heavy—it darkened the sky, and the apartment and the rest of the world—and since I never liked working in other people's gardens in such rain, I decided to reschedule all my work.

"I could use a hand," I said again, nodding toward my crotch, right hand still thrust down the front of my pants.

"How do I look?" he asked and turned so I could get a look at his arse in his suit pants, then turned again to face me. He looked great, with sexy close-cropped salt-and-pepper hair and his Paul Newman eyes. His chest pressed tight against the light blue fabric of his shirt as he tied his tie.

"You're a bit too sexy, I think."

"That's always going to be a problem. Not much we can do about it."

We both smiled, and Ivan gave my cock and balls a squeeze and me a kiss before he headed out the door.

I lay on the sofa listening to the rain fall before eventually pulling my hand off my cock, and then I set out candles on the altar, crossed my fingers and toes and prayed to the stars and the universe that Big Ben would give me a call, invite me round to his place, fuck me silly and then punch me in the head.

He called as soon as I lit the last candle, and the clouds cleared and the sun broke through.

I'm not sure why I said yes, when my real life proclivities—just like my porno predilections—tend toward the very first movements, toward intention and nothing more.

Pause

I floated up Spencer Street in the rain, uphill, upstream in the downpour, aware of my surroundings, of the lines laid out across the landscape of the city—tracks, footpaths—of the flashing orange lights on the green and yellow trams, of the colossal oversized-egg-carton roof of Southern Cross Station, of the umbrella-wielding mobs. I kept inside my own private rectangle, upright on solid ground, watching the lines intersect and diverge, diverge and intersect. Serpent trams hissed and rattled.

Ben lived at the top of a tower at the bottom of Latrobe Street. I looked at my ugly face in the mirror as I went up in the lift, smiled at the devil in it and at my crooked nose. You'd think I'd recognize the guy I saw, but he was always an interesting stranger with a confused look.

Big Ben answered the door in baggy sweatpants, shirtless, with a serious case of bed head that suited the young, thick, brute. He was about as wide and thick as I was tall, and a good foot and a half taller. We sat on his balcony while he smoked a cigarette that almost disappeared in a hand the size of a dinner plate. It looked like a little redhead matchstick.

The rain had stopped, but his balcony was wet. While he

smoked, I tended his potted plants, a veritable garden—herbs and tomatoes, flowering shrubs, poinsettias and even a couple of frangipani. I couldn't help but do the gardening thing.

The sky had turned purple, the temperature had risen and something was brewing in the sky. I leaned on the air-conditioning unit next to Ben's giant body while he watched me, cigarette between his thumb and forefinger, and wished I could push pause at that exact moment. He breathed out the cigarette smoke, which hung in the air like a cloud far above my head. I watched it circle and storm like the clouds just beyond the balcony rail, then saw the big fella begin to lean his dark scruffy face toward mine.

I'm not sure when it started, this pulling back, this desire to stop everything at just that moment. It's much more beautiful, though—the pending moment. So I looked at his thick lips, breathed in the air (rainfall, frangipani, cigarette smoke, recent sleep, a young man's breath, neck sweat), negotiated his unshaven jawline with my eyes (big as a sisal doormat as it got closer), saw out of the corner of my eye his big hand flick a cigarette over the balcony rail before starting on its way toward my waist or my crotch, saw his lips opening, saw the tip of his thick tongue, breathed his recent sleep scent again and sensed my cock stirring in my jocks. I watched it all and felt it inside me, smelled it, saw him moving in slow motion, his red lips, the red ember of his cigarette tumbling over the side of the balcony.

I think it's safer to stop there and somehow more satisfying. It always has been, in my life. There's no free-fall that way, only solid ground, and it all felt very solid just then, in the big man's grasp, on that balcony in the sky. I paused for one more beat, watched the purple clouds moving behind Ben's shaggy brown mane, and then the storm started. He landed a kiss and we breathed the same air, his mouth tasted like sex, and I felt it inside me and at the tip of my cock, and then the cyclone started.

I swear to god that's exactly what happened. His bucket-sized heart beating against my chest, my own heart filled like a bucket, my cock knocked against his through my jocks and jeans and his tracksuit pants.

Left Fist

And then Ben punched me in the head just like I thought he would, the big giant. I saw a flash of light and my head exploded. I should've known not to climb up into the giant's lair looking for the golden egg when I knew he wanted to go toe-to-toe with me, to tell me what an ugly fucker I was. *Now why'd I have to go and do that?* I thought as my knees buckled.

It was another pause moment, the bright white light, the sound of something popping, and the brief flash of pain before my body collapsed and blood flowed. I thought of Ivan, his big chest under his blue-striped tie, his blue eyes; thought of the time I got hit by a cricket bat at school; thought of my own fear of everything, of my inability to get really close to another man; and then the blood poured more, a lot of it, and I tasted it, and Big Ben caught me in his full-size arms.

Only a few minutes later, I woke up in Ben's bed, inside his arms, my startled head against his slab of a chest, my neck cradled by his tender left hand. He was a gentle nurse, cleaning up my bloody head, my angry eye. *Ouch.* It was only then, looking up at his chunky head as he looked after me, that I started to work out what had happened—he'd saved the hailstone that had clocked me, and he showed it to me before chucking it out the window.

"Won't be needing that," he said, winking at me.

Big Ben had a heart the size of a bucket, and he was filling me up with love. He tended my wound and we had a tender fuck and the big fella pumped me full of big love, while the rain continued to fall.

Outside the city was in chaos, we heard nothing but sirens and alarms. Ben was gazing at me sideways with a curious look on his face.

"And I thought you were a dog before!" he said, giving me the once-over, pausing at the damage. "You're a sexy fucker, and those bruises just help to make you look better. You got some character, you ugly bastard."

I laughed, kept laughing while I dressed, looking at my purple face in the mirror. Ben caught my eye a couple of times and winked.

"Sexy," he said.

I was still wobbly, and the world was blurry, so Ben offered to walk me home. Feeling tenderized, I said yes.

Heart

We had to splash through knee-high water part of the way, under cataracts and around broken glass, and at one point the big fella threw me over his shoulder like a rag doll while he waded through waist-high water up Clarendon Street. A kayaker passed us by just then, and we gave each other a wink and a smile, appreciating the other's choice of transportation.

It looked like the drought was over, and I was pleased to see Melbourne this way, liquid, underwater, softer.

We waded through thigh-high water just to get into the lobby of my building. The lift was out, so we climbed seven flights of stairs to my apartment. My balcony garden was destroyed, my terra-cotta pots broken and scattered, soil twirled in an eddy, mixed with a world of brilliant white hailstones and thousands of bright, shredded emerald leaves.

"It's a mess, but it's kind of beautiful, innit?" Ben said, watching the mess swirl in the wind.

He left me with my bucket on the balcony, to salvage my plants.

Ivan found me on the couch later, nursing my throbbing head.

"What the fuck happened to you?" he asked as soon as he came in the door, shoes and socks off, pants rolled up to his knees.

"God gave me a big punch in the head."

"What the fuck?"

"A hailstone the size of your fist clocked me."

He's a doll, my Ivan, and he fell straight onto the couch where he could hold me in his arms and plant a kiss on my damaged head, inspecting it up close.

"You're going to have a serious black eye."

I told him it was killing me and he insisted on the hospital, but I was more obstinate than he was and instead we curled up on the sofa. He told me that I should probably get stitches, and that I would probably have another scar to add to the map of ruin across my forehead, cheeks, chin.

"No one can say you don't have a lot of character written all over your face," he said.

"Good thing you've still got your movie-star looks," I said, and pushed myself farther into him.

We stayed like that, pouring love back and forth while the rain landed outside, until night fell.

I eventually asked Ivan to turn the television on, with the sound down. Lying in the blue TV light, I was comforted by the sound of the rainfall and even the sirens outside. Ivan's face looked serene and beautiful in the muted light, and I took pleasure in watching it until I fell asleep in his arms.

The Big Fella

The next time I saw Ben, he was bigger and shaggier than ever, and he circled me just like before. The rays of his smile fell upon my heart, filling me with delight. We were on the banks of the Yarra, as before, though the river was thicker and muddier this time, after all the rains. He circled in close to get a look at my face, at the purple- and mustard-colored bruise surrounding my eye.

"Sexy," he said, then turned his head to look upriver, before turning back to look at me with a big gap-tooth smile, his unkempt lion's mane surrounding his head like sunshine. He seemed more shy this time, but really pleased to see me. I liked the attention. We stopped like that in the cool autumn breeze, sharing space, smiling, enjoying the sight of each other while breathing the same air.

I took it all in: his cigarette smell, the green leaves on the trees, the muddy river, the buskers, the shape of his smile, the size of his hands, the clouds swirling behind his head.

"So we going to go another round?" he asked, looking sheepish, turning his gaze toward the painted Prince's Bridge, purple in the evening light.

"Absolutely, champ," I said, feeling good, as though I was underwater.

"That's good," he said, looking me up and down. "Gee, you're an ugly fucker aren't you?"

"You can't even stand to look at me, can you?"

He laughed, his thick lips parting slowly as leaned his shaggy head down toward mine.

PRECIOUS JADE

Fyn Alexander

I was beautiful in 1885 when Queen Victoria was on the throne, and I still am, according to someone who loves me. I was paid far more attention than I deserved by both men and women, and was, frankly, rather vain. At eighteen years old I was slender with sun-colored hair that was much too long and skin like an unblemished peach.

I had grown up in the theatre as an angelic boy soprano. But, much to my chagrin, my voice changed at fourteen, and along with it, my ability to earn a living. Consequently, that warm day in May the very thought of having to attend an interview for a job I did not want at a house in Belgravia made me as sullen as a spoiled prince.

Money I wanted, a place to live I needed, but work! I wanted to cry out to God to save me. Why could I not be rich and free and live in some foreign clime where it was always warm and no one cared that I, a boy, preferred men to ladies? I favored girls when it came to chitchat, gossip and whispering about men's bodies. But I had always wanted a man to overpower me, to master me, to fall madly in love with me and make me his own. Since I was to be a servant of sorts, a secretary, you would think I'd be happy, but no! Any master I would end up with would be either some doddering old man I did not want near me, or some nasty married gentleman who would treat me with utter disdain, if he noticed me at all.

It wasn't fair.

I suppose I must have looked disgruntled when I was shown into the study and made to stand in front of a broad oak desk whilst being looked up and down by an elderly woman dressed in black silk. She never invited me to sit. She fired questions at me while acting as if I had brought a smell of refuse into the house with me. All in all, I felt like reaching across the desk to slap her cadaverous cheek. I found my left eyebrow lifting as it often did when I was affronted. Remembering my mother's admonition before I left that morning—"Keep that haughty look off your face, darling boy. An employer will not take kindly to it"—I lowered my eyebrow and attempted to look meek.

"Your mother is on the stage? She calls herself Amethyst Swift?" Mrs. Wynterbourne asked. From her tone she might as well have said, *Your mother is a prostitute, she has sex for money with perfect strangers.*

"My mother is a singer, a coloratura, and that's her *real* name." My eyebrow shot up again of its own volition.

"And she extended the family tradition of naming infants after stones by calling you Jade?" She actually sniggered, a very unattractive sound.

I was outraged. I clasped my hands behind my back to control them. "Jade is very expensive. It is the same color as my eyes." The first man who had ever taken me on his knee and petted me had told me my green eyes were *fit to die in.*

"Is it indeed?" Mrs. Wynterbourne's eyebrows both rose perilously close to her receding hairline. "Watch your tone, my lad! Why are you not on the stage yourself? You might be better suited to that life." She was obviously referring to my long hair and velvet jacket.

"My mother wants something better for me," I said quietly, ashamed to admit it.

"Does she indeed? Well, I suppose the job is yours."

"Thank you," I muttered, taken by surprise. The sun shone through the window behind her directly into my eyes, making me hot and crotchety. I wanted desperately to get away from her. "May I see my room please? Then I can go and fetch my belongings."

"You will not be staying here," she said as if the very thought was repugnant to her. "You are going to the country to work for my son, Mr. Marcus Wynterbourne, who fancies he is writing a book. He wants me to send him a young lady, but I don't trust him with one."

Not to be trusted with young ladies? Just my luck!

The journey to East Sussex on the public coach was hellish, to say the least. Squashed in for the first half of the journey between a fat, dirty woman and her farting husband, then for the second leg, alone in the carriage with a man with roving hands and halitosis, my senses were outraged along with my very person. The first I ignored as best I could: the second I slapped, then bit when he refused to accept my firm refusal.

I arrived eventually in the pitch dark at a vast country estate, tired, hungry, dejected and wanting my mother. None of my needs were met except for a bed, and I retired hungry and miserable, bursting into tears under the covers. Sometime later I paused in my pathetic weeping, swearing I heard a step outside my door. I drew the eiderdown up under my chin like a maiden defending her virtue, though my virtue was long since trampled upon, and I was more disappointed than anything when no one entered my lonely chamber.

Over breakfast with the servants, who never spoke directly to me, and looked at me as though I were a recent escapee from a traveling freak show, I fantasized about my new Master as I had done since first hearing his name: Marcus Wynterbourne. Since childhood I had dreamed of a man, cold and haughty, whose icy heart could only be melted by me. But Mr. Wynterbourne liked the ladies, it seemed, and he was probably ugly anyway.

At length I was shown into a sunny morning room, where a man stood at the window with his back to the room, ignoring me. I remained standing by the door until he deigned to turn around. When at last he did, the sight of him captured my breath as I had dreamed it would.

When he approached me, I observed a man nearly as slender as myself, though far taller and more masculine. He had black hair beginning to be streaked with silver, intense dark eyes and a frenetic presence. I stepped back, afraid for a moment he would grab me to examine me more closely. Instead he pulled a letter from his pocket and held it at arms' length to read it. "James Swift," he pronounced. "Eighteen years old, well read, hand-writing excellent."

"Jade," I corrected. "Sir, my name is Jade Swift."

He laughed, an almost frightening sound, then stopped abruptly. "Jade? My mother changed your name. She wants you to be James while you work for me." He looked me up and down, a sarcastic smile playing about his mouth.

"Well, I won't be," I said, petulantly. I had had quite enough. "My name is Jade. I insist upon it." My heart fluttered as I spoke.

"Do you?" He stepped closer, looking down at me. He really was very tall.

"Yes, Sir," I whispered, not quite so sure of myself now that I could feel his breath against my cheek. He smelled wonderful, nothing fancy, just expensive, masculine soap and a splash of Bay Rum. He was clean-shaven in a time when whiskers on a man were all the rage. I could not admit him handsome with his strong jaw and thin face. In fact he was a bit scary looking. However, it would not be a lie to call him attractive.

"Jade," he said, as if mocking me. "I am writing a book and you will take dictation and fetch any volumes I require for my research, though most of my writing is a memoir of my extensive travels. Go to my office at the end of the hall and wait there for me."

As I trotted down the carpeted hall I experienced a violent excitement in my stomach. *Love at first sight* is what they call it, and a romantic boy like myself had passed many a happy hour envisioning such an event. I had felt attraction at first sight so many times it did not bear scrutiny. Indeed, there were times when a wink from a pretty boy or handsome man was sufficient to have me following him like a puppy into the first dark corner available. But this weakness of the stomach, this unfathomable desire, was new to me. Several minutes later my Master entered the room, threw himself into the chair behind the desk and began to dictate.

That was it for the next month and a half. He dictated while I transcribed. He ignored me completely while I sat bored stiff and longing to be noticed. He marched up and down the room speaking into the air, hands clasped behind his back. I caught my breath every time he walked too close, which he did increasingly as the weeks passed until I was driven insane with yearning. I entered my room each evening, my cheeks drenched in tears of frustration, to write a missive to mother about how desperate I was for London, the Theater and her.

I was completely infatuated with my Master and I had a suspicion that he knew. I had a great tendency to fall easily in and out of love, and every time I did, I thought it would last forever. But what I was beginning to feel for Mr. Wynterbourne was different. The usual intense emotions were there, but it was as if something deep-rooted had begun to grow inside me. I sought a communion with him I did not understand and could not have put into words even if I had wanted to.

One afternoon he leaned over my shoulder so closely that his body touched mine and said, "Let me see what you have so far, boy." The feel of his warm breath against my ear caused my cock to rise. I swear he chuckled as he walked back to his desk. Sometime in early July he caught me distracted and staring out into the grounds, which had grown beautiful with the fullness of summer. I had missed several lines of dictation.

"Am I keeping you from something you would rather be doing, boy?" His sarcastic schoolmaster tone snatched me from my reverie. I turned to him, my ire raised. I was sick of the job and sick of pining for a kind word or a warm look from him. I would rather he slapped me than offer this total negation of my being.

"I should never have left London!" I burst out like a ridiculous child.

Very calmly he asked, "What would you have done had you remained?" With one hand, he pulled the chair from behind his desk, plumped it in the middle of the room and sprawled in it, elbows propped on the arms, fingers steepled, long legs stretched out before him. His intense gaze rested upon me and my cheeks began to grow warm. The only thing I hated about being so blond was the tendency for every emotion to show in my face. He beckoned me to stand before him. "Speak," he demanded. "Tell me all about yourself."

I was in shock. Moments ago I was bored to tears and resentful that he ignored me. Now I stood before him, all his attention focused on me, and I wished myself a mile hence. I had no idea where to start. "My mother is on the stage. I too worked on the stage."

"What did you do on the stage?" His eyes looked serious yet his mouth tilted at the corners and I was certain he wanted to laugh.

"I was a magician's assistant for a time and sometimes I would dress up to take part in skits, but I want to be a singer again. I sang on the stage when I was younger. I was billed as *Amethyst's Angel*. But then my voice broke."

"That does tend to happen. Sing for me," he ordered.

I trembled. I stood only a few feet from him utterly exposed in this small venue. I clasped my hands before me and raised my voice in an old music hall love song. When I was done the silence filled the room with far more intensity than my singing.

At last he spoke. "Why did you leave the theater?"

"My mother insisted I do something more respectable." I hated saying that, but it was what she told me.

"Your mother wanted you to do something you could make a living at because you will never again make a living with that voice. It's awful," he said calmly.

I turned from him quickly to hide the hot tears coursing down my pink cheeks. I hated him! I wanted to strike him and run from the house back to my mother. How could he treat me so cruelly?

"Boy," I heard him say. I would not face him again, but stood at the window with heaving shoulders, crying silently. Then he was behind me, wrapping a strong arm around my waist, pinning my body to his. With his other hand he wiped my tears and drew me round to face him. I pressed my hot face into his chest and felt his hand on the back of my head, caressing my hair.

"Jade. Precious Jade," he whispered my name. "Don't cry, beautiful boy." Thrilled and shocked by turns at this unexpected intimacy, I dared not move for fear he would become sensible of his madness and let me go. "Your voice is dreadful but I was rather cruel in saying so. Your writing on the other hand is excellent. You take fast dictation and your skill at research is impressive. You are a clever boy. Well spoken and with a fine vocabulary."

"Thank you, Sir," I replied through my tears, thrilled at the praise, yet still feeling limp and stupid.

"I have grown very fond of you," he said quietly. Then he held me at arm's length, gazing down at me. "And you are beautiful."

I was so confused. For weeks he had been distant, calling me Swift or boy, mostly boy. Now he called me precious Jade and held me in his arms. Was he toying with me? I threw myself at him and wrapped my arms around his waist as if I would never let him go. "Sir, Mrs. Wynterborne said you are not to be trusted around young ladies," I ventured. "Yet I have never seen a lady in your company."

"Yes, I know. It is me who belongs on the stage, not you, boy. I'm a fine actor. But what choice do we have?" He smiled kindly for the first time in all those weeks and his voice was tender when he said, "May I have you?"

I nearly fainted. Was it really that simple? Had he really just offered to make me his own, or had I misheard? "Yes, please, Sir," I said without hesitation, assuming he would sweep me up in his arms and carry me to his bedchamber, much to the shock and horror of any servant we passed on the way.

My Master was a very strong man despite his slender build, possessing tight, sinewy muscles, and now he put his strength to good use. Before I could react, he had my trousers down and threw me over the back of a chair.

It seemed the virtue I thought I had lost long ago was still intact, because I had never dreamed of what he did to me next. I was an innocent. I was a virgin! All my kissing and fumbling in various cobwebby corners of London theaters was nothing but childish play, preamble to this moment. Mr. Wynterbourne reamed me good and proper, then fastened his trousers and sat down again behind his desk. I turned to look at him, myself still in dishabille, and he merely started to dictate again. Utterly humiliated, I dragged up my trousers, grabbed my pen and ink and attempted to keep up.

That night in bed, I cried my heart out. Master had pretended to want me, then he had done no more than use me like a piece of meat from Smithfield Market. My sobbing was so loud and indulgent that I did not hear him enter my room. At some point I looked up to find him standing silently beside my bed. I sat up at once and did the eiderdown thing again, which made him laugh. "You're cruel!" I burst out, and began to weep once more, before crying, "I love you." How pathetic I must have sounded.

"Yes," he agreed. "Of course you love me. I expected you would the moment I saw you with your peach-perfect skin and overly long hair." He cocked his head to one side, looking down at me from his great height. Then he sat on my bed and took my trembling hands in his. "Do you wish to be my boy, precious Jade?"

I drew his hands to my mouth, smothering them with kisses. "Yes, Sir, yes please, Sir."

Solemnly, he nodded. "I knew you would accept." Had he been anybody else I would have wanted to teach him a lesson for being so smug. But he was not anybody else. He was my Master. All I felt was gratitude and a desperate desire to please him.

Disappointment flooded me when he stood and walked to the door. I thought at least he would invite me to his chamber. "Be prompt in my office in the morning as usual and in the evening we will talk about my expectations for your new position."

My confusion must have been obvious; still, he waited for me to ask. "New position, Sir? I am still working for you, aren't I?"

"You will continue as my secretary," he agreed. "Indeed, I could not do without you for my book. But now you are more than that. Now you are my slave."

"Yes, Sir, thank you, Sir," was all I could say.

The next morning I reported for my day's work in Master's study, my heart pounding. I expected him to greet me with a kiss and an embrace. He did not. As always, he waited for me at his desk, and the moment I entered the room, he pointed at my escritoire. I sat down, and he began to dictate before I could pick up my pen.

All night I had hardly slept, sick with anticipation and excitement, and for what? This? Being ignored as usual. Being treated like a piece of furniture as usual. As the day wore on, so did my unease. Had I imagined him coming to my chamber last night? Had I wanted him so desperately that I had imagined the entire scene?

At six o'clock, just as I thought he would have me writing far into the evening, Mr. Wynterbourne stopped speaking and walked to the window. I watched him stand silent for a while, and then he looked at me with his intense gray eyes. "Come here, boy."

In my excitement to get to him, I dropped my pen to the floor, then moaned in fear that I had splattered ink onto the beautiful Persian rug. I stooped to pick it up, fumbling stupidly, and returned it to the pen case. He watched, smiling, and waited patiently until I stood before him. I wanted to throw myself at him but dared not presume.

He held out his arms to me, and I fell into them with such relief that I feared I might weep again. "Sir, I thought you had changed your mind," I mumbled into his lapel.

"Not at all, dear boy. When I decide upon something, I always know I have made the right decision."

My instructions were rather simpler than I had expected. My Master said, "Obey me in everything. Obey me at once. I will always be fair with you. I will never let anyone hurt you. Be humble and be proud at the same time. Do you find that confusing? Don't worry, boy. I will show you what I mean. Nothing will be expected of you that is beyond your ability to achieve."

Later that week they came, the men and women of The Hellfire Club. Never in my short life had I beheld such an assemblage as gathered in the drawing room that evening, and I had grown up in the theater! I had seen boys dressed as girls and girls dressed as boys. I had met a good number of both ladies and gentlemen who preferred their own sex to the other. My mother had a friend who was born with two penises, which he insisted on showing me one evening, and I must confess I was fascinated. But these people who knew, and clearly loved, my Master, took the cake.

Whilst the butler served brandy, which I was not offered, I was ordered to sit on the carpet at my Master's knee. I felt the great weight of this honor and was frankly rather smug about it. *Do they all know I'm his,* I wondered. It seemed they did because a number of very haughty men and women looked down on me and asked, "Is this your new boy, Marcus? Isn't he pretty."

At one point I responded, "Yes, I'm Jade Swift," and received a slap across the back of my head for my trouble.

"The only thing swift from now on will be retribution if you speak again without permission," Master told me firmly. Burning with humiliation I learned a sharp lesson, the first of many, and sat in silence eyeing the party.

The Masters and Mistresses were unmistakable because they walked about freely or sat on the beautiful furniture while talking and laughing. Many wore clothing that designated some sort of rank—heavy, leather belts with metal studs and high leather boots. More than that it was their attitude, the authority with which they carried themselves, that set them apart from their minions.

The slaves, though, sat on the floor, some naked under their cloaks and with various chains and restraints upon their persons. They were silent unless spoken to, kept their eyes lowered for the most part, and remained very still beside their Masters and Mistresses. I became fascinated by a man, quite a bit older than myself and wearing what appeared to be a muzzle, who sat beside a woman's knee, panting like a dog and suffering constant, exacting correction. I looked up at Master, and when he noticed me, I nodded at them. He leaned down, saying, "That is a puppy in training."

My mind was in a whirl.

Soon enough I followed my Master and his guests down into the extensive cellars of the great house. A sign on an immense barred wooden door read DUNGEON, and my heart began to pound. The dungeon was lit by flaming torches set in wall sconces. The corners were dark and cavernous. There was a general air of revelry; the slaves bright-eyed, their chests heaving; the Masters and Mistresses sure of themselves and in control.

I was ordered to strip as were all the slaves, male and female, young and old and every age between. Master, who dazzled my eyes in his black trousers, black leather boots and snow-white shirt, watched me and smiled as my nipples and cock reacted to the cool air.

"Precious Jade, tonight you will be tested," he said. Overwhelmed with excitement, I was led to a post by the wall where I was bound like Christ on the cross, ankles together, hands above my head. I was a picture of angelic beauty with my blond hair about my shoulders and my slender body stretched out for all to admire. And admired I was for about five minutes by my Master's friends, gathered about to gaze at me. It was my moment in the spotlight. Then it was over. "Observe everything, beautiful boy," were Master's last words to me. After that I was left alone.

For the remainder of the night I witnessed scenes that enthralled and delighted me, yet I was miserable. I went from boredom to tears of frustration, from horror to fascination as the hours wore on. From my ignominious place in a dark corner I watched floggings and spankings that I wanted to experience. I saw slaves restrained and gagged in a myriad of different positions and styles, with everything from rope to leather thongs to iron manacles, and I was jealous. I saw hot wax poured over sensitive body parts making me wince while wanting to experience the sensation. I saw a life I wanted and I was provoked to insane jealousy of every slave my Master touched, flogged, punished or smiled upon.

When at long last my Master came over to me. I wanted to scream at him in frustration, but I was clever enough to know that that would be a mistake. "Master, you said you would test me," I said quietly.

"You have been tested, precious Jade." With care he released me from my bonds. "Your patience has been tested and you have made me proud." I all but swooned with joy. He took my face in his hands. "You are an impatient, demanding boy and I am going to tame you. Everything is a lesson. Now come with me." He led me to the middle of the dungeon and to my delight spanked me soundly while everyone watched. I was in the spotlight again.

Afterward he hugged me close and I whispered, "I love you, Sir," and waited for him to respond likewise. But all he said was, "And so you should. You should always love your Master."

In the days that followed I learned that I held a cherished place in my Master's heart. While he was teaching me the basics of being his slave I was showered with praise, kisses, scrumptious hours in the dungeon—and my favorite thing in the world—the privilege of being allowed to sit in Master's lap. At night I was permitted to sleep beside him in his bed. But he never declared his love for me, if he had any.

I began to get quite full of myself, I admit. The euphoria I experienced from being tested to the limits of my endurance can only be compared with the heightened awareness I got from sharing my Master's best opium, which on a few rare occasions I was allowed, and which I sometimes thought made me invincible.

It was this invincibility which led me to thinking it my right to take advantage of an offer from a handsome, sun-browned gardener, only a little older than myself, whose sole desire one hot afternoon was to suck my admittedly small cock behind the stables. He was on his knees and I had my eyes tight shut, moaning openly when I felt the stinging flick of a whip across my bare belly. My eyes shot open. My handsome friend screamed as he too took a lash from Master's single tail, across his bare back. The pair of us stood with our heads hung like schoolboys before an enraged headmaster. The gardener was sent back to his duties whimpering after several more lashes and I was slapped hard across the cheek and ordered to pack my bags.

* * *

In the days that followed, in my mother's dingy lodgings, I poured out the whole tale of passionate love and delicious subjugation. Mother held me close in her big bed at night while I sobbed for all I had lost. I pressed my face into her ample bosom and was able to keep my sobs down to merely pathetic while she stroked my long hair, twisting it into ringlets round her finger, saying "Mother's darling boy." It was when she called me her *precious Jade*, my sobs rose to truly melodramatic heights. "He calls me that!" I wailed.

I had always thought a broken heart was something to aspire to, something that would set a boy apart, making him purer and nobler. I never expected a broken heart would leave me weak and empty. Snot dribbled down my face as I sobbed; I pissed in my mother's bed two nights in a row. She forgave me, god bless her, but after a week she told me in no uncertain terms that there was a job available at the Adelphi Theatre cleaning the dressing rooms and that I had better take it and bring in some money.

I was humiliated to the very core of my being after my first day as a broom boy. I lay thoroughly exhausted, curled up in the middle of mother's bed, watching her ready herself to go back there to "warble for the punters," as she put it.

"Visitor!" was screamed up the stairs by the landlady whenever one arrived. I did not move from my prone position, not expecting anyone would want to see me. Mother opened the door and invited the visitor in.

"Get up when I enter a room, boy." I heard my Master's voice and reacted like a starved dog. I leapt to my feet, stumbled to my knees and kissed his black leather boots. Mother raised her eyes to the damp-stained ceiling, proclaiming, "Good god," and sat down again to arrange her hair. "If your intention was to humble my sweet boy, you've done it. Now will you please take him back?" she said calmly.

I sat back on my heels waiting for his answer, looking up into the face I had grown to love and had missed desperately these empty days. I waited, afraid to breathe. "How do I know he is sufficiently humbled?" Master asked.

Mother swung around on her stool. She was in her silk corset and lace-edged pantaloons, her face half made up, and was not the slightest bit abashed by my fine gentleman. "He cries for you every night. He calls out your name in his sleep. He hardly eats." *Please don't tell him I pissed in the bed,* I thought desperately. "And he wet my bed the first two nights he was home," she added for good measure.

I hung my head in shame.

"Excellent," Master stated, smiling at mother. "I see where the boy gets his beauty."

Mother was not averse to flattery even from a lover of men, and smiled back. "Too bad he didn't get my voice. He has the face of an angel and he used to sound like one, but the minute he turned fourteen..." She shook her head sadly.

"Yes, I've heard him sing," Master said. They continued talking as though I were absent.

"What made you come to get him back?" Mother asked.

I gazed up at Master adoringly, wanting him to say, *I miss him, I love him, I need him.* Instead he said, "I always intended to come for him. This was just another lesson. I could have flogged his bare arse until he screamed as a punishment for taking liberties, but I thought the gentler way might be better on this occasion." He looked down at me, wagging a finger. "Pack your bag and come home. And this time, behave yourself."

"Do you love me, Master?" I whispered. "Do you love me as I love you?"

After a long pause, during which mother turned her back to allow us a modicum of privacy in the small room, Master said loudly and firmly, "Yes, Jade, I love you. I love you very much."

I smothered his boots with kisses and still do whenever I am overcome with gratitude that Master noticed me all those years ago when I was eighteen years old, presumptuous and foolish. He still calls me his *precious Jade* and he still tells me I am beautiful.

VIVA LAS VEGAS

Max Pierce

I stood at the top of a grand staircase suitable for a classic MGM musical, but feeling less like Cyd Charisse and more like Debbie Reynolds: an eternal boy next door. Perennially cute, but seldom sexy. I forgot that sometimes cute wins over sexy.

It began as the *worst* date ever: a comic misadventure of epic proportions. If one was reading *TV Guide*, the log line would read something like this: Romantic Comedy; Boy travels to Sin City and finds nothing is as he expected yet discovers love in the process.

However, I hadn't the luck to read the log line. Three hours before I stood on that staircase, located in the swankiest hotel in town, I only knew I'd been invited on a potential romantic voyage and it was sinking faster than the Titanic, with no lifeboats in sight. Cue up Celine Dion.

Notice I wrote *potential*. I paid for my airfare but Tom insisted he'd pay for the hotel and we would be sharing a room. He was cute, I was cute, and it *was* Vegas, right? I'd read the literature.

This was my first visit to Las Vegas and I'd jumped at the chance to go. Showgirls! Roulette wheels! Ninety-nine-cent shrimp cocktails! If I were feeling particularly decadent, I might even smoke a cigar. So what if I didn't smoke? And the kicker: meeting Ann-Margret after her concert. Sexy, age-defying Ann, who'd rocked with Elvis, pined for Birdie, and was iconic enough to appear in animated form on "The Flintstones." Tom had a connection who had guaranteed we'd get backstage after the show. The time: early November, Halloween was out of the way but holiday thoughts hadn't taken over. The setting: Caesars Palace. And for the next eighteen hours, I rolled the dice and had the best date ever. And it wasn't with Tom.

Reality had kicked in shortly after I stepped off the United flight from Los Angeles, overnight bag in hand, and found I was being whisked *away* from the glittering Las Vegas Strip to the more moderately priced downtown area. Our hotel was no grand resort, more a glorified hostel with a room the size of a closet and the smell of an old humidor. It was perfect if you'd lost your pagoda at the Pai Gow table and needed a place to slash your wrists or swallow a handful of Seconal: precisely the reason why none of the windows opened. The presence of two twin beds in opposite corners, no less, squashed any idea of romance, as I'm not one for shoving beds together. Our $3.99 dinner in the hotel restaurant, a necessity due to our late arrival, made me eager to find a McDonald's—or a bathroom.

I had taken great care in dressing to meet Ann, perhaps a tad over the top, only to be informed by Tom that he had only secured *one* backstage pass. Setting a new record for the transformation from romantic possibility to platonic nobody during the cab ride between downtown and my dramatic Caesars entrance, I felt like the Christians being introduced to the lions. Suddenly trapped

in a black-and-white RKO budget picture, I was a plucky hero
pining for Technicolor, Cinemascope, and Stereophonic Sound.
When a lonely boy knows he's different, but *doesn't* know there
are at least ten percent more like him in the universe, and is raised
on a steady diet of old movies, he can't help but aspire to glamor.
I knew I didn't belong in downtown Las Vegas. I belonged in
Caesars Palace, hobnobbing with the high rollers.

Ann, thank goodness, did not disappoint. Seated close
enough to the stage that if she'd taken another tumble, as she
did in Lake Tahoe in 1972, we could have caught her—and the
eye of any press photographer in the pop of a flashbulb. After
watching her sing and gyrate for two and a half hours, and
guzzling one vodka-infused drink after another, my now-former
date went around to the back with his original *Bye Bye Birdie,
The Pleasure Seekers,* and *Bus Riley's Back in Town* posters,
leaving me to my own devices. Exploring the casino, I plunked
myself in front of a slot machine, accepted a complimentary
cocktail from a woman dressed as an extra from *Troy,* and lost
twenty bucks in ten seconds flat. Not sure how long Tom's assig-
nation with Ann would take, and not having enough money to
keep losing, I wandered out of the casino and into the hotel.
In a rather obscure passageway linking Nero's all-night buffet,
Cleopatra's disco Barge, and an exclusive restaurant named
Bacchanal (which plugged toga'ed attendants massaging sacred
oils into your neck while you ate), rose a marvelous staircase,
all gilt rails and plush ruby carpet, stretching to where I wasn't
sure; but my inner Nancy Drew had been activated and I was
eager to find out. Never being one to pass on an opportunity
to make life more like the movies, I climbed the stairs two at
a time, paused at the top, whirled in a dramatic fashion, and
began descending, arms outstretched, visions of Lana Turner in
Ziegfeld Girl swirling in my head.

About two tap steps down, I remembered that Lana's character died in that film, so I wasn't drawing upon the most positive movie reference. Nor was Norma Desmond's close-up in *Sunset Boulevard* a good role model. *Hello Dolly!* and *Mame* were too obvious and far too queeny, even for a musical queen like me. I had no Rhett Butler to whisk me up, and there were too many steps to effectively re-create Bette Davis gunning down her lover in *The Letter*. I went back to Ziegfeld. Rewinding, I became Hedy Lamarr slinking downward to a chorus of "You Stepped Out of a Dream" that played in the soundtrack of my imagination. Halfway down, I eyeballed a cute guy in a black tuxedo at the foot of the staircase, looking like he stepped out of a dream. About this same time, a slot machine in the casino rewarded a Midwesterner with a jackpot.

Ka-ching!

"Yee-haw!"

The guy looked back up at me, and burst out laughing.

I mentioned earlier I had dressed a bit over the top: I was wearing a tux. And why not? I'd had one for years with no occasion to put it to use, until now. To me, Vegas means Sinatra, Steve and Eydie, and Bugsy Siegel, with well-heeled patrons tumbling from casino to showroom along the Strip soused on martinis and chewing cigars, garbed in fashions from Armani and Versace. Or in my case, Calvin Klein, whose tuxedo design I'd nabbed at a department store clearance sale. After partying into the wee hours, I'd expected Tom and me to stagger into our room and consummate the evening with a tumble onto the requisite circular bed while the mirrors on the ceiling reflected our every decadent act. Roll credits, end of story.

Of course, our hotel room was nothing like that, and even if there had been a second backstage pass, I don't think I'd have consummated anything. Right now, however, I was alone and in my element—glamor and just a hint of mystery with a stranger at the foot of the stairs. And whoever he was, he was about to join my movie, whether he liked it or not. Nicely draped in his own tuxedo.

Except he was still laughing at me. No longer Hedy Lamarr, I marched down the remaining steps, now in tough-guy Jimmy Cagney mode, hoping he wasn't a house detective about to bounce me from the joint.

"What's so funny?"

He said, "You look like you're having a good time."

"I am," I replied, as if I made a living walking up and down hotel staircases. At the last step, and to my amazement, I discovered I stood two inches taller than him. I didn't think there could be anyone shorter than me, yet he was, although what he lacked in height he made up in muscle, apparent from the thick forearm exposed as he extended his hand, and covered with a healthy amount of body hair of the Robin Williams variety. Behind us, another jackpot echoed in the casino.

Ding-ding-ding-ding-ding-ding-ding-ding!

"I'm Bill."

I shook his hand and lost myself in his eyes, which were hidden behind glasses. I'd popped my contacts in before I left the hotel, but left the all-essential drops in the room. The smoke in the air was making me squint, and I wondered if Caesars' amenities included an all-night drugstore.

"Did you see Ann-Margret's show?"

"Yes. I especially liked the number where she sang and danced with her old film clips." Oddly, I now pointed out, Ann had looked younger now than she had in her *Birdie* days. After saying that, I hoped Bill didn't think I was too bitchy.

"Have you seen the pool?" It was a charming non sequitur.

I shook my head and we, two penguins, walked outside. The

deserted pool was oversized, like everything at Caesars (except my new acquaintance), and decorated in a *Roman Holiday* motif. The fresh November air, dry as vermouth and windy and warm, had the same effect on me as a bushel of raw oysters. I eyed Bill much like a cat does a canary.

"Where are you from?" we both said at the same time.

"Los Angeles," we both answered.

This was an incredible run of luck. Had I not been so interested in continuing my conversation with Bill, I knew I could have run in, plopped a hundred on the roulette wheel, and doubled my bet.

"My friends are backstage getting her autograph." Bill said.

With that, I might as well have been Cinderella—wearing a watch with a dead battery—who hears the village clock strike midnight. Tom! My date-in-name-only. He had paid for the show tickets. Yikes.

I was glad the pool area was discreetly lit, as I knew my eyes had bugged out. "My...friend is probably looking for me."

"Boyfriend?" Bill asked.

I shook my head. He too had mentioned friends. I prayed that was plural.

"Boyfriend?" I queried, holding my breath.

"No. Let's go back in." And there, in the stillness, beside the shimmering pool reflecting faux-ancient columns and pseudo-classical statuary, with the lights of the Strip illuminating the sky above us in a Technicolor rainbow, Bill leaned over to kiss me, and there was nothing faux or pseudo about it. Bingo.

Okay, so he wasn't *that* much shorter than me.

During the walk back into the casino, my sense of honor attacked me. I had come to Las Vegas with Tom, and even if things hadn't worked out, manners dictated I should remain with him. I'd been on the receiving end of being dropped more often than I cared to remember, and it wasn't a pretty feeling. The polite thing, the honorable thing, would be to get Bill's number and call him later.

Or I could tell Tom *See ya* and drag Bill to the nearest poker table. We'd fit easily under the green tablecloth.

For years I'd been the good boy with the straight A's. I was entitled to a little selfishness. And if Bill turned out to be a mass murderer, well, so be it. It wasn't the first time I'd gambled on romance and come up short—make that lost.

The casino was swarming with activity, except around Tom, who stood tapping his foot impatiently where we had parted earlier. What a difference twenty minutes can make!

"Where have you been?" he said, eyeing Bill as if his lamb had come back to the pen accompanied by a miniature wolf.

I can be pretty quick with my back against the wall. I did a double take. "Oh! Why, this is...Bill. He's from...Los Angeles. Small world, isn't it? Bill, don't you know...Tom?" I hoped this cocktail party chatter made it seem as if we were all old friends.

I needed to go no further with my charade. Bill's friends Ray and Greg, also tuxedo-clad, popped over clutching programs. Never before or since have I felt as if I'd fallen through a film screen and right into a classic screwball comedy. If Carole Lombard and William Powell strolled up, I would not have been surprised.

"I've been invited to go with some of Ann's friends—" Tom said, his voice fading out after *go*. Just where they were going escapes me now. Maybe Ann-Margret herself had seen Tom in the front row clutching his posters and was spiriting him away for a private screening. Whatever the destination, I knew providence was removing Tom. I needed to offer a novena, at my earliest convenience, to thank the patron saint in charge of romance. "I have my key, so I'll see you back at the hotel," I answered, hoping *back at the hotel* meant tomorrow around the time we caught the cab to the airport. It probably was not the most tactful dump, but I didn't care. This was a magic moment, and I was going to hope for a royal flush. I could blame it on the staircase and the Stoli.

With Tom conveniently removed, I got acquainted with Bill and his friends. He was the chief financial officer for an upscale Century City firm. Ray was an entrepreneur who owned a variety of successful businesses. Greg was Ray's boyfriend of the moment, and didn't appear to have any job other than placating Ray, which appeared to be a full-time job. Ray wanted to play baccarat, so we went into the high roller area, the one cordoned off with velvet ropes. We were ushered through by burly yet impeccably groomed guards as if they had been waiting for us.

Ray lost five hundred dollars on his first bet. As I saw him toss another chip down, my mind reeled with the thought that his chip could pay my rent. To my relief, Bill was much more frugal with his money, and we watched Ray lose, and lose, and lose. In fact, Ray and Greg became so absorbed in their game that we were able to casually fade into the background.

Bill asked if I was hungry and I nodded, so we took the moving sidewalk out of Caesars to the street, then strolled over to the Flamingo. The wondrous thing about Vegas is that if you get tired of ancient Rome, just nearby are Paris, Venice, Egypt, Manhattan, and so on. The Flamingo was the brainchild of Bugsy Siegel, who, it is said, buried a few enemies in the hotel flower garden. We had a late supper at the Peking Market, a bustling restaurant replete with an enormous aquarium, lanterns, roasted ducks hanging in the window, and mandolin music echoing off the teak walls. In the excitement of the evening, the ill effects of my cheap dinner had worn off, and having been fueled only by vodka for the last three hours, I was starving. But a bowl of egg drop soup, followed by a platter of moo goo gai pan and combinations of beef, broccoli, and Szechwan shrimp restored me.

We left the Flamingo and went to the MGM Grand. This was my kind of hotel: I could spend hours looking at the photos of the stars. I kept an eye on my camp-o-meter; no sense scaring Bill off by reciting movie lines for the balance of our evening. After a stroll through, we skipped out and explored the Imperial Palace. The Palace was a little down market after the pizzazz of Caesars, the MGM Grand, and the Flamingo, but we did have some clever drinks served in little ceramic skulls. We talked the whole time, about our jobs, our families, and our dreams as if we'd known each other for years and not just an hour. I'd never met someone I connected with so quickly and so well.

By three A.M., after such a glorious evening, there was no way I was going back to my closet-sized cigar box with its twin bed. Bill was staying downtown too, but at the Golden Nugget, with its clean-smelling rooms and decidedly more upscale atmosphere. I walked him to his room and as he opened the door, he shyly looked at me. The room was large and well air-conditioned. There was no mirror on the ceiling, and the bed was square. But it was California king-sized. We tossed our tuxedos and snuggled under the covers, but not before making sure the heavy drapes blocked out the approaching sunrise. I was glad I'd taken a bet on love. *Roll credits.*

CODY BARTON

Martin Delacroix

Cody Barton tried killing himself, but he failed.

Then Cody came to live with us.

His dad dropped him off on our driveway. No hugs good-bye. Dr. Barton only waved from behind the wheel of his Audi before he drove away. This was days after Christmas. The after-noon was overcast and a damp breeze fluttered Cody's shoulder-length hair while he strode up our walkway.

I met Cody at the doorstep. The rope mark on his neck looked like a violet snake; it passed beneath his Adam's apple. Dark smudges appeared beneath Cody's eyes and a few zits dotted his cheeks. He carried a suitcase the size of a portable television in one hand, his skateboard in the other. A backpack hung from his shoulders.

"Are you all right?" was all I could think to say.

Cody wouldn't hold my gaze. He stared at his feet and shrugged.

"The Bartons' housekeeper found him hanging from a rafter

in their garage," my mom had told me the night before. "There was some sort of family argument beforehand."

Family argument? What's new?

Cody was my best friend; I'd known him since middle school. I had spent much time at his house and I knew his parents. Dr. Barton was okay: soft-spoken and reserved. But Cody's mom, Barbara, was a complete bitch. She hounded Cody about everything: his school grades, personal grooming, even his posture. Her voice was nasal and flavored with a Georgia drawl. I winced whenever I heard it.

When he was younger, Cody weathered his mom's insults silently. But once he reached high school, Cody started talking back. He'd argue with his mom in front of me. They would shout and sometimes throw stuff across the room. It made me so uncomfortable I avoided their home. Whenever Cody would ask me to visit him there, I'd suggest another meeting spot: my house, our neighborhood skatepark—anywhere but the Bartons'.

Finally, Cody stopped inviting me over altogether.

Weekends, he'd often spend Friday and Saturday nights with us, sleeping on an army cot in my bedroom. My parents didn't mind; they liked Cody, especially my mom. Cody and I would sit on the family room sofa—we'd play a video game or watch a movie—and Mom would enter with two glasses of iced tea. She'd run her fingers through Cody's rust-colored hair; sometimes she'd call him "sweetie" or "handsome." Cody would grin and his cheeks would redden.

"Your mom's the best," he'd tell me.

Now, Cody followed me into the house, his suitcase banging against his leg. In my room, the cot was already set up, equipped with sheets, a pillow and blanket. I pointed to a battered chest of drawers my dad had borrowed from a neighbor the day before.

"You can put your stuff in there," I said, "and there's room in the closet, too."

While Cody unpacked, I sat on my bed and watched. He placed his socks and underwear in the bureau's top drawer, his T-shirts, jeans and shorts in others. He tossed two pairs of athletic shoes into my closet, along with his skateboard. Then he draped a hooded sweatshirt and a jacket over clothes hangers.

The last thing Cody removed from his suitcase was a framed, five-by-seven photograph of Dean Barton, Cody's late brother. Dean had died the previous spring, victim of a hazing mishap at his University of Florida fraternity house. Just nineteen, he died of heatstroke while locked in the trunk of a car. The beer-sotted brothers who'd put Dean in the trunk forgot he was there, until it was too late.

I had known Dean before he left for college. He captained our high school's swim team, made National Honor Society, was elected to the homecoming court. Tall and blond, with a perpetual suntan and a mouthful of white teeth, Dean was the guy all of us aspired to be. Over three hundred people attended his memorial service.

After Dean's death, Cody changed: he talked less and rarely laughed. He avoided the few friends we had. Our passion, mine and Cody's, had always been skateboarding. In the past we'd spent countless hours grinding on the streets of Clearwater. But now Cody hardly skated at all. He smoked marijuana most every evening, spent hours alone in his bedroom listening to music or wandering the Internet on his laptop computer. His school grades worsened, and some days he actually smelled bad, like he hadn't showered or washed his hair for several days.

When I confronted him about these things, Cody only scowled.

He said, "Leave me alone, Zach."

So I did.

I waited for Cody to phone me, and sometimes I wouldn't hear from him for a week or more. He rarely slept at my house. The cot remained folded up in my closet, and I wondered if our friendship had reached an end.

Now, in my bedroom, Cody placed the photograph atop the bureau, next to his toothbrush and wallet. He stowed his suitcase in a corner, along with his backpack. The box springs wheezed when he sat next to me. Sunlight entered through a window above my headboard; it reflected in Cody's green eyes, highlighted freckles on his nose.

"Go on," he said, looking at me. "You can ask whatever you want; I don't care."

"Tell me why you did it."

He gazed into his lap. "I couldn't take her shit any longer."

"Your mom's?"

Cody nodded. He spoke in falsetto, mimicking his mother, complete with Georgia drawl. "'Dean made Honor Roll every term, why can't you? And why aren't you dating? Dean had a girlfriend his sophomore year.'"

Cody puckered one side of his face. "Why go on living with *her* in my life?"

I scratched my head, thinking, *I smell bullshit.*

Cody's explanation didn't ring true. I was pretty sure something else had driven Cody over the edge—exactly what I had no idea—but I didn't say anything.

According to my mom, Cody's therapist had insisted Cody *not* return to the Bartons' home after his brief stay in a psychiatric facility. Arrangements had been made between Cody's folks and mine. Cody would live under our roof, at least until the school year's end, when Cody and I would graduate. Each month the Bartons would write my parents a check for Cody's food and incidentals.

Now, in the bedroom, I looked at Cody and wondered what thoughts dwelled inside his head. Was he angry his suicide attempt had failed? And how did he feel about living with my family?

Cody glanced at his wristwatch. He rose and plucked a bottle of prescription pills from his backpack. Placing one tablet on his tongue, he swallowed.

"What's that?" I asked.

"Antidepression medication."

When I made a face, Cody raised his shoulders and puffed out his cheeks.

"Sorry, Zach; I guess I'm kind of crazy."

The day we returned to school, a band of thunderstorms spread across central Florida. Charcoal-colored clouds filled the morning sky. Raindrops stippled the surface of mud puddles. Cody and I sat in my car at a stoplight, both of us dressed the same: beanie caps, faded T-shirts, jeans and skateboard shoes. Our backpacks rested on the rear seat.

Cody's T-shirt did not conceal his rope marks. My mom had offered Cody a tube of cosmetic cover up, but he declined it. "Everyone knows," he told her. "Why try to hide it?"

Our school had its fair share of assholes, guys who reveled in making other people miserable. I wondered what might happen during the hours ahead. How would people react to Cody? To *me* when they saw us together?

Cody stared out the windshield at passing traffic. His voice quivered when he spoke.

"Will you walk to first period class with me? I don't think I can do it alone."

"Sure," I said. "No problem."

In the school parking lot, a few people pointed and stared. One jerk grabbed his throat; he made loud, strangling noises and his antics caused other people to laugh. Cody and I pretended not to notice. We entered our monolithic, two-storied school through glass doors. Inside, a crush of voices echoed in the hallways. More people pointed at Cody; at me too. They stared and whispered. My pulse raced and the tops of my ears burned. I kept my gaze straight ahead, avoiding eye contact altogether.

Just get Cody to class...

Things went okay until we reached Cody's locker. Someone had fashioned a full-size noose from a length of cotton clothesline; it hung from the finger hole in Cody's locker door handle. Cody's face turned ashen when he saw the noose. Down the hall, two guys cackled.

"Ignore them," I whispered.

A tear trickled from one corner of Cody's eye.

"I *hate* this fucking place," he said.

On a Thursday afternoon, I drove Cody to an after-school appointment with his therapist. The therapist's office wasn't far from Oleander Park, a green space fronting Tampa Bay. After dropping Cody off, I drove straight to the park.

I'd visited Oleander two dozen times at least, and I'd always sit on a particular bench in an isolated spot. Then I'd wait for something I sorely needed: sex.

The park was a notorious cruise area for gay men; I'd learned this through articles published in the local newspaper. I'd go there after school, when my folks were at work and my whereabouts wouldn't be questioned. I met guys at Oleander who would never patronize a gay club, attractive but closeted men, some of them married.

I was queer, no question about it. I craved the feel of a man's muscles, the weight of his cock on my tongue and the taste of his semen. For some guys my age masturbation was enough, I guess. But not me; I needed another man's flesh. Of course, nobody knew about my visits to Oleander. I'd have died of embarrassment if they had. I considered gay sex sordid and nasty, but still I craved it like some folks needed illegal drugs. Too young at eighteen to visit gay bars, I satisfied my urges at the park. I didn't feel good about myself after these encounters, but my guilt didn't keep me from frequenting Oleander.

This particular Thursday, a warm breeze blew and the sun shone, casting shadows of slash pines onto the park's sandy soil. I strode down a sidewalk, hands in my pockets, till I reached my bench. Shrubbery surrounded me on three sides and pine needles carpeted the ground. Few people were about. I crossed a knee with an ankle, sucked my cheeks and gazed at a squirrel hopping about the limbs of a turkey oak. Checking my wristwatch, I saw ten minutes had passed since I'd left Cody at the therapist's. At best I had a half hour to kill.

I squirmed on the bench, glancing here and there. Would I fail to meet someone this visit? Would I leave dissatisfied?

Be patient; give it time.

Minutes later someone cleared his throat. I glanced toward a clump of saw palmettos. A man stood among the bushes, a decent-looking guy with dark hair and eyes, probably in his late twenties. I'd never seen him in Oleander Park before. When my gaze met his, he grinned at me and crooked a finger.

Go on, get moving.

Up close, the guy looked even better: a bit of stubble on his cheeks and chin, muscles bulging under his T-shirt, another bulge in his blue jeans. I followed him to a clearing where passersby wouldn't see us. Used condoms and damp wipes littered the ground.

He turned on his heel to face me. "I'm Todd," he whispered.

"I'm Zach."

"You're cute, Zach. Do you suck cock?"

I nodded. Already, my pulse raced. I salivated like a starving man invited to a feast.

Todd tapped his zipper with a fingertip. "I have eight inches. Want a taste?"

Eight inches? Fuck, yeah...

I sank to my knees. Hands trembling, I reached for the button at the waist of Todd's jeans and popped it open. I couldn't wait to get my mouth on Todd's cock. While I lowered his zipper, he reached into his back pocket. I figured he wanted to play safe; I assumed he'd offer me a condom, but I was wrong.

Boy, was I wrong.

Todd flashed a badge in my face instead.

"You're under arrest, Zach."

An explosion went off inside my head. *He's a cop, stupid; you're screwed.*

Then I thought, *What will Mom and Dad say?*

Oh, shit...

The ride to County Jail was awful. Todd and another officer sat in the cruiser's front seat, discussing banalities, while I sat in back with my hands cuffed before me, listening to their radio bark. I'd never felt more scared or humiliated in my life. I stared out my window, shaking like a sapling in a storm. Tears rolled down my cheeks. How could I have been so careless?

Things worsened when we reached the jail. The intake officer was someone I knew. Her son had performed in a school play with me and we'd rehearsed at their house a few times. She had seemed nice back then, but now she arched an eyebrow and scowled.

"Zach, what are *you* doing here?"

I lowered my gaze while my cheeks flamed.

I spent three hours sitting in a windowless cell, along with a couple of tattooed street thugs and a pale, skinny guy hallucinating on LSD. The skinny guy wouldn't stop babbling nonsense. We all wore orange jumpsuits and slip-on sneakers. I felt lower than pond scum. The cell stank of ammonia and human sweat. Above us, a fluorescent ceiling fixture hummed and flickered. I sat on a bench, staring at the concrete floor while my stomach churned. The enormity of my arrest had settled over me like a leaden blanket.

You're fucked, I kept telling myself, *totally fucked.*

My dad posted bail for me. After I changed into street clothes, I met him in the jail's reception area. He stood there with his hands in his pockets, staring at the floor with his shoulders hunched.

"Dad?"

He lifted his chin and his gaze met mine. I trembled like a kid in a spook house, feeling fear, disgust and shame. Why had this happened to me? Would my parents hate me for what I'd done?

Dad didn't say anything. He took me by a forearm, guided me through the exit doors and into the parking lot. The sun was down and stars appeared in the night sky. Crickets chirped among the trees. Standing next to our car, I fell apart and wept like a four-year-old.

"Daddy, I'm so sorry."

He took me in his arms and held me close.

"It's okay, son. It'll be all right."

* * *

The night of my arrest, my parents didn't lecture me. When Dad and I got home, my mom hugged me and asked if I was okay.

"I guess," I said. "Can you forgive me?"

"We love you, Zach; this doesn't change a thing. Go take a shower."

I felt filthy from my stay at the jail. Warm water raining on my skin soothed me and helped me feel human again. But I couldn't get memories from jail out of my head: the stink, the creepy prisoners, and the sordidness of it all.

Afterward, Cody and I sat in my bedroom with the door closed. I told him everything: how many times I'd visited Oleander Park, the sex acts I'd performed there, how I'd known I was gay since I was twelve, and how badly I craved intimacies with men. The words poured out of me like water from a spigot. I guess I'd always wanted to share my secrets with someone, and now I could.

Cody listened without comment. When I'd finished talking, he tapped his chin with his fingertips. "I don't understand something," he said.

"What's that?"

"How come you didn't tell me these things before? I thought we were best friends."

"We *are*," I said, "but sucking cock's not something I'm proud of. I wasn't sure how you'd react if I told you I was queer."

Cody made a face. "That's how little you trust me?"

His remark got me angry. I spoke without thinking first. "You're a fine one to talk: you've lived here three weeks but you still haven't explained."

"Explained what?"

"The reason you tried killing yourself. And don't give me that crap about your mom. It was something else, I know."

Cody looked away and rubbed his lips together.

"Come on," I said, "tell me."

Cody went to the cot, climbed under the covers and turned away from me.

Most everyone at school used Internet social networking, so it didn't take long for news of my arrest to spread. Altered photos of me appeared online: I'd have a cock in my mouth or a dildo up my ass. I received dozens of insulting emails, a couple of threats too. In the school parking lot, someone spray-painted FAGGOT on my car.

I was shoved and kicked numerous times in our school's hallways. Guys called me every name in the book: *fairy, fudge-packer, sissy boy, pervert* and *cocksucker*, to name a few. They made kissing sounds behind my back. People I'd *thought* were my friends ceased talking to me altogether. Suddenly I was a leper.

The only person who stuck with me was Cody. We'd walk to first period together each morning, eat lunch together in the cafeteria. Each afternoon we'd walk to my car together. None of this was easy for Cody, I'm sure. Guys called Cody and me "asshole buddies"; they accused Cody—right to his face—of being my boyfriend. But none of it dissuaded Cody from standing with me.

"If someone tries to beat you up," he said, "they'll have to fight me too."

After a couple of weeks, guys grew tired of harassing me. The insults tapered off and people stopped staring. My arrest became yesterday's news. But my former "friends" still avoided me. My cell phone rarely chimed and my text message inbox remained empty. Socially, I was a complete pariah. I went through my school days speaking to no one but my teachers and Cody.

Thank god for Cody.

Since moving to our house, he'd become more like his old

self. He had emptied his bag of marijuana down the garbage disposal. He took more pride in his appearance, put more effort into school. Each afternoon, we'd study in my room. In our free time we played video games, rode our skateboards and watched TV. Or we drove around town in my car, not talking much, just cruising the streets.

Our misfortunes had brought us closer together, I think. We'd both been shamed before our peers and socially ostracized. Lesser boys might've gone crazy—maybe even jumped off a bridge—but together we managed to survive. On campus we kept our grades up, our chins as well.

"Fuck people at school," Cody said. "Who needs them?"

You're right, I thought.

All I need is your friendship.

I woke to the sound of Cody's whimpering. I'm a fairly sound sleeper, but he made plenty of noise. He lay in fetal position, under the blanket on his cot. I glanced at my nightstand clock; the time was three a.m. Cody's knees chugged; his feet kept thrusting from beneath his covers. Silvery moonlight poured into the room through a pair of double-hung windows. I knelt beside Cody and shook his shoulder. When Cody didn't respond, I poked his ribs.

"Wake up."

He turned toward me and his eyes fluttered open.

"What is it?"

"I think you're having a bad dream."

He flipped onto his back and didn't say anything.

"What were you dreaming about?"

"The same shit as always."

"What?"

Cody looked at me. Then he returned his gaze to the ceiling.

"Tell me," I said. "I'm staying right here 'til you do."

He drew a breath, released it. "I dreamt about my brother."

"Dean?"

Cody nodded. "In the dream I stood next to the car he died in. I heard him kick the trunk lid and holler for help. He knew I was there; he even called my name. My parents watched. They shouted at me to do something but I didn't have a key to the trunk. It was...awful."

"Have you dreamt this before?"

"Many times, Zach."

Jesus, I thought. *Poor Cody...*

Spring break arrived in late March. Cody and I had performed well in school, so my folks agreed to rent us a room at the beach for three nights.

"I'm trusting you," my mother said. "No drunken parties."

And I thought, *Parties require friends, Mom. We don't have any, remember?*

But I only nodded.

The motel manager puffed on a cigarette while he checked us in. Students from assorted high schools and colleges occupied most of the rooms. Kids were all over the place, on the pool deck and in corridors. Boys guzzled beer, girls sipped wine coolers. The scent of burning marijuana was pervasive.

Our first night there, while swimming in the motel pool, we met a couple of guys from University of Florida. Ten minutes into the conversation, one guy told us the name of his fraternity and Cody's face turned white as an egg. He glanced at me and shook his head, very subtly. I cleared my throat. Changing the subject, I asked the UF guys if they might buy us beer, since Cody and I were underage.

An hour later, Cody and I sat in our room on our lumpy beds

while a case of Budweiser chilled in our mini-fridge. We sipped
from cans, both of us wearing only board shorts, while Cody
spoke of the boys from UF.

"I can't believe it. Of all the guys we had to meet..."

"Look," I said, "they don't know you're Dean's brother."

"True, but still it's weird. They could be the ones who—"

"Let's talk about something else."

While we gabbed, I studied Cody's physique. Like me, he
was skinny and pale, with a smooth chest and a narrow waist.
Copper-colored fuzz dusted his calves. In one leg of his shorts,
his cock bulged and the sight of it made me hunger for sex.

By midnight we had killed most of the beer. We lay on our
respective beds, listening to reggae music on my portable player. I
didn't drink alcohol too often—neither did Cody—and both of us
slurred our words. When I rose to visit the bathroom, I staggered
and nearly fell. I stood before the toilet, swaying. Half my urine
ended up on the floor. I didn't even bother flushing or zipping up,
I just stumbled out of the bathroom with my cock hanging out of
my board shorts. Then I fell backward onto my bed.

Cody looked at me and rolled his eyes. "You're shit-faced,
you know. You forgot to put your dick away."

The alcohol emboldened me, made me feel reckless. I looked
down at my groin, then at Cody.

"Why don't *you* put it away for me?"

Cody made a face and snickered. "Are you making a pass at
me?"

"Maybe," I said. "I'm so horny I could fuck a goat."

Cody made a bleating sound. "You sure know how to flatter
a guy."

I jabbed at my mattress with a fingertip. "How about it?"

Cody drew a deep breath. He swung his feet to the carpet
and placed his hands on his knees while my pulse pounded in my

head. This was uncharted territory for me and Cody. We were best friends, sure. But what would he say?

Cody licked his lips. He looked at the door, then at me.

"Tell you what, Zach: I'll sleep in your bed and we can do whatever you'd like. Just don't tell anyone, okay?"

Holy crap...

My cock stiffened—it looked like a runaway banana—but I felt a tinge of guilt. Would I regret this once I sobered up? Was I taking advantage of Cody?

"Look," I said, "you don't have to do this."

Cody put his hands on his hips and a little smile played on his face.

"I *want* to, Zach. I really do."

Cody locked the deadbolt, engaged the door's security chain. He went to the bathroom and used the toilet. After flushing, he switched off the lights. Our drapes were thin. Glow from the motel's corridor lights entered the room, enough so I could see.

Cody stood beside my bed. Looking down at me, he loosened his shorts' drawstring and let them drop. I'd never seen Cody's cock before. It was long and pale, with a head shaped like a strawberry. His pubic bush was copper colored.

"Hey," Cody said.

I looked up into his face.

"How come I'm the only naked guy here?"

Chuckling, I shoved my board shorts down my legs and kicked them away. Then I scooted over, making room for Cody. The bedsprings sighed when he lay beside me. His skin and hair smelled like pool chlorine. I lay on my back and Cody placed his cheek on my chest. He draped an arm across my waist, brought a knee to mine. His leg fuzz tickled my leg fuzz while he seized my erection in his fingers. He worked my foreskin back and forth. Then, shifting position, he took half my cock into his mouth and sucked it like a regular at Oleander Park.

I crinkled my forehead, thinking, *Huh?*

We were both drunk, of course. But something didn't feel quite right. I told myself, *This is* far *too easy.*

"Cody?"

He let my cock slip from his mouth. "What?"

"Have you done this before?"

He chuckled. "Lots of times."

"With who?" I said.

"You *don't* want to know."

"Of course I do."

"Are you sure?"

"Yeah, go ahead and tell me."

Cody let out his breath.

"Zach, I was my brother's lover for the longest time."

Huh? Dean and Cody?

I felt like someone had punched me in the stomach. My vision blurred and a flash went off inside my head. My cock went limp as a dishrag. I pushed Cody away, sat up straight and flicked on the nightstand lamp. Cody's lips shone with spit. Both of us squinted in the brightness while our chests heaved.

"I don't believe this," I said. "How come you never told me?"

He raised a shoulder. "How come *you* never told me about Oleander Park?"

I fell onto my back and studied the popcorn ceiling, while questions flooded my brain. How long had Cody's affair with Dean lasted? What kind of sex acts had they performed and how often? Was Cody gay like me? Had he enjoyed lovemaking with his brother? Or had he simply submitted to Dean's will? Dean had dated girls in high school, real beauties. Had it all been a cover?

I didn't ask Cody about these things; they could wait.

I had something more important on my mind.

"As long as we're getting secrets out of the way..."

"What?"

"Tell me why you tried killing yourself? I want the truth this time."

Cody dropped his gaze and nodded.

"Turn off the light," he said. "Then I'll tell you."

Details of Cody relationship with his brother weren't all that complicated. When Cody had been fourteen, and Dean a year older, they'd experimented sexually while the Bartons vacationed in the Bahamas. The boys started with mutual masturbation, advanced to oral sex, then anal.

"Dean was great in bed," Cody told me. "He'd done it with guys before."

Both brothers felt enthralled by their intimacies. They made a pact before returning to Florida: they'd become lovers, but no one, *nobody*, must know.

"Dean said if anyone found out, he'd have disaster on his hands. His reputation at school was important, he said. He had definite plans for his future: college, law school, and politics."

I lay there in darkness with Cody's head resting on my sternum. I didn't say a word.

"It was crazy," Cody said. "I'd pass Dean in the school hallway and he'd be talking with some girl he dated. He'd give me a wink and then I'd ask myself, 'What would the girl say if she knew?' Or I'd overhear Dean talking on the phone with his swim team buddies. He'd mention fucking this girl or that one, and I'd recall him fucking *me* the night before."

I rubbed the tip of my nose. "Did you love Dean?"

"Of course I did. When he left for college, I thought I'd lose my mind. I kept calling him during fall semester—to see if I could come up to Gainesville for a visit—but he always said no 'cause he had no privacy there.

"Dean told me, 'Wait for Thanksgiving, little brother. I'll come home and we'll be together.'"

I twirled a lock of Cody's hair around my finger.

"Of course," Cody said, "Dean never made it home. When he suffocated in that car trunk, I grew so depressed *I* wanted to die. Why go on living if I didn't have Dean in my life? I bought a length of rope, learned how to tie a noose from the Internet. It took me many months to work up the courage, but I finally did it. I figured death would bring me peace."

I shuddered, thinking of Cody hanging in his garage. "My mom told me there was an argument at your house, just before—"

"We had a blowup all right, on Christmas Day, at the dinner table. My mom said it wasn't the same without Dean during the holidays, how we'd never understand the loss she 'felt in her heart.'

"It made me want to puke. I thought of the last time I'd made love with Dean, the night before he left for Gainesville. I told my mom, 'You didn't even *know* Dean. I was closer to him than you or Dad or anyone else. I'm the one who's suffering here.'

"My mom said something like, 'If you loved Dean you wouldn't have disappointed him so often. You never lettered in a sport; you never dated girls, were never popular like Dean. He felt embarrassed by you and your slouchy friends.'

"When she said that, I...*exploded.* I stood up and threw a gravy boat across the room; it hit the wall and shattered. I said, 'Dean wasn't just my brother, Mom; he was my boyfriend. Do you hear me? He was my *lover.*'"

"Holy shit, Cody."

He chuckled deep in his throat. "Yeah: holy shit. At that point, the toothpaste was out of the tube. I'd disappointed my parents before, of course. But now they knew about me and Dean. They'd hate me forever, I knew, 'cause I'd destroyed their vision of who Dean was."

Cody rearranged his limbs and cleared his throat.

"I had no one left to love me, Zach. It was time to die."

We lay there in silence for a bit, just breathing and thinking. I tried to imagine how lonely Cody must've felt Christmas Day and how badly he must've missed his brother.

Cody turned his head and looked at me.

"Any more questions?"

I shook my head.

Cody and I didn't have sex at the beach motel. His revelation about his brother had shocked me so badly I couldn't *think* of touching Cody. I kept seeing visions of Cody and Dean in my head, the two of them surreptitiously making love while the rest of us remained clueless. I felt foolish, like the last guy in the room who's let in on the joke.

I imagined how Cody's parents must've felt when Cody thrust reality into their faces.

No wonder Cody couldn't return home.

During the remainder of our motel stay, Cody and I busied ourselves with walks on the beach, dining at fast-food joints, and sunning ourselves by the pool. We bought a bottle of Canadian whiskey, courtesy of the UF boys, and our last two nights we drank the stuff mixed with ginger ale until we both passed out. We didn't discuss Dean or sex or anything remotely personal again.

I wasn't ready to.

Spring break ended. We returned to school and our empty social life. Cody slept in his cot, I in my bed. We'd both been accepted to University of Central Florida, but attending there wasn't an option for Cody. At the dinner table one night, he said his parents had refused to pay for his education.

"I'm on my own after high school," he told me and my folks. "I'll find a job, attend community college part-time. It'll be okay."

My mom looked like she would cry. She told Cody, "You'll always have a home with us."

My dad nodded in agreement.

I signed up for fall semester at UCF. My folks sent them a deposit check. Then, during the last week of May, Cody and I walked across the school's auditorium stage, looking ridiculous in our disposable caps and gowns. We both shook hands with the principal while my folks smiled and applauded. My dad took photos with his digital camera.

Cody's parents did not attend.

In mid-August, Cody's mom died unexpectedly, from an "aortic aneurysm." A blood vessel near her heart burst. In the space of ten minutes, she bled to death at the Bartons' country club, after collapsing on the putting green. Her obituary described her as a "loving wife and mother." When Cody saw it in the newspaper, he shook his head.

"Bullshit," was all he had to say.

I went to the funeral only because I felt I should be there for Cody. We both wore starched shirts, neckties and khaki pants. The day was overcast, with a smell of rain in the air. At the Bartons' family plot, a breeze ruffled Cody's hair while they lowered his mom's casket into the ground. Cody, I noticed, wasn't observing the goings-on. Instead, he kept his gaze on Dean's headstone.

That night, lightning flashed outside my bedroom window.

Thunder rumbled so hard the house shook. Cody's cot frame creaked.

"Zach, are you still awake?"

"Yeah, this storm's keeping me up."

"Me too; I can't sleep."

We decided to play cards. I flicked on my nightstand lamp and Cody joined me on my bed. We sat facing each other, legs crossed at our shins, both wearing boxer shorts. I shuffled the deck and dealt. Then we played gin rummy, arranging our tricks on the blanket and saying little.

All summer long, Cody and I had power-raked people's Bahia lawns for cash. It was hard, sweaty work but paid well. In ten weeks we'd earned more than we could have bagging groceries an entire year. We were both tanned and fit, but skinny as ever. The muscles in my back and arms ached from the day's labors and I shifted my weight on the mattress, trying to get comfortable.

In a week, we'd return the power rake to the rental place. Then my dad would drive me to Orlando with my belongings and my college days would commence.

"Promise you won't pledge a fraternity," my mom had begged me.

I promised. What fraternity would pledge a guy with tooth-pick limbs and hair past his shoulders?

Now, in my room, Cody drew from the deck. "I'll miss you when you go," he said.

I nodded. How would it feel, not waking next to Cody each morning?

I told him, "At least you won't have to sleep on the cot. You'll like this bed."

After discarding, Cody looked up. "Will you do something for me, before you leave?"

I asked what.

He placed a hand on my knee and squeezed.

My eyebrows gathered. I looked at Cody's hand, then his face.

"Just once," he said. "It's been a rough day and I don't want to sleep alone."

I didn't know what to do. I thought of Dean's perfection. He'd been *way* out of my league; there was no way I could measure up to him and what he'd meant to Cody.

Say something.

"I'm not your brother," I told Cody. "I'm just a skater with zits."

Cody reached for my cheek and stroked it with his thumb. "It doesn't matter, Zach. You're my best friend; my *only* friend."

I hadn't touched a man sexually since my arrest. Already my cock was stiff and my pulse quickened.

Do it, stupid; do it for Cody.

Do it for you, too.

We lay naked on my bedsheets, Cody and I, each guy gripping the other's erection. Our lips smacked and our tongues rubbed. My heart thumped while my belly did flip-flops. I kept running my fingers through Cody's hair, marveling at its thickness and texture. I kissed his eyelids, his forehead and the tip of his freckled nose. When he took my cock in his mouth and sucked the glans, I groaned so loud I'm surprised my parents didn't hear me.

Actually, I think they did.

Cody worked my cock with his tongue and lips. It felt heavenly. His mouth was warm and wet, so sensual. I shifted position so I could return the favor. Then we both slurped away. I loved the scent of Cody's crotch. How *different* this was from sex in Oleander Park. I was making love with my best friend, the guy who'd stood by me when no one else would.

What a fool I'd been, turning down Cody at the beach motel. Sure, I'd been angry because he'd hidden his sex life from me all those years, but hadn't *I* done the same to Cody? Now that he was in my bed, I couldn't get enough of him. I wrapped my arms around his waist and squeezed as hard as I could.

Okay, I wasn't Dean Barton—I didn't have his looks or his athleticism—but at least I was there for Cody. I found Cody's lanky frame sexy; I liked touching him intimately. Maybe I could offer him a small measure of what he needed. Not just tonight, but in the future, if he'd let me.

UCF's only a ninety-minute drive from Clearwater. Maybe—

"Zach?"

"Yeah?"

"Will you fuck me?"

I greased my cock with lube from the nightstand drawer. Then I greased Cody's. He straddled me and sat on my erection. It was like nothing I'd ever experienced. I felt the clench of his pucker, the warmth of his gut when I entered him. Moonlight let me see the expressions on Cody's face while I thrust inside his body and he stroked himself. He looked drugged, as though he were far removed from reality.

A shiver ran through me when I came. My lungs pumped and my body jerked each time I shot. I closed my eyes while fireworks exploded in my head. Moments later, Cody cried out my name when he blew his load. His semen sprayed my chest and collarbone; it felt warm and viscous, teeming with his life force.

My cock still inside him, Cody bent at the waist and kissed my eyebrows. "That was wonderful, Zach. Is it okay if I tell you I love you?"

Tears leaked from the corners of my eyes. Snot crowded my nose and my lips quivered. I felt completely overwhelmed.

This is all you've ever needed: Cody's love. Screw Oleander

Park and screw the kids who bullied us at school. Screw Cody's parents, too. They never deserved him, but I do.

I've earned Cody's love by being his friend.

My mother called to me from beyond the bedroom door.

"Zach, are you and Cody okay?"

I wiped my eyes and sniffled. Then I cleared my throat.

"Yeah, Mom," I said.

"We're both fine."

ONE

T. Hitman

Lyle was already feeling like a pariah when Mike leaned over him to grab another stack of corrugated boxes off the shelf. He tried his best not to gawk or react, difficult feats to pull off given the closeness of the other man's bare legs, so solid and furry; the hypnotic scent of him, a trace of fresh, masculine sweat mixed with the deodorant Mike had slapped on earlier that morning; the meaty fullness packed into the front of his camouflage cutoffs—all tempting Lyle to steal a glance.

The atmosphere in the warehouse was tense enough and growing worse with every day that passed since Kevin Collins had pointed out the bear paw-print sticker on the back bumper of Lyle's truck. It wasn't a rainbow flag, but it hadn't taken much after that to polarize the men. Even Mike had been less of a buddy in recent weeks. The handsome, late-thirtysomething go-to guy that Lyle had fallen in crush with on Day One had gotten colder and quieter since Collins spilled the news about what the sticker meant to the rest of the warehouse crew.

"Help me a sec?" Mike's deep, powerful voice shattered the spell Lyle had fallen under—but not the temptation to look, to draw in a deep breath of the Mike-flavored air, thus taking at least a part of the other man inside him. Penetration by proxy, Lyle thought.

"Sure."

Together they lugged two more stacks of unassembled corrugated cardboard boxes onto the pallet, filling the first of the morning's orders.

Unable to resist, Lyle let his eyes wander for a few dangerous seconds, just enough time to drink in Mike's unrivaled magnificence. His dark hair, in a neat athlete's haircut, was going silver around the edges, right above his ears. An old T-shirt bearing the logo of the local pro baseball team showcased the muscles of his chest and arms to perfection, the pits damp with sweat, the collar near his throat prickly with a thatch of dark hair that trailed up into the days-old scruff coating the lower half of his handsome face.

Mike's ass was high and square, a leftover from his years in the army that he'd maintained by playing all of the Big Four sports—baseball in the summer, ice hockey in the winter, pigskin and hoops in the seasons between. His old construction boots flashed a hint of clean white sock at the top. When you factored in Mike's blue eyes, which looked wounded even when he smiled, the dimple on his right cheek, and his no-bullshit, easy-going blue-collar work ethic, the end result was almost blinding to behold.

And impossible to ignore.

Lyle picked up the work order. "Anything else I can help you with?"

"Nope," Mike said.

Lyle forced himself to look away as the other man grabbed

the pallet jack's hydraulic handle and gave it a few firm pumps, ignoring the ache in his stomach signaling that Kevin Collins and the other straight, intolerant yahoos who toiled in the aisles of the cavernous State Street Warehouse had turned Mike against him. He was alone now. One.

Despite the endless succession of jerk-off fantasies that had sustained Lyle over the past few months, he had no illusions about the truth of the situation. He was twenty-eight, living by himself in a one-bedroom apartment a few miles and a pair of right turns up the road from State Street. Mike was straight, ten years older, a lone wolf if the snippets and sound bites Lyle had collected turned out to be true. Wasn't married, but most likely kept at least one if not a bunch of lady friends at the ready, because he was a man and men had needs.

Lyle understood a man's needs better than he gave himself credit for.

That afternoon, about an hour before the jarring buzzer would sound, releasing them all from what sometimes felt like modern-day slavery, Lyle spotted Mike standing alone on the loading dock, leaning against the wall, one giant foot crossed over the other. He was staring off into space, his blue eyes—bluer than even the sky—oblivious to Lyle's presence.

The knot in Lyle's stomach pulled tighter. He wanted to march over, to ask Mike how he was doing, was everything all right between them, any chance he could explain his side of what Kevin had turned into the biggest scandal to hit State Street Warehouse since the previous year's Christmas party, which was still spoken about occasionally during lunch breaks by the other knuckle draggers. But his sneakers wouldn't obey his heart, and he kept right on walking.

The next day, Mike didn't show up for work. Nor did he the

day after that. By Friday, Lyle was feeling isolated and shunned by the rest of the warehouse. The last of his kind.

"Hey, Kevin," Lyle said.

The other man took a step back, coughed to clear his throat, and said, "Not so close. I don't want to get what you have. What up, homo?"

Lyle gaped, " 'Scuse me?"

"Homes. What up, *homes*?"

Lyle let it slide. The under-the-breath comments, snickers, and stares had gotten too obvious to blame on simple paranoia. Lyle didn't eat lunch with the rest of the warehouse workers any more, and rarely spoke to any of them, except on an as-needed basis. Even approaching Kevin to ask about Mike had taken more effort than not allowing his gaze to linger too long on his hunky supervisor, before Mike had gone missing.

"Have to ask you something."

"What about—sports? Pussy?"

Lyle ignored the snark. "Mike—where the hell is Mike?"

"Big Mike?" Kevin parroted. "He didn't tell you?" Lyle shrugged. "Hate to be the one to break the news, seeing as how much guys like you love another man's balls. Mike had to have one of his lopped off. Cancer, dude. Bet that ruins your day almost as much as his."

Kevin walked away, leaving Lyle frozen where he stood. From the corner of his eye, Lyle saw the other man yank the leg of his loose-fit shorts up. He turned in time to see Kevin's balls spill into the open. Kevin wagged his hairy sac at him, chuckled, and continued on his way.

The rest of the afternoon passed in a blur. Lyle felt numb, going through the motions, only partially aware of time and space. The few times he tried to press his coworkers for more information, he was met with apathy and condescension. Mike's boss told Lyle he couldn't discuss the situation due to medical privacy laws.

With no other option, Lyle consulted a reliable fallback: the telephone book in the junk drawer in his kitchen.

Heart galloping, he approached the apartment block's front door. The building was an ugly, square, brick throwback to the 1970s with zero personality. The kind of place that unleashed a feeling of despair in Lyle whenever he saw one, a place where hopelessness was a tenant. Not fitting for the caliber of a man like Mike.

For days, Lyle had picked up the phone only to hang it up again before dialing past the first few numbers. Driving to the place, parking his truck with its bear-paw bumper sticker in the spot right next to Mike's rugged SUV, Lyle felt like a stalker. He almost backed out and drove away, but killed the ignition and pocketed the keys before he chickened out.

There was no denying the fact that Lyle was attracted to Mike. That mysterious chemical spark had flared the moment they'd first shaken hands in the warehouse. Hell, he hadn't pumped his cock thinking about anyone else for months, hadn't slept with another warm body for much longer than that, was sustained only by his fantasies because contrary to what Kevin and the others thought, Lyle wasn't the kind of guy who slept with a different dude every night. He was a romantic at heart—and his heart had been captured by one man and one man only, Mike Logan.

Sometimes, Lyle would do a crazy trick he'd performed when he was younger: lay in bed with his spine braced against the headboard and his legs over his head, jerking his dick until he shot into his open and hungry mouth. In those moments, he pretended the juice was Mike's as he devoured it, jealous and envious of every mouth that had tasted the legit thing in the real world.

But as much as he lusted after Mike's body, he also really liked Mike, the human being. And being a good friend meant helping a person out when he was down, even if he hadn't asked for it.

Lyle grabbed the bag containing a six-pack and a package of cookies off the passenger seat and tromped up the brick stairs to the door, his heart pounding in his chest. He found the right apartment and buzzed, then waited. After several interminably long seconds, the squawk box squawked.

"Yeah?"

"Hey, Mike," Lyle said, his already-dry mouth draining of the last of its spit. "It's Lyle. From work."

He added the last part in haste—quantifying his identity spared him from how he knew it would feel if Mike asked *Who?* Then he thought, *How many Lyles can the man know?*

The intercom died. The squeak of a door's hinges from somewhere deep in the apartment building's dark interior sounded, alerting Lyle to a flash of motion from beyond the security door's glass. Mike. He appeared and opened the door.

"Hey, man," Lyle said, smiling widely.

"Dude," Mike greeted him, indifferent.

It took the greatest effort not to stare at Mike's clean white T-shirt, blue jeans, and bare feet. Lyle did, however, notice that Mike's puppy-dog eyes looked even more wounded than usual.

"Hope you don't mind me dropping in like this."

"Why are you here?" Mike growled.

Lyle shrugged. "Thought you could use a friendly face. The baseball game's coming on, and I brought beer."

Mike smiled, but the gesture contained little humor. "You know?"

Lyle nodded.

"I'm off the beer for a while."

"I also brought cookies."

Mike drew in a deep breath, his annoyance—hell, his anger—obvious, barely contained. But just when Lyle figured he'd made a mistake in coming here, Mike's furry mouth curled into a smile that was more convincing than its predecessor. "What kind of cookies?"

"Chocolate chip. The soft, squishy kind, from the bakery," Lyle said. "Only the best for you, man."

The apartment was a typical bachelor's cave, with mismatched furniture. A soft and overstuffed chair in front of a widescreen TV hooked up to the usual gadgets and games, a baseball poster tacked to one wall beside it. Mike's familiar work boots sat just inside the door, a discarded pair of sweat socks bunched inside them. Several pill bottles littered the top of the kitchen table, along with stacks of unopened mail and a stroke magazine.

"So how are you doing, big Mike?" Lyle said, drawing in a deep breath of the Mike-scented air.

"How do you think?"

Lyle shrugged. "Probably not too good."

"No, probably not," Mike said.

Lyle set the bag down on the counter and pulled out the cookies. "I wanted to bring you something, but I didn't peg you as the flower or fruit basket type."

Mike snorted, slumped into his big chair, and thumbed the remote. Lyle tossed the beer into the fridge, which was populated by a threadbare collection of protein shakes, yogurt, and bottles of sports drinks. He picked up the cookies but wasn't in the mood to eat them any more than Mike seemed to be.

"So when are you coming back to work?"

"Don't know. Depends on how I feel. Next week, maybe."

"Good, because it isn't the same there without you."

Mike sighed, flipped through channels to the pregame show, then continued on through the dial. The air in the apartment, except for the hollow cadence of channels flying past on the TV screen, fell oppressively silent. At the periphery of Lyle's line of sight, he glimpsed thick black leg hair poking out of the cuffs of denim, right above Mike's ankles, and the undeniable sexiness of the other man's enormous bare feet. If he forced his eyes to roam higher, he'd easily be able to track his way up to Mike's crotch. Lyle desperately wanted to look but couldn't make himself do it. It grew harder by the second to breathe.

"Kevin Collins still being a dickhead to you?" Mike asked, bringing Lyle out of his trance.

"Huh?"

"I warned him, last day I was on the job. Told him to cut the shit or I'd show him some serious harassment."

Lyle waved a hand to dismiss it. "He is, as you've said, a dickhead. But don't worry about it. You've got bigger things on your plate."

"He *has* been harassing you? Fuckin' asshole," Mike sighed. "I know about you. About what, you know, you're into."

Lyle choked down a heavy swallow. The words he planned to offer in his defense died somewhere in his throat.

"You got a guy?"

Lyle shook his head. "You got a girl?"

"Naw," Mike said. "I haven't gotten laid since...shit, like a hundred years before the surgery. Don't even know if I can still perform."

"Course you can," Lyle said. "Can't you?"

"Not exactly been in the mood. Haven't felt much like trying, being as I'm half the man I used to be."

"Are you kidding? Look at that dude Lance Armstrong. Losing a nut didn't stop him from being a stud. That handsome fucker was screwing the hottest chick in rock and roll for a while."

Mike shrugged. "I appreciate you saying that, but I'm not much of a stud anymore."

"Oh, man," Lyle chuckled. "Lance ain't got nothing on you...."

Eyes narrowed, Mike said, "Shut the fuck up."

"Seriously, you're the whole package."

"Bad choice of words," Mike said, pointing at his crotch.

"Heart, soul—and with a super-sized dose of handsome thrown in."

Mike's face went red as he broke their gaze, but his smile persisted. "But with half the balls."

"There's more to a man's being sexy than whether he has two balls or one," Lyle said. "Case in point, Kevin thought he was being funny the other day when he wagged his raisin-nuts at me in the warehouse."

Anger flashed across Mike's face. "He did *what?*"

"Trust me when I tell you, the joke was on him. Kevin may have both his balls, but he's nowhere the man you are," Lyle continued. He realized that he'd started to ramble, but now that it was all out on the table, he couldn't stop himself, and probably wouldn't have if given the choice. "If you're asking, I'll tell you. Tell you why. For starters, those puppy-dog eyes of yours. How you don't shave for a couple of days, and you get all that scruff. It's so sexy."

"It's *lazy.*"

"It makes you look like a pirate, a palooka," Lyle said. "And when it's a hundred fuckin' degrees in that warehouse and your arms are dripping with sweat, you still look like a million bucks. Those hairy legs of yours...fuck, even your big feet."

"My feet?" Mike snorted again.

"Yeah, in those old work boots. It drives me crazy to see you strutting around in them, especially when you wear your camouflage cutoffs. Makes your butt insanely hot. And, of course, your bulge. So you got one nut less now, big deal. I bet your one is still fatter than most other dudes' two."

The knowledge that he was blathering and had crossed the line finally struck Lyle.

"Shit, I'm sorry, man. I shouldn't have said all that."

Lyle stood. He started for the door, but Mike's voice stopped him from retreating.

"Wait," Mike said.

Lyle hit the brakes and revolved.

"Since this happened, you're the only guy from work who's made the effort to ask how I'm doing. Thanks for saying it, for making me feel good about myself."

"Any time," Lyle said. "I think you're a hell of a guy."

"My feet," Mike repeated, lifting up one of his giants and examining it. "You think they're sexy?"

"Oh, very much so," Lyle said. "Most men don't know it, but their feet are their most underrated sex organs."

Lyle couldn't believe what happened next, any more than Mike seemed able to comprehend just how incredible the unthinkable idea could feel. With the baseball game droning on low in the background, Lyle sat Indian-style between Mike's legs. Mike reclined in his big chair, offering his feet, one at a time, into Lyle's hands.

"*Dude...*" Mike moaned.

Lyle applied gentle but firm pressure and massaged Mike's naked foot from ankle to instep, sole to topside, eventually reaching toes. Starting with the small one, Lyle rubbed them in order, all the way to the big toe.

Mike shifted in his seat and groaned, signs that Lyle at first assumed were due to the other man's discomfort.

"Want me to stop?"

"Hell, no," Mike sighed, closing his eyes. His hairy throat knotted with a difficult swallow, something not lost on Lyle. As aware of Mike as he was, Lyle didn't realize his cock had gotten stiff until he shifted to accommodate the man's other foot.

"You're sure?"

"Feels great, pal," Mike said, his voice barely above a whisper.

Lyle drew in a deep breath. "I can make it feel even better... if you want."

Eyes still closed, Mike nodded.

Lyle raised Mike's foot to his mouth and began to suckle his big toe, as though it were a smaller version of his cock.

"Fuck," Mike growled. "Aw, fuck..."

Lyle continued nursing on Mike's toes, but worried he'd gone too far, that the realization of the line they'd crossed would hit fully home to Mike, sending a man who had already been sorely tested by life in recent weeks into a blind rage.

"*Fuck*," Mike repeated.

Lyle glanced up to see Mike's eyes were open, as if tele-graphing that he had, indeed, come out of his trance, had landed hard and found another dude touching and tasting him in a way most straight men would find unthinkable.

Lyle spit the toe out of his mouth. "Mike?"

"I don't fuckin' believe it. Dude..."

For several tense seconds, Lyle was sure Mike was going to deck him. But then Mike snaked both hands down to his crotch and hastily unzipped his blue jeans. He fished out his dick and let it hang in clear view, gloriously hard.

"I haven't gotten a boner since this whole fuckin' nightmare started," Mike said, a wide smile breaking across his handsome face. "Not since…fuck…thanks, man."

Mike eased his foot away from Lyle's mouth and leaned forward, cupping his cheeks in both powerful hands. A mix of relief and giddy excitement flooded Lyle's insides.

"I told you there were other parts of your body more important, you know, than balls," Lyle said, smiling back.

For a moment, he wondered if Mike, overwhelmed by excitement, might actually kiss him, crush their mouths together, perhaps wrangle Lyle's tongue into submission with his. The look in Mike's eyes said all that his lips could not, that Lyle had pulled him back from the dead, had saved him body and soul, and that Lyle had given him a better gift than any woman—any *person*—ever had.

"So how about you help me out with this part, now," Mike growled, releasing Lyle's face and giving his cock a shake.

By the time Mike returned to the job, Lyle had revealed other secrets about his body Mike hadn't considered before the surgery, that toes and earlobes, throat and armpits, legs and asshole could also give a man an amazing erection thanks to the licks of another male's tongue, if he simply opened himself up to the possibilities of finding love in unexpected places.

Lyle didn't see Kevin's elbow coming at him. Lightning quick, the powerful jab collided with his shoulder, knocking him into the nearby shelf.

"Sorry," Kevin said. It was obvious by the chuckle he added that he really wasn't.

Lyle straightened. Less than a minute later, Kevin was on his knees in front of him, held in place by a powerful armlock.

"Apologize," Mike ordered.

"Let go of me, fucker!"

"Oh, dude, I'm *this close* to letting you go—right out the fuckin' door, unless you make good with your esteemed coworker and cut the shit."

"I was just joking around," Kevin pleaded.

"Nobody's laughing. This guy you've been fucking with has more balls than you, me, and the rest of the warehouse combined. I see or hear one more deliberate attack against him, I'll clean house. You and your pals got that straight?"

"Yeah," Kevin muttered, surrendering. "I'm sorry."

Mike released him. "Now prove it. Get the fuck back to work!"

Kevin grumbled a blue streak of curses under his breath, but none of them were directed against Lyle.

"You okay, pal?" Mike asked.

Lyle rubbed his shoulder. "Sure am."

Mike nodded and turned to go, but then pivoted back in Lyle's direction. "You up for hanging out tonight?"

"Always."

"Game's on, and maybe you could stay over. You know…"

"Love to," Lyle said.

As he turned to continue filling the order he'd been picking when Kevin side-armed him, Mike gave Lyle's butt a friendly pat. Lyle cast a look at the prominent bulge in Mike's camouflage pants, no longer afraid of stealing glances because permission had been granted.

The ones had become two.

THE FALLS

Natty Soltesz

Randy Perletti came out of the closet when he was nineteen. His mom cried. His dad stayed silent and retreated to the backyard shed. A few hours later his older sister, Becky, called from her apartment in Pittsburgh.

"How could you do this to them?" she said with all the righteousness she could muster from her three-and-a-half years as a psychology major. "You're their only son, Randy. Can't you understand how this would affect them? Don't you want to get married and have kids someday?"

Randy sighed. For much of his first semester at college he'd been holed up in his dorm room exchanging blow jobs with his well-hung roommate, Chuck. Chuck had undergone a Christian reawakening just a week before, though, and had asked for a room exchange.

Randy was no stranger to curious straight boys and their post–blow job blues. Usually he'd ignore the pain, but this one had left him feeling weirdly courageous. If God took stock in the fact that you liked the smell of your lacrosse-playing roommate's sweaty balls, well, what did that say about God?

"Love is the most sacred thing you can experience," Becky continued, "and you want to write it off, just like that."

"Give me a fucking break, Becky. Just 'cause you have a boyfriend now after, like, eight years of crying into your pillow and listening to Karen Carpenter doesn't make you an expert on relationships." Becky didn't say anything. "I'm gay. Get the fuck over it." He hung up the phone and headed upstairs.

"Where are you going?" his dad called from the couch.

"To my room," Randy said, exasperated. His parents watched him, as though fascinated that gay people ascended staircases to rooms.

Fortunately his parents were still in shock that spring when Randy dropped his second bomb and told them he wasn't going back to school. They even let him move back home. He got a job washing dishes at the diner and another job cleaning buildings on Market Street. He was saving money (he wasn't sure what for) and still had enough for gas and a weekly lid of pot. He was happy at home in Groom, Pennsylvania, where things were safe and familiar. Most of his high school buddies were still around. A few of them were more than pleased to have him back, for Randy was as discreet as he was up for anything.

Randy met Becky's boyfriend, Dominic Posvar, for the first time on Memorial Day at his parents' house.

"I've heard a lot about you," Randy said, shaking Dom's hand which, like the rest of him, was thick and strong.

"Me, too," Dom said, and he blushed. Becky was engaged to Dom by then and was in the midst of planning an insanely elaborate ceremony, wringing as much stress and drama from the process as she could. Randy figured it was her punishment to the world for not having noticed her sooner.

Randy was asked to be a groomsman, but stuck to the side-lines as the wedding date neared, grateful that the family's atten-tion had been diverted from him. Dom seemed glad to acquiesce to Becky's whims and go with the flow. He wasn't unfriendly to Randy, nor did he reach out, but as the weeks went by Randy started noticing things: glances that lasted too long, nervous tics whenever they were together in a room. A telepathic dialogue was manifesting itself.

Dom bunked at the Perletti house the night before the wedding, while Becky stayed with her bridesmaids across town. Randy was up late watching TV when Dom came downstairs, wearing a white V-neck T-shirt that hugged his muscles, and blue pajama pants.

"Hey," he said to Randy. Randy hadn't expected anyone to be up this late and was wearing just his boxers. He didn't mind showing off his thin, defined body, which was tanned a golden brown.

Dom seemed half asleep. He rubbed his hands over his close-shorn, sandy-haired head, then shuffled to the kitchen and poured a glass of milk. He sat down on the couch next to Randy.

"What are you doing up?" Randy asked.

"Just jittery I guess. What about you?"

"Too much coffee at the rehearsal dinner. Well, that and I'm nervous too. First family gathering since...well...you know." Dom's head snapped to the TV. He took a too-quick drink of his milk and it spilled down the sides of his mouth.

"Crap," he said and lifted his shirt to wipe his face. Randy couldn't help but look. Dom's stomach was thick but tight, with a blondish happy trail that disappeared into his pajama pants.

"I guess it's normal to be nervous," Randy said, shifting his gaze. "Anyway I'm sure Becky would understand if you changed your mind." Dom smiled. He took another swig from the glass, this one more successful.

"I just wish it was over," Dom said. Randy gave him a sympathetic smile. After a moment, Dom lifted his shirt again. He wiped his mouth even though there wasn't anything there, and he did it slowly. He watched Randy gaze at his body as he tugged his shirt back down, until their eyes met and they realized they'd caught each other in the act.

So Becky got hitched and Randy got drunk. The new couple bought a house in Groom just a few blocks from the Perletti house. Dom, who had a bachelor's degree in communications, took a job managing the Groom Motor Lodge on the highway while Becky looked for work.

One night after the newlyweds came for dinner at the Perletti house, Randy fell asleep in the easy chair while Dom watched TV from the couch. The first thing Randy noticed when he awoke was Dom watching him. Dom quickly averted his eyes back to the TV, his face flushing. Randy reddened himself when he realized what Dom had been staring at—a conspicuous tent in his sweats from the industrial-sized boner he'd sprung in his sleep.

The next Friday Becky recruited her brother to help paint the new couple's bedroom. When he arrived Dom was already rolling paint onto the walls, and Becky was getting dressed for a job interview in Latrobe.

"They called me at the last minute," she said. "Hopefully you guys will be all right?"

"I'm sure we can manage," Randy said. Becky looked to her husband.

"Dom? You'll be okay with just Randy here?"

"Why wouldn't we be?" Randy said again. Becky ignored him.

"Sure, honey," Dom said, and Becky said she'd be back in a few hours.

There was some brief awkwardness after she left, but small talk was one of Randy's strengths, and he easily maneuvered them into friendly waters.

"Is married life all it's cracked up to be?" he asked as he loaded up his brush with periwinkle paint.

"I wasn't expecting anything, I don't think," Dom said. "It's nice though. You know—comfortable. I don't have to wonder about, like, going out on a Friday night, looking for whatever, getting drunk. That gets old."

"You don't like to drink?" Randy said.

"Well, sometimes I do."

"Good, cause I brought a six-pack. We can split it." By the time they finished painting they had two beers left. They were cleaning off their brushes and rollers in the utility room, the close quarters heady with the smell of sweaty bodies.

"Wish the pool was still open," Dom said.

"We should go up to Bolivar Falls," Randy said. "You ever been?"

"No," Dom said, then hesitated. Into the vacuum of his silence rushed sexual tension. Randy hadn't intended it, but there it was.

"I've heard of it," Dom continued, whacking a brush off the side of the sink. "We could take the rest of the beer."

"Sure," Randy said, his heart picking up speed. "Becky won't care, right? We can leave her a note or something."

"Don't bother," Dom said.

After a ten-minute drive they started the two-mile hike into the woods. They were soaked in sweat again by the time they got to the falls, a forest glen with a creek that dropped off into a deep pool. There was graffiti on the rocks and some strewn-about trash, but it had a secretive charm.

"I guess we can go in in our underwear?" Randy said.

"Sure," Dom said, emboldened by the beer and the beauty of the place. He stripped down and Randy followed suit. Dom's tighty-whities hugged the generous curves of his muscular butt and acted like a sling for his beefy cock. Randy was embarrassed to reveal his patterned bikini briefs—a purchase he'd made out of boredom and horniness one night while stuck at the mall with his mom.

Dom swept his eyes up and down Randy's body and Randy did the same to Dom. Before either could register anything Dom turned and ran for the ledge, springing himself over the waterfall and into the air, crashing into the pool below.

"It's freezing!" he called. Randy approached the edge. He felt the slick rock beneath his feet. He jumped, fear and release rushing through his body for a drawn-out instant before he plunged into the water.

"It feels fucking amazing!" Randy said, his breathing short and shallow. They laughed with exhilaration.

Later they lay on the warm rock above the waterfall.

"Did you have a good time at the wedding?" Dom asked.

"Yeah, man."

"It wasn't awkward for you? I mean, you said you thought it might be."

"Well, the open bar helped." Dom laughed. "I don't care what people think of me, anyway," Randy said. Dom drank the last of his beer.

"You mean the fact that you're..."

"Gay. Yeah. That."

"Yeah," Dom said. Birds squawked in the trees. "I was wondering... Like, how did you know you were? I mean, did you ever date girls?"

"Yeah I dated girls. I even had sex with a few of them."

"Really?"

"Yeah. But I always did stuff with my friends, too. And eventually I realized that stuff was more interesting."

"You messed around with your friends?" Dom said.

"Yeah."

"Like what kind of stuff?"

"Like, you know. Kissing. More than kissing," Randy said. Dom brought the beer bottle to his lips, tipped it back even though it was empty. Randy took a deep breath. "Did you ever do stuff like that? Like before you met Becky?"

"No," Dom said. He turned his head to Randy and smiled. "Not even kissing."

"Kissing's easy," Randy said. "You know—noncommittal."

Dom laughed. "I'd try that. Kissing a guy."

"It's not much different from kissing a girl," Randy said, nervously plugging his thumb into the mouth of his beer bottle.

Dom stood up. He tossed his empty bottle into the weeds and turned toward Randy. His half-hard cock tented his transparent briefs. Randy set down his bottle and stood up next to him, his hefty dick also visibly at half-mast.

"You want to?" Dom said.

"Kiss?" Randy said.

"Yeah," Dom said. They moved toward each other, their cocks hardening. When they came together an involuntary, almost reflexive force took over. Their mouths locked and their tongues dueled, desire passing between them thick and hot as molten rock. Randy moved his hands to Dom's back. Dom placed his hands on the smooth sides of Randy's torso. Making out with Dom felt natural and breathtaking, but it was just too much. Randy had to break away.

"Thanks," Dom said, looking at the ground, and the word

was a hollow thud. They dressed and headed to the car. The world, having disappeared for a moment, rushed back like a tsunami. They rode home in silence, each mile getting them closer to the lives they'd upended.

The strange thing was that after that day, hard as they tried to avoid each other, Becky seemed to do all she could to bring them together. She went whole hog in enlisting Randy's help with their house, making dates that Randy always managed to blow off.

"I saw they just opened a record store on Market Street," she said one night over dinner at the Perlettis'. "You and Dom both like music—you guys should go down there together!"

"Sure," Randy said, and Dom nodded politely, while Becky eyed them like they were lab rats.

"Do you like Dom?" Becky asked her brother one night after dinner. Randy was washing dishes while Becky sat at the kitchen table. Dom had already gone home.

"Of course," Randy said. "Dom's a good guy."

"I think he's about the best-looking guy I've ever seen," Becky said. "Don't you think he's good looking?"

"Yeah, he is," Randy said. "He's got a handsome face."

"Are you happy for me?"

"Of course I am. I'm happy for all of us, 'cause if you hadn't gotten laid soon you would've drove us all nuts."

"Hush up," Becky said. "I hate it when you talk like that." She dipped her finger into a candle, coating the tip with hot wax. "I never thought a guy like Dom would *look* at me, let alone *marry* me."

"Don't say that," Randy said.

Becky shrugged. "I know I'm not the cutest button in the box. But there was Dom, sitting across from me in my Shakespeare class, and he just...I don't know...*listened* to me. Made me feel like I was worth his time. I asked him to go out, and he did. I'd never asked a guy out before. Can you believe that?" Randy toweled off a plate and stacked it with a clink.

"I can," he said, turning toward his sister. "You don't give yourself enough credit, Becky. You've always been shy, but you're great. People just don't get to see it." Becky smiled and cast her eyes downward. Randy went to bed that night with a heavy heart.

On Labor Day Becky arranged a picnic at their parents' house. Dom wore a pair of thin khaki shorts that made his ass look like wrapped cantaloupes. In the chaos of aunts and uncles and cousins Randy lost track of his brother-in-law. He had to piss, so he entered the quiet house and went up the stairs to the bathroom. The door was closed and the shower was running. He figured it was his dad, so he walked in and shut the door behind him.

"I gotta pee," he said after he'd already unzipped. He heard the shower turn off. "Just gimme one second." The curtain pulled back and Randy turned his head. There was Dom, naked, wet, and already half-hard.

"Shit," Randy said. "Sorry." Dom, who'd needed to clean up after knocking whiffleballs around with the kids in the ninety-degree heat, locked eyes with Randy. He didn't move a muscle except for his cock, which lurched like a thing from the dead until it was standing straight up.

Randy could've left the room. It was probably the right thing to do. But instead he stepped forward and wrapped his hand around Dom's fat cock. He raised his face to meet Dom's mouth. As they made out their hands moved like wildfire, Dom ripping off Randy's clothes, Randy feeling every inch of Dom's body. Randy knelt down, his shorts around his thighs and his hard cock jutting out. He took Dom's cock in his mouth.

Dom's lungs deflated. A few passes of Randy's mouth and

throat around his cock and Dom was almost juicing. Randy licked his way up his brother-in-law's body, munched on his pecs and nipples, then trailed his tongue down Dom's thigh. He flipped him around. Dom braced himself against the shower wall. Dom's ass was a gift, big and perfect, and Randy dove in. His pink, deep asshole seemed to invite Randy to dig deeper with his tongue. Dom whimpered and pushed back harder.

Randy stood and dropped his shorts so that his buckle clanged against the floor. He grabbed a bottle of shampoo and lubed himself up. He pressed his cock to Dom's asshole and in moments he slid inside. Dom stifled a cry but didn't protest as Randy porked him balls-deep. A minute or so of thrusting and Randy was blasting inside Dom's virgin butt and Dom was spraying the shower wall.

They didn't talk as Randy slid out, pulled on his pants, and left. He went to his bedroom and locked the door, caught his breath. When he came back out Dom was with the rest of the family on the patio, freshly showered and freshly fucked. He had a noticeable glow, and even nodded to acknowledge Randy's entrance.

"It was like you tripped a switch in me," Dom would say years later about that afternoon. "I instantly knew how sex was supposed to feel. I felt so relieved." Randy had apparently fucked the fear right out of Dom, and Dom got bold. Two days later he came knocking on Randy's bedroom door. Randy tossed his liquid-crinkled issue of *Mandate* on the floor, zipped up, and answered the door.

"What are you doing here?" Randy said, ushering a wild-eyed Dom inside.

"I told Becky I was borrowing a record," he whispered. Dom impulsively leaned forward and kissed him, knocking their mouths together so hard it hurt. "Here," he said, and handed Randy a key. The plastic, diamond-shaped key ring had the number *428* imprinted on both sides. "I got this room for tonight."

"For us?" Randy said.

"You don't want to come," Dom said, his face falling.

"No, no, of course I do, it's just...Jesus. Okay. When?"

"After two. I'm supposed to be doing paperwork in the back office but the night clerk won't notice." Randy took the key. Dom made it halfway down the hall before Randy thought to call him back. He grabbed the first record off his stack and shoved it in Dom's hands. Dom looked at it: Abba, *Arrival.*

"I already have this one," he said.

Sex at the hotel that night was less furtive than before but even more frenzied. Randy dropped three loads into his brother-in-law in less than two hours—one down his gullet and two in his increasingly insatiable butt.

"I love your dick in me," Dom admitted as they lay beside each other watching the blank TV, the Zen-like hum of the motel room thrumming through them. Then, "Becky wants a baby."

"I'm supposed to be saving money to move to the city," Randy said.

"You're moving?"

"That was the plan. I don't know what the fuck I'm going to do now."

"Me neither," Dom said. They fucked again.

For two more weeks they met at the motel, until Randy couldn't take it anymore and put all he'd saved on a security deposit for an apartment in Pittsburgh. He moved in the middle of the night, telling no one until he called his parents the next day.

That October, Randy heard from his mom that Dom was leaving his sister. No particulars were offered. Randy sensed his mom knew—or at least suspected—more than she was letting on, but he didn't press the issue.

He lay low all winter. He hadn't spoken to Dom since he'd left, though on several occasions he'd driven all the way back to Groom just to see if Dom's car was still parked outside the motel, which it always was.

That spring Randy came home to visit. The divorce had gone through. Becky was even dating a guy named Hugo that she worked with at the state mental hospital in Torrance.

"He likes bird-watching," Randy's mother reported. Randy was weeding her garden. "That's what they do together in their free time, watch birds."

"He sounds nice," Randy said. He'd tried to call his sister the week previous and she'd hung up on him.

"Your Aunt Mary called. She wants the whole family up for the Fourth of July. A reunion, she says. It's a ridiculous idea but you know how she gets."

"Hmm," Randy said, yanking plants.

"Did I ever tell you that your father used to date your Aunt Mary when they were in high school?"

"Huh? No," Randy said.

"They were in love—so *she* said. I suppose she must have felt they were—"

"Her and Dad? How long did they date?"

"Oh, a few years, I think. Even after high school. In fact they talked about getting married at one point."

"You're kidding," Randy said, sitting up to look at his mother, who was gazing into the distance.

"Even today I catch her looking at him. Maybe I just think I do. Who knows?" She shrugged. "Love is love and it doesn't care about anything but itself."

With that she walked away, leaving Randy with a head full of questions and his knees in the dirt.

THE PRISONER

C. C. Williams

I surveyed the items arrayed on the stark, utilitarian bedspread of the guest room: khaki T-shirt; camouflage fatigues; a sandy, dun-colored officer's cap. Tucked neatly beneath the bed stood black combat boots so highly polished it was as if they were carved from obsidian. *I guess we're doing some paramilitary scene.*

Charley waited for me in his bedroom; he'd approached me earlier that night.

I had stopped by Tony's Bar & Grill after a late night at work and sat nursing a Tanqueray while a bored go-go boy gyrated to Lady Gaga's "Born This Way." At first I hadn't recognized Charley; he'd changed so much from our days at the academy. Gone was the vulnerable boy's face, shadowed with inexperience and bright with expectation. His face had filled out; ten years of life lay like a mask across his features. But the voice, soft and insistent, had remained the same. I had a hard time listening to him. While he spoke of joining the Marines and doing several tours of Iraq and Afghanistan, I shut my eyes. And there I saw his young eighteen-year-old face as it had been when we had lain together in the dark—intelligent and beautiful but innocent of the evil that men do.

Stripping off my jeans and polo, I began to don the military gear. Pulling the fatigues up over my thighs, I was surprised to find that we now wore the same size pants. In college I had always out-massed Charley, but our bodies had fit just right; his wiry sprinter's form merged with my wrestler's build, like muscle and sinew entwined on bone. The shirt stretched tight across my more muscular chest and biceps; a tear on the right shoulder opened wider as I pulled on the shirt. Lacing up the combat boots, I noticed a few milky stains around the toes. The spots marred the glossy blackness, and I thought of wiping them off. But I considered they might actually be part of the scene that awaited me. I put on the starched, sweet-smelling officer's cap and tucked some stray hairs behind my ears. I recalled the last time we had been together—a beautiful night, an awful night...

I had returned to our dorm room, worn out after wrestling practice, wanting just a shower and some mindless TV. I switched on the lights, tossing my gym bag on the floor.

"Leave 'em off." Charley's voice was thick and emotional, clogged with something raw. "Please."

Clicking off the fluorescent fixture, I looked to his bed where he lay on his belly, naked. The parted curtains let a splash of moonlight fall across him. He looked like an artsy postcard—except for the welts and livid bruises on his lower back, arms and legs.

"Oh, my god!" I rushed forward and knelt at his bedside. "Are you all right? What happened?"

"Nothing. I don't want to talk about it."

"Can I get you something? Water? Aspirin?" I blurted out, panicked, concerned. "We should go to the infirmary—"

"Shut up, just..." Charley sighed and broke down.

I fought a creeping sense of distance, a feeling of abandonment that pressed on my heart. "Should I leave you alone?"

He reached out, grabbing my hand. "No! Please don't." He squeezed my hand hard.

"What do you want me to do?" I climbed up and sat on the edge of his bed.

After a painful silence, he whispered, "Show me you care."

Just like so many times over the last eight months, I laid my hands on him, marveling at his satiny skin, pressing my fingers into the lithe muscles of his shoulders. I rubbed his back, and he moaned softly. My long fingers crept up his neck to tangle in his dirty-blond hair—it was longer than regulation and needed a trim. I massaged his scalp. Lowering my lips to the small of his back, I kissed around the red, inflamed skin, a crawling sense of dread nibbling at my mind. Dark thoughts invaded me, gray worries of the unknown scudded across my mind like clouds before the moon. Usually, I was breathless with wonder as I reveled in the sensations of his body, awash in a mixture of fear and joy, that stomach-fluttering feeling when you stand on the diving board, before surrendering to the cool breeze and the water that swallows you up.

My hands came to join my lips at his waist. Before I massaged his gorgeous butt, he winced. "Not there—not...tonight."

Sitting upright, I wiped his forehead. "Tell me what happened." I kissed his cheek, nuzzling at him, loving the softness of his day's growth of beard.

"Not yet," he breathed. "Love me everywhere, but not there tonight. Just love me, Jake."

Still dreading the silent unknown, yet moved by the aching

need in his voice, I took him in my arms and picked him up from the bed. Cradled like a baby, he clung to my neck and shoulders, embracing me as tightly as he could. We kissed, our mouths open, panting into each other. We drank from the saliva we exchanged; our tongues dueled for supremacy.

Breaking from the kiss, I licked at him, running my tongue over his lips, his chin, tasting the salt on his tear-stained cheeks. With pursed lips I pecked his cheekbones and eyebrows, blew cool air on his closed eyelids. I covered his nose with kisses, lapping at the bridge, his nostrils, again tasting the saltiness of his pain.

My passion increased as I worshipped him, fired by the feel of soft skin covering solid muscle. Entranced, I bit his neck, licked his shoulders and swallowed up each of his nipples. Straining my back and biceps, I covered his chest and belly with wet, hungry kisses; then lowered my mouth to his erect cock.

"Oh, *yeah!*" Charley gripped my hair. "Eat me up, man, eat me alive."

I sucked at his swollen cock head, swirling the tip of my tongue around the slit and nipping at the curve, clean cut around the edges. He bucked his eight-inch cock against my face, begging with his body to fuck my mouth. I'd become a pretty good cocksucker in the last eight months. Having had only fantasies, I had been inexperienced, but my slightly more experienced roommate had proven to be an excellent teacher.

"Put me down, Jake. I don't want you to hurt yourself." I obeyed, lowering him to the floor. Charley leaned against our dresser, spreading his thighs with a wince. His pale cock stood tall, curving out from his sandy bush. Grabbing his sinewy legs, I dove for his crotch, taking him in with every gulp of air I inhaled. Charley withdrew to some place in his head, arms behind his back, legs spread. Once he stroked my cheek. Once he grabbed his briefs and wiped my nose before snot ran down and mixed with my spit and his precome.

Jerking his rod, I gnawed on his hips and thighs; my nose pressed into his crotch. He smelled like woodsy air, boy sweat, and sex. Testosterone fired my brain, burning away my worries with bright desire. I still wore my wrestling singlet, and my stiff cock strained for release from my jockstrap. Like a dog I rubbed my dick against his calf.

"Yeah! Hump my fucking leg, boy. Hump away while I fuck your hand with my cock. Don't stop, asshole. Don't you dare stop."

Charley was unusually aggressive in his love talk, so I wondered what was playing out in his head. *Who are you talking to?*

"God, I want so much for you to fuck me right now. To bend me over and spread my white ass. Hock a big gob of snot down on my crack, and poke it in me with your thumb—running that thumb around my hole, opening it up for your big, veiny cock. You thrusting in and fucking me harder and harder. I'll pretend, yeah, pretend that you're going to fill me up for the rest of my life."

Unsure of what I was hearing, I looked up. "Do you want me to?"

His body writhed, and he grimaced in the moonlight. That meant he was getting close. "No! Just keep loving me hard like you're doing now. Aww, shit—"

Shuddering, he collapsed against me. His dick erupted, shooting a ropy load up onto my neck and shoulders. He continued to orgasm, letting go a second and third time, thickly coating my hand with his white cream. Never had I seen him shoot more than twice. Before I could grab for a towel, Charley was licking me clean. He seemed to have returned to the moment; he sighed. "I'm sorry. I was selfish. Let me suck you off."

"No," I replied. Standing, I pulled him up and hugged him. "I just wanted to make you feel good,"

"You sure did that!" He licked my jaw. "You'll never know how much."

Pushing away from him, I held him at arms' length. "Charley, tell me what happened—now!"

"I need a drink first." A moment later, dressed in his tattered bathrobe, he sipped whiskey from a Dixie cup. Contraband whiskey I kept far back under my bed. His fingers tapped on the cup as he paced the room. I stood by the dresser, confused, feeling embarrassed, still smelling of sex and wrestling practice. He took a deep breath. "You know Trey Hauser."

"The dumb-ass bully? Of course!" Hauser, a rich, legacy senior, regularly sought out and bullied the scholarship guys. He and his little gang were two years ahead of us.

"He's been harassing me for a while now—most of the year."

"Shit." I sat on my bed and poured myself more whiskey.

"He's been leaving notes in my books, my gym locker, even under the door. Notes that say things like *Cocksucker* or *Ass Licker*. He's cornered me after lunch, between classes, grabbing at my uniform and messing it up. He'll say, 'You're mine, fag,' or 'One of these days, I'll get you.'

"A couple of weeks ago he and three of his friends came at me. He called me a pussy and grabbed my nipple. They just laughed and watched me squirm. Then Trey said, 'Come on. Tell me what a pussy you are and I'll let go.' He squeezed so hard I had to obey or he'd have torn a hole in my fucking chest!"

That explained the ugly bruise; Charley's story about stabbing himself with a marking pen had been pretty lame.

"Well, a few days ago, I'd had enough. I told Trey I was going to report him to the Commandant. I don't know how much good it would do—Trey's father graduated with him, so they're like best buddies. But I threatened to tell him everything.

"'You'll be dead,' Trey said.

"'Fuck you,' I said. In fact, I was going to tell the Major tonight. But when you went to practice, Trey and his buddies showed up." Charley held out the paper cup, and I splashed in more liquor.

"The four of them grabbed me outside the front door, dragged me down to the boiler room and stripped me." Charley's hand shook as he sipped at the liquid. "Trey had brought along his razor strop—that pretentious fuck with his old-fashioned shaving kit! His friends held me down. I struggled and struggled; I just couldn't get away.

"He said, 'Bend him over.' They held my arms and legs, while Trey beat my ass with his strop. He said he wouldn't stop until I begged him to fuck me. I wouldn't." Charley shook his head, reliving the memory.

"I didn't even cry at first. He just kept hitting me and hitting me—god, it must've gone on for ten, fifteen minutes. Maybe longer! I could hardly breathe; it was like my ass was on fire. I finally broke down—I let out a scream and cried and cried. Trey and his buddies just laughed. I couldn't stand it anymore. I...begged...for it. And Trey...Trey gave it to me." He dashed tears away with the back of his wrist. Sniffling, he took a shot of whiskey.

Bile rose in my throat, burning away the mellowness of the whiskey. My heart ached with rage. My arms tensed; I wanted to pound something, pound on something again and again until there was nothing left.

"I..." I had no words.

Charley didn't move, just stood sipping from the crumpled paper cup. "It wasn't like us, Jake. It was...ugly, violent. Then...they...did it...too... I closed my eyes and imagined that

I was somewhere else, making love with you."

My anger gave way to sorrow. I remembered the first time we'd made love: how Charley had guided me to fuck him, nice and slow, tempering my pent-up desire into slower-burning passion. How each day I would anticipate the wavelike rhythms of our lovemaking at night, the way we would breathe into each other's mouths.

"I feel so ashamed." He choked back a sob.

"You have to report this." I touched his shoulder. "I'll stand with you, be your witness."

"What good would it do? Trey spotted me as a butt licker the minute I walked into this place." Charley shrugged off my hand and moved to face the window. Silvery light highlighted the tracks of tears on his face. I wanted to dry them, make the whole episode go away.

"It was just a matter of time before it came out." He leaned on the windowsill, swirling the cup, and then downed the rest of the liquor. "You know, people feel sorry for you, having to room with the likes of me."

"I said that I'll stand with you—I'll admit everything about me too."

"Why should you? Nobody suspects you're a fag. You're a wrestler. You're a man." He hurled *man* as if it were an obscenity. "I'm just the nelly little runner. Fuck. No matter how fast I run, they always catch me." He sat on his bed, cradling his head in his hands.

I wanted to show him that this time was different, to prove to him that not everyone was against him. But I didn't know how; in my heart I feared I was wrong, feared that my love wouldn't be enough. Apprehension throttled me and I had nothing supportive to say, so I sat on the floor, resting my head against his thigh, and stroked his calf. "Then we'll leave. We'll transfer out of here and go to a better school. I'll protect you. I'll never—ever—let anyone hurt you again."

Charley's hand stroked my hair. We held each other for a long time, cuddling together in the dark. He said only two words the rest of the night: "Thank you."

The next morning I awoke to find Charley gone.

In the following days nobody would tell me where he went. His parents hung up when I called; my letters were returned unopened. Confusion and heartache turned to bitterness as I finished out the year and then transferred to State, giving my folks a cock-and-bull story about the "lousy politics that prevented me from fulfilling my athletic potential."

Feeling sullen and rejected, I had sex with no one until three years later, when I took a lover in grad school. By then my broken heart had scabbed over and Charley entered my thoughts only rarely, usually when I buried myself in my lover's ass, rocking against his smooth back and listening to him purr with contentment.

Before leaving the guest room, I shook my head, clearing away the memories. I'd been so transported that now more than ever I regretted not standing up for Charley. *I should have gone after that fuckhead Trey, taken his strop and beat him senseless in front of his shitty friends.* I wondered what Charley thought. He'd not said a word about that night.

Entering Charley's room, I found myself transported into a different scene. The bedroom was austere: a gray-sheeted double bed against the wall, no rug, the only other furnishing standing opposite the bed—a wooden construction composed of a sturdy upright and a crossbeam; it resembled a crucifix. Desolation filled the room; the air itself felt devoid of any happiness, and that depressed me.

Leaning against the cross, Charley held his hands behind his back. Barefoot, he wore torn camouflage pants and a stained green tank top that clung to his well-developed torso. Dog tags hung from his neck, resting in the valley between his pecs. His hair was mussed, and he had smudged soot or something across his nose and cheeks. He stared at me, his eyes daring me to pass judgment on him. Again I was struck by how he had changed. Not just older, he'd become different: he was not the adult that my Charley would have become. His arc had been altered.

"I'm your prisoner of war." His voice sounded flat, matter-of-fact. His eyes never left mine. "You're responsible for interrogating me. I may have information vital to your cause. You've had me locked up for a week, starving me, but I haven't said shit so far. That's why you've brought me here. I need additional... persuasion."

He flashed me a reassuring grin and the young Charley shone through for a moment. "Don't worry, Jake. I'll guide you through this."

Just as quickly the grin vanished, replaced with a sneer. "See those cuffs above my head? Put my hands in them, turn the key and place the key in your pocket."

Part of me wanted to say, "Let's cut the theater, get naked on the bed and fuck like we used to." But another part, a part I thought long healed, wanted to go where this was going, wanted revenge. Maybe Charley knew that, maybe he wanted it too. I obeyed.

Stepping back, I studied him, now spread-eagled before me. He pulled against the restraints, apparently judging the seriousness of my participation. The muscles of his arms and shoulders bulged as he strained against the handcuffs. A trickle of sweat ran down his arm, darkening the edge of his tank top. I wanted to lick him, wanted to taste the salt on his skin. That realization drove blood straight up my cock. I was hard.

Charley gestured toward the bed with his chin. "Now go and get some nipple clamps."

I turned to the bed; laid out upon the gray sheet were implements I had only seen on porn sites: clamps, cock rings, a riding crop, items I didn't recognize. I picked up some clamps with jagged edges, like sharks' teeth.

"See that chain? Attach each of the clamps to the chain. Good. Now put them on me." He inhaled and his nipples pressed at the thin cloth of the shirt; already he was aroused. His breathing sharpened when I fastened the mean-looking pincers onto his chest. "Now twist." I gave each of the clamps a cautious turn.

"Harder!"

I hesitated, thinking of what Trey had done to Charley in school.

"Pull, you lazy bastard!"

His attitude raked at the scar tissue on my heart, angering me. I grabbed the chain and yanked hard, twisting his swollen nipples. I watched him squirm and arch his back; his body's reaction to the pain aroused me even more. I released the tension then pulled again and again. Charley groaned and panted, but said nothing.

Panting myself and frightened by my growing excitement, I let go of the chain. That obviously dissatisfied my old roommate.

"I love it," he sneered, a cruel smile playing across his lips. "They send a boy to do a man's work."

"What the fuck is that supposed to mean?"

"You heard me." Again our eyes met. The belligerent glare bore into me, picking at scabbed hurts. His aggression fanned my anger, really pissing me off. "Pussy."

I backhanded him, snapping his head to the side. "Enough of this shit!"

Turning back to face me, he licked at a smear of blood on his lip. That sight quelled my anger, and I wanted to comfort him, to stroke and soothe his face. But Charley laughed at the taste; the sound was cruel and stoked my rage again. He glanced down between us. "Look at my crotch, bud."

I followed his gaze. Beneath his khakis, his dick formed a ridge across his groin; a dime-sized circle of precome stained his right hip. He cocked his head, raising his reddening cheek toward me again.

"Come on, coward; do it! Hit me again!" Before he could repeat *coward*, he got it across the face. Twice I struck him—this time with my open palm. I'd hit him with such force, I knew that at least one side of his face would swell up soon. My palm smarted too. Charley continued to smile, leered at me even. "By the way—look at yourself."

I knew without looking: my own cock threatened to push out of my uniform.

"Admit it, Jake. This turns you on as much as it does me."

Shamed by my blatant arousal, I turned away. "God, you've become a bastard."

"We're not kids anymore, playing doctor with the lights out."

Growling my inarticulate humiliation and grief, I spun around and grabbed at his crotch. "You like fucking with people's minds, do you?" Grasping his balls, wanting to deflate the reproach of his erection, I yanked—hard. "Have you always liked screwing with their feelings?"

"Feelings?" he grunted. "Bullshit!"

I pulled harder. Charley gasped and didn't reply. Closing his eyes, he seemed to concentrate on the pain that must have throbbed through his gut and down his thighs.

"Was it just playing for you? Was it some sort of game?" I twisted his nuts and he moaned. "Was I just some dumb jock you manipulated into loving you?"

"I'm your prisoner," he deadpanned, unmoved by my admission.

Hurt and despair welled in my chest, firing the fury that burned within me. Letting go of his balls, I grabbed him by his hair, pulling his head close. "You were my lover!" My voice rasped; surging emotions threatened to choke me.

"Lover, ha!" He scoffed, spitting the words at me. "I'm your prisoner and I have information you want—and will get—if you have to beat it out of me."

Now I practically shook with rage. Reaching over to the bed, I picked up the biggest piece of leather I could lay my hand on. I raised it to his face.

"You're damn right I want information." I stroked the leather along his cheek, tracing the livid print of my hand along his jaw. "And I want you to give it to me now."

Charley panted, his shallow breaths wafting the smell of bourbon over me. "No."

"Yes, you will." My anger had mutated into a hard resolve. No longer did my hands shake when I caressed his neck with the piece of cowhide, following the rapid pulse of his jugular down to his chest. "I want you to tell me why you left." I flicked the leather against the clips that still chewed on his nipples.

His nostrils flared, but he gave no other sign of discomfort. "No," he whispered.

I moved the cowhide down his torso to press against his accusing hard-on. "Tell me why you deserted me without a single word. Not one word. Not one!" I smacked the leather against his khaki-covered thigh.

He gasped. "No."

"Tell me!" I whacked him again.

Licking his lips, he pursed them and swallowed. "No."

I beat the leather against his hips. He shook his head.

"Wasn't I worth at least a god...damned...good...bye?" Emphasizing each word with the leather, I struck him, swinging at his legs, his back and his butt.

Charley's body glistened, coated with his sweat. Mine poured from my forehead, running into my eyes, stinging them with salt. The longer he held out, the harder I hit him. A decade of pent-up frustration poured forth, became pure aggression against the man I had caressed and kissed in the dark. Now, under the bright, harsh light in this desolate, little room, I punished him for the pain he had caused me.

"Stop!" Charley cried out, breaking down at last. "I'll tell. Just wait."

I stopped, gulping air as my heart raced. Dropping the piece of leather, I grabbed his hair, gently this time. "I'm waiting," I panted.

To my surprise he leaned over and stuck his tongue in my mouth. We kissed deeply, our sweat mingling on our cheeks. Our lips and tongues entwined, each tasting the other as if for the first time. I ground my groin against his, wanting to fuck him.

He nuzzled my sweaty, beard-stubbled chin. "Forgive me... for holding out on you. I have a lot to tell."

"Go ahead." I nibbled on his earlobe.

"First, pull off my pants and grab a condom. I want you inside me."

Still cuffed to the cross, he grabbed hold of the chains and levered up his legs. I entered him, gripping the underside of his thighs. He rode me with his legs locked behind my back and humped his butt on my aching erection. He resembled a country boy on an old tire swing.

"I'm so sorry." He kissed my mouth. "I was so young. I was scared." He pulled me in close, impaling himself on my cock. "I wanted to forget it all ever happened. Everything. Even you."

"I loved you," I whispered in his ear, reveling in his musky scent. Still he stroked his ass on my cock.

"I loved you too." He licked my cheek. "But I was so hurt I couldn't even think about facing anybody or doing anything. Plus, I didn't want...how can I say this?"

I bit his neck. "Just say it."

He licked around my ear. "I didn't want anyone at school to know about you. I wanted to protect you. After all, you weren't a fag like me."

I pulled back and slowed the fucking. "Who do you think blew you at night?" My mouth found his again. "I was just as into it as you were."

"And you were great! And good for me. But..." He sucked on my tongue until I thought he'd pull it from my throat. "But... you never paid for it...the way I did."

I cradled him, carrying his weight the way I had that last night, a decade ago. "Did you ever talk about it? Get counseling or anything?"

He laughed a strained, taunting laugh. "Lots. You saw all that stuff!"

"What do you mean?"

"Look at the piece you grabbed." Charley kissed my forehead in a soft, feathery kiss.

Glancing down, I spotted the leather at my feet where I had discarded it. I had taken a razor strop from the bed. Probably identical to Trey's at the academy, the leather appeared alien and ugly to me. I felt weird—both repelled and turned on—and never closer to Charley.

"Don't stop fucking me," he urged, as if he sensed my

withdrawal. He tenderly kissed my cheek. "It's you who's working me over now. You—the one I always loved." He tightened his hole on my cock. I swelled inside him. "Love me, fucker. Love me hard the way I need you to."

Our bodies entwined, our sweaty hips slapping together. Naturally, I obeyed him.

Later in the shower, Charley knelt before me and soaped up my legs, kissing my hips and drinking the water that ran in a thread off the head of my cock. The intimacy revived my hard-on.

I leaned against the wall, spent both physically and emotionally, yet never had I felt more alive. Charley picked up my left foot and lathered soap all over it. "I have one more thing to tell, but I'm scared you won't understand."

"Tell me anyway." I sighed, aware of nothing but the touch of Charley's fingers.

He kneaded and rubbed my toes, washing away my weariness with the suds. "About what happened with Trey. I was so ashamed because...because..."

I listened for an explanation. It was the least I could do.

"Because...I had sort of wanted him."

He waited for a response. I weighed the admission against my memories and remained silent.

Charley continued. "I always hated him—always. But I hated myself more." He moved to my right foot, lathering and caressing my toes. "I hated that I loved you and loved being with you, but, in spite of that, I was hot for him—all along."

I drew him up to face me. Tears streaked his face, little hidden by the spray. "I know. I probably always knew, even then. But I wasn't sure until tonight."

Charley rubbed his face; my handprint had begun to fade. "The humiliation drove me away. That night you were so caring, so gentle, I couldn't bear to face you after that. I was sure that you'd see through me, see my ugly secret."

Taking him in my arms, I kissed him long and hard. "Now will you let the shame go?"

He grinned. "Do you mean it?" His relief lit up his eyes, brightening his face so much that I laughed too.

"Absolutely!" I bit his ear and spoke loud enough so that he would hear every word and never forget. "I am claiming my captive, and I am never going to release him."

He laughed, dousing our heads under the steamy spray. "Promise?"

"I promise. You're my prisoner."

JULY 2002

Jameson Currier

"I'm not convinced two men can have an honest relationship,"
I said. I had not said anything at all during dinner, remaining
quiet and listening to the mix of political and sexual banter
bounce between the other guests and our hosts, as Eric deliv-
ered one elaborately prepared dish after another to the table.
My neighbors Eric and his lover Sean, a gay couple in their
midfifties, threw little soirees biweekly in their Chelsea apartment for a combination of their single and coupled gay friends,
in order to be matchmakers or therapists as the necessity of
their friendships required. I was twenty-four that summer
and staying in my older brother's apartment down the hall; it
was often impossible to escape Eric's attentions as I came and
went from the building, and I once amusingly accused him of
installing a spy cam because he was so knowledgeable of my
comings and goings—or lack thereof—particularly my desire
for hibernating for long stretches on the sofa watching movie
after movie, the titles of which he also seemed to know.

But it was my comment on the inadequacies of gay relation-ships that immediately stirred up my host that evening.

"Of course they can!" Eric answered me. "You've just had a bad experience." And then to his other guests: "Teddy is just talking nonsense. He's too young to really believe that."

"Think about it," I continued. "Two men. In a relationship. How much truth can there be?"

"As much as you can accept," Eric answered. "Not every relationship is the same. And sometimes just because a man has secrets, doesn't mean that he is not an honest man and truthful to his partner. Sometimes it's a matter of compromise, not truth."

"Maybe you just haven't met the right man," Sam said to me. Sam was a friend of a friend of Eric's. He worked in a foreign service program and had returned to the States and New York because of "family business," which none of us had asked him to elaborate on, respectfully considering it another off limit issue that evening. "Family business" could mean either a parent's illness or a sibling's marriage or divorce. Or it could be a deeper secret, a way to disguise one's own truth. Perhaps Sam had been in some kind of legal or financial trouble. Perhaps he was bisexual and married and had a child—or had fathered an illegitimate one. It was a mystery Sam was not ready to explain or reveal to anyone that evening.

But I was grateful that I didn't have to elaborate any further on my own disastrous personal experiences, and that the others around the dining table were now drawn into the conversation.

"Or perhaps you're too focused on sex being an equivalent of love," Sean said to me, jokingly. Sean was a psychiatrist, so everyone always gave his words more weight than those of his stockier partner, though Eric, a respected commercial photog-rapher, relished being the foolish and more socially frivolous of the two. "I certainly had that problem when I was your age," Sean added. "Of course, I'm wiser now because my sex drive is not what it once was. But I don't think that sex should be the sole basis of a long-term relationship with another man. Too much disappointment."

"Are you saying I'm not sexy?" Eric whined across the table. "Or lousy in bed?"

This was followed by nervous laughter from everyone.

"Of course, as Eric said, every relationship is distinct," Sean added.

I was glad that the topic soon shifted back to Sam, who until recently had worked in Afghanistan, and as dinner progressed from drinks to salad to entrees to dessert, the tale of Sam's work in a clinic in the Bamiyan province unraveled as he recounted his experience aiding a television journalist who had been injured in an accident. The journalist was a mutual friend with Eric and Sean. And in the odd set of connections and circumstances of those at dinner that evening, the journalist who Sam had helped had once lived in my brother's apartment, before my brother had assumed the lease. Eric was particularly proud that he was able to join together all the pieces of this puzzle over a three-course meal.

I was tired that evening and after a rich and heavy dessert of Dutch apple pie and ice cream, I excused myself from the party and the other guests and went back to my apartment. I had found it increasingly difficult to be social with other guys, which Eric had noted, of course, and which had been the catalyst for the dinner invitation. That week I was also watching another neighbor's dog, Joe's black cocker spaniel named Inky, while Joe was away in Los Angeles. Inky was a beautiful dog, a princess who padded about softly and tossed her curly head and floppy ears at me; one of her unacknowledged blessings was that she pulled me in and out of the apartment so that I did not completely lose contact with the outside world. I was greeted with a whoosh of affection as I stepped through the apartment door, tiny paws landing just below the faded white of the knees of my jeans. I snapped on her leash and we went to the end of the hallway to wait for the building's sluggishly slow-arriving elevator.

As it finally arrived, Sam was leaving Eric and Sean's apartment, and I held the elevator door open while he said goodbye to the two men with handshakes and kissed cheeks. He joined me for the ride to the ground floor and Inky's brisk sprint through the lobby to the sidewalk.

I liked Sam. Unlike our hosts, who were forever filling empty spaces with nonsensical chatter and opinions, he was not much of a talker. He was a tall, handsome, masculine man, a guy's guy who always seemed to be well put together and admired, about three or four years older than I was, so I felt a more generational bonding with him than I had shared with our older hosts, who had, in the eleven months that I had lived in my brother's apartment, tried to step into the roles of mentor, parent or guide for me. There was also a quiet modesty to Sam, as evinced by the personal story he would not disclose at dinner—he had been as vague in many of his statements as I was that evening about my ruinous love life—and there had been no ounce of bravado when he had recounted his assistance of Eric's friend in Afghanistan. I admired the fact that he had boldly stepped into foreign service after graduating college, something I had not been able to do myself, and I envied him for having already amassed a handful of anecdotal adventures that he could recount to strangers over a meal. But it had also made me feel rather inconsequential in the fabric of gay life and that perhaps I had been wasting my life in the city. In the elevator I was bashfully shy—or rudely disinterested in him—but Sam gruffly complimented Inky's beauty and funneled me questions about her and her owner which kept both of us looking down at the curly black mop of her and not at each other.

It was a warm summer night in mid-July, and the day's heat still seemed trapped close to the sidewalk. I broke into a light sweat as I moved away from the air-conditioning of the building and into the city air. We walked silently together to the end of the block and were about to shake hands as we reached Eighth Avenue where Sam would head toward the subway stop to begin his journey back to Long Island.

On the street, a bike messenger—an Asian guy about our age in a tank top and bright green cycling shorts—suddenly rode across a pothole he had not seen in his path. He went flying over the handlebars and landed on the street, unconscious. From the angle where we were standing we had both witnessed the accident. The messenger had not been wearing a helmet for protection. Sam touched me on the shoulder as the guy was rising up in the air, over the handlebars of the bike and onto the pavement, as if to keep me in place and out of harm, and once the fellow had landed on the ground, Sam rushed into the street to aid him.

"Do you have a cell phone?" There was blood on his shirt from where he had leaned into the Asian boy's head to check his wound.

I did, but not with me. I stepped farther away from Sam and the accident and stopped another guy who was walking by and talking on a cell phone, and I tapped him on the shoulder and asked, "Could you call nine-one-one for us?"

He was a beefy sort of guy, wearing a formfitting T-shirt and carrying a shoulder bag, and I gathered he must have just been at one of the gyms that dotted the neighborhood. He nodded at me, hung up on his call, called the emergency line and explained to the operator where we were.

Before he had hung up, a police car arrived, followed by an ambulance, and soon the messenger was being lifted onto a stretcher.

I thanked the beefy guy, and he disappeared as Inky's restlessness tugged me to one end of the block and back so she could sniff around and do her business.

When the ambulance and officers left and the street was cleared of gawkers, it was just Sam and myself and the dog. Sam's clothes were soiled and his hands were caked with dried blood. The messenger would be all right—more blood and broken bones than serious internal damages, the medical workers seemed to think. His blackout had only been for a minute or so. But he was being taken to the hospital for stitches and further tests.

"You can't get on the subway like that," I said to Sam. "You can wash up and take one of my brother's shirts."

We walked back to the apartment building and self-consciously waited for the elevator. I tried to commend Sam on his quick actions, but it felt strained and awkward and I was tired and ready to be on my own for the night, and Inky was restlessly tugging at the leash because she knew she would soon get a treat when we were back in the apartment.

In the elevator I unhooked Inky's leash and she leapt down the hall when we reached my floor. Inside the apartment, I pointed to the bathroom—the layout was not much different from Eric and Sean's apartment—and went to give Inky a treat and then find a shirt for Sam to wear.

A few minutes later he emerged bare chested and asked if I had a plastic bag he could use to carry his soiled clothes back to Long Island. It was impossible not to take in his body's military athleticism—thick, muscled shoulders and arms and a nicely developed chest covered with black hair curving into a thin, dark line that traveled down the middle of his solid stomach and widened again above his navel. I handed him the shirt I had found in my brother's closet and went into the kitchen to find a bag.

Sam was in the living room wearing my brother's shirt when I handed him the plastic bag and, as he stuffed the soiled clothes inside it, he asked, "Do you think they were trying to set us up?"

"I know for a fact that they were trying to set us up."

He nodded and smiled and stepped a little closer to where I was standing.

"You're a nice guy," he complimented me. "It would be a shame to disappoint them."

I smiled and bowed my head, accepting the approval, and he kissed me on my forehead.

He was a big guy and it was a brotherly gesture, but it made me feel vulnerable. I lifted my eyes up to him, which was when his kiss fell against my lips.

Slowly, clumsily, as if being awakened from a deep sleep, I put my arms around his waist. His hands slipped around me and settled at the belt loops of my jeans, where he hooked his fingers as I moved my hands beneath his shirt and around to his chest. I had wanted to kiss him since I had met him at Eric and Sean's, and I held my lips open as he forcefully moved his tongue into my mouth, as if to prove that he had been interested in me, after all.

He tugged the bottom of my T-shirt and slid it up over my arms and tossed it behind him, and his hands moved to my waist as he pressed his mouth against the center of my chest. His lips rode up my neck, and I let him linger there till the pleasure was unbearable, and then I took the edges of his shirt and pulled them toward his head.

We stood bare chested now in front of each other, deep-tonguing and stroking each other's bodies. I rubbed his nipple between my thumb and forefinger while he moved a hand to my crotch and grasped the erection beneath my jeans. Then he unzipped my fly, pressed his hand inside and clutched my cock through the fabric of my underwear.

My hands moved to unbutton the top of his khaki pants and as the zipper gave way his trousers fell off his hips and puddled at his knees. He was wearing a pair of light blue boxers, tented from the head of his cock, and I reached my hand to his thigh and slipped my fingers under the hem of his boxers until I found its wide, mushroom-shaped head. His cock was warm and hard, and I clutched it and gave a few strokes, then found his testicles and cupped and squeezed them.

He pulled away from me as if to find his balance and breath, and I took the opportunity to slip out of my jeans. He sat on the arm of the couch and undid the laces of his shoes and stepped out of his trousers. He had a nice smile and I leaned over him and kissed him, and we fondled each other for another few moments, then I drew him up by his arms and he followed me into the bedroom.

We were rougher now, stroking, kissing, tweaking, nibbling. In the darkness of the bedroom I could see his smile, and he made soft noises of astonishment as we twisted and rolled around. I expected him to withdraw from my rising intensity, but he accepted it and pushed it farther. I wanted him to love me because I found him, in spite of whatever secrets he might possess, a good, honest man—and to love him in a way that could transcend the need for sex but would also embrace its deepest desires. I thought that if I could prove to him that I was a good sexual partner then he would also see that I could be a good boyfriend or husband for him, a mistake I continually made with every man I found my way into a bedroom with.

He asked if I had lube and condoms, and I rolled away from him and found them in the drawer of the nightstand. I thought he wanted to fuck me, but it was the opposite. I took it slow, fingering him till he was ready to accept my cock. He gasped and his chest flushed as I entered him, and I pulled out until he hungrily urged me back. He wanted to hold my neck as I fucked him, and I obliged until I realized I could curve my spine and take his cock in my mouth as I remained inside him. I felt entirely innocent and genuine with him, as if this were the first time I had ever done this with a guy and we were to do this together the rest of our lives. He was full of puffs of astonishment, and I could feel the muscles of his stomach clenching and shifting and I kept at him, unrelenting.

He pushed my lips away as his orgasm arrived, and I withdrew from him and finished myself off. I left him and toweled myself off in the bathroom, regarding the satisfaction of my smile and the raw, red patches on my shoulders and neck where his jaw stubble had burned my skin. Back at the bed, Sam toweled himself off, and there followed a long period of lying together cuddling, holding each other, rubbing our hands and fingers along skin and hair. I mentally reprimanded myself for pushing myself so emotionally into the sex and for stepping into what I really knew was to be another one-night stand. I knew it wouldn't go any farther with Sam than this pleasurable moment, and I felt the hurt and disappointment of it before he had even left the apartment.

"You must have been starved for affection there," I said, as I lifted myself out of his embrace, referring to his time working in Afghanistan.

"No," he answered. "Just the opposite. There was a local boy," he said, then quickly clarified, "...young man. He was a handsome young man."

He rolled over so that he looked out the window, away from me, and I followed him, wrapping my arms around his waist in an effort to keep us together. I could feel his voice vibrating through his skin and into my fingers as he talked. "It began innocently enough. Eye contact. Flirting. Holding hands."

"Holding hands?" I said and lightly laughed.

"Casually," he explained. "It's a gesture of friendship between men. Muslim men are openly affectionate toward each other in a way that would be regarded as odd—or gay—here, and it's easy to fall into their habits."

"I was working at the clinic," he said, after a pause, as if he had been reviewing a memory before he attempted to describe it. "Dispensing medicines at the makeshift pharmacy. Tending to walk-in emergencies. Trying to patch up all these problems with aspirin and Band-aids."

Now he laughed as I had, lightly, then continued. "The young boy showed up one day looking for work. I shooed him away because there was nothing for him to do but get in the way, and there was nothing to pay him with. But he returned about an hour later. He was really looking for food, and I gave him some bread and a chocolate bar I had saved since I was in Kabul. He was ecstatic. He knew a little English. They all know a little English there."

"Hello, Meesturh," Sam mimicked the accent. "I lihcke you. You lihcke me?"

We both laughed at the imitation, and Sam continued. "Like I said, it started with flirting. He was always smiling at me and he had a terrific smile—dimples on his left cheek you just wanted to drop your tongue into. He was always happy to help me with whatever I was doing. He made me smile. I gave him food every day. Bread I had taken from the guesthouse where I was staying and taking my meals. I would be grumpy in the mornings until he showed up, ravenous, and I watched him eat. He was sleeping in the caves up on the cliffs."

"The caves?"

"The grottoes on the hillside, carved by the Buddhist monks centuries ago. Where the ancient giant Buddhas had been. They were cold, nasty places, and I have no idea how he stayed warm at night, because it could get very cold. There were many families living in the caves, and I can only imagine that their body heat was what was warming them—when they had food to fill their stomachs. The boy had been separated from his parents at a refugee camp, and he was staying with his older sister's family—her husband and a little baby girl. He wouldn't eat all the food that I gave him. There was always something that he tucked away in his pocket that I knew he would give to one of them later. It was heartbreaking if you stopped to think of it, but there was so much to think about, that this was only one minor thing. Every day there was another casualty or a patient with a problem—an abscessed tooth or a broken toe. *Something*. It was such a cold, harsh place. Beautiful. But *hard*."

He continued. "One night I was able to bring him to the guesthouse to dine. It was owned by a local Muslim man and his wife, and they had always objected to my suggestion of him eating with us, in spite of my offer to pay extra to have the boy there, then one night they changed their mind. He ate with us—the rest of the MSF staff in the clinic and a few of the Red Cross guys who were also in the house—and they all knew him and were glad to have him with us. He helped the owner carry out the dishes of food and clean up—we ate on the floor, sitting on pillows and using our hands most of the time. There were three or four of us staying in each of the rooms, and instead of having the boy walk back in the freezing dark to the cliffs I had him sleep beside me on the floor. It was a simple, polite gesture. I was just trying to be a good Samaritan, but I knew it would create trouble for me one day. He stayed with me every night after that. Each night he slept closer and closer until we were sleeping together. It was just so natural. One day I knew I was in love with him."

"This was the fellow who drove the van?" I asked. "To the hospital. To Kabul?"

"Yes," Sam said. His body was tense, frozen into thought.

"How old was he?"

"I don't know."

Then again, after a pause, he added, "It was part of why I left. He was too young. I wasn't sure what I could give him. So I ran away."

"You ran away?"

"I left him in Kabul. I told him that I had to return to America for a while, because of a family problem; that I would be back soon. He took it okay, because I convinced him that I was coming back. There was no family problem."

"Are you going to go back?"

"I've gotten a new assignment. Working in Tunisia."

He lay still for a while, breathing slowly in and out. Then we both rose and showered together, stroking each other to another orgasm beneath the warm flow of water.

Clean, exhausted and back in the bed, I drifted off to sleep in his embrace. I sensed him stir hours later, rise out of bed and begin to get dressed. The activity aroused Inky in the other room, and I groggily stayed awake until Sam was dressed and at the door.

"Good-bye and thanks," he said, as he left. "I hope you find him."

I nodded and closed the door, petting Inky and groping my way through the darkness of the apartment and back to sleep. I was by then too tired to miss him, but I knew I would in the days that followed.

WHAT WE LEAVE BEHIND

Shanna Germain

There is a dying dog the size of a small horse in my kitchen. She is nearly as tall as the kitchen table. Nearly as wide. With a hell of a lot more long white hair.

"I'm sorry," I say to the man who brought her here. "There's been a mistake."

The man who brought her is on his knees on my kitchen floor, rubbing the dog's brown- and gray-tipped ears. He has bits of gray in the dark hair above his own ears.

"It's okay, Annie," he says to the dog, who lets her tongue fall from her mouth and tilts her head sideways to listen. "This is gonna' be *sooo* good for you. Okay, girl, it's all good."

He doesn't seem to care that he's talking baby talk to this polar bear–like creature in front of me. He doesn't seem to hear me saying that the polar bear cannot stay in my kitchen.

When the man stands, his knees pop on the way up. "Ack, getting old." He shakes his legs out and laughs. "Too much bending down to dogs is more like it."

Even standing, he can't seem to keep his fingers out of Annie's fur. They nuzzle the pads of her ears while he pulls a clipboard from his shoulder bag.

I want to touch Annie, too. She's almost all white, except for those ears. From here, her fur looks like soft fuzz all over. But I don't touch her. I can't. It's not that she's dying. That, I'm used to. It's that she looks so damn healthy.

By the time Bella came to us, she was already missing her back leg from the knee down and was getting oral pain meds twice a day. Her owners had tried to save her by cutting off the tumored foot. But when the cancer spread, they decided it was too much and turned her over to the shelter. That's when she came to Thom and me.

It had been Thom's idea to take in a dying animal. A few years back, our local shelter had joined with a group of vets to start a hospice program for animals—some strays, some abandoned—who were dying, but still had quality time left in their lives. The goal was to get the animals into a good final home, a place where they could die with love and compassion. "We can still do something good," Thom had said when he'd heard of it. "Think of it, these animals, having to die alone."

He was thinking of himself too, of me after he was gone. That was after he got sick, but before we realized what it was. We'd thought it was AIDS, of course. As a gay man, you spend your whole adult life running from the thing you fear most, so fast that you don't see the other things on the way by. Until you get sideswiped by them. Car accidents. A guy in the alley with a knife. With Thom, it was lymphoma.

I'd said yes to the first dog—Bella, a lab-something-or-other—because I loved Thom, and I wanted to give him whatever I could, even at the end. Especially at the end. It made his skin ache to feel anything on it, but even so, it was Bella he let in the bed at night, Bella he reached for when the pain was bad. It was helping Bella toward her death that gave us something to focus on, that helped us move toward Thom's death in a way that felt, if not normal, no, never normal, at least like we were working with some kind of plan.

I didn't know that somewhere between those last days at home and his final trip to the ER he'd signed us—no, signed me—up for another dog.

I try again with the man in my kitchen.

"Really, I can't take her," I say.

He has finally let go of Annie's ears and is signing a clipboard with a big flourish. He holds the clipboard out to me.

"Of course you can," he says.

There is something in his dark eyes, a glimmer around the edges that shows he doesn't have any doubts. I signed on for this dog. She is here in my kitchen with two months to live. Of course I can take her.

I push the clipboard back at him. The ID tag clipped to his shirt pocket says, I'M A PAWSPICE VOLUNTEER! Beneath that it says, SETH.

"Listen, Seth," I say. "I can't take her. My partner signed us up and…" It is too complicated, too much to say. The words pile into my throat like bones and stick there.

Seth stays silent for a moment. Annie whines for the first time and pushes the side of her face carefully into his palm.

I feel like I have to say something, so I say, "I can't do it alone."

Seth holds the clipboard as though it's a Frisbee he'd like to wing at my head. I can understand the impulse. He probably sees this all the time—people who sign on for this venture and then decide they can't see it through.

But he doesn't wing the clipboard. He just says, "You wouldn't be alone. You'd have Annie."

At the sound of her name, Annie pushes her cheek harder against Seth's hand. When she doesn't get a response, she turns her head my way. The kitchen is small, and she's so big that she nearly touches my thigh with her nose. Her eyes are so dark in all that white fur. I think what it would be like to have footsteps in the house again, noise at the door when I get back from errands. Somebody who needs me again.

I need time, so I ask, "What...what is she?"

Seth doesn't seem to notice my change in subject. Or perhaps he's content to ride it through.

"Great Pyrenees," he says. "Full-bred and papered." He doesn't say it with anger. He doesn't shake his head like I would have, to think of someone dropping off an animal, any creature, papered or not, just because it was terminal.

"Pyrenees?" I've never even heard of it.

Seth smiles for the first time. It's a half smile, shy enough to bring out dimples on both cheeks. "It's Norwegian for small horse," he says.

Annie wags her tail as though she gets the joke, and then drops herself to the kitchen floor at my feet. Her body makes a thud that's so loud I wonder if she's hurt herself, but she just puts her head down on her paws.

I stare at her. She looks so healthy. Thom and Bella both showed their illnesses. They were twins in the way their bodies responded. Losing weight no matter how much I fed them, until their knees were bigger than their thighs, until I could count every vertebra and rib with my fingers. Thom's fine blond hairs shedding on blankets next to Bella's dark curls. Neither of them said anything, not by mouth, but at the end, their bodies knew no language but pain.

This is what I think: *I can't do this again.*

This is what Seth seems to think: *He's going to do it.*

He is unpacking her things from his bag onto my kitchen table. The bag says, PAWSITIVELY PAWSPICE, in green letters with a big paw print on it. Like some kind of bizarre Mary Poppins, he pulls out two leashes, cans of dog food, an unopened package of very large bones, and a bottle of meds that rattles like maracas and makes Annie open her eyes warily.

"She doesn't need the meds very often," he says. "I don't think she likes the way they make her feel."

I nod. Thom complained of that all the time. The pain, he said, was easier than the disconnect. But then the pain would come on, hard, and he would let me open the IV, watch the liquid drip-drip him into semiconsciousness.

"She looks so healthy," I say. I don't even realize I'm going to say it.

"Nasal cancer," he says. "It's all on the inside."

"Nasal?" I'm not sure I know what that even means. I mean, I know what it means, but, "How does nose cancer land a dog on the hospice list?"

"It spreads," he says.

Seth keeps his eyes on Annie, who is, for the first time, starting to sound like a dog who might have something wrong with her. Her breath whines in, just a bit, only if you're listening in a quiet kitchen.

Seth reaches into his canvas bag and pulls out a tennis ball punched full of holes. Then he goes down on his knees next to Annie. I'm getting used to seeing the top of him like this. Even though it's not my own instinct, I like a man who will get down on his knees. Thom was a gardener, always in the dirt. Even near the end.

I realize that Seth is talking to Annie and to me at the same time.

"C'mon, girl, open up," he says. Then, to me, "Now, you'll

want to catch her just before she falls asleep, and get the ball in her mouth. The holes help with the stridor, so she can breathe. She's used to it, so if you just ask her to open, she will. A bone works too, if you're out of tennis balls. Anything big enough to keep her mouth open while she sleeps."

Annie takes the ball in her mouth and drops her head back down on her paws. Her breathing is noticeably quieter.

Seth is still on his knees. I try not to look at his hands across her back. He has good wrists, muscled enough to chop vegetables and lift weights, soft enough to hold books and wineglasses by the stem.

Seth is still talking about Annie. "You could give her one of the pain pills, too, if she's having an especially hard time, but the tennis ball usually does the trick."

I realize I'm not listening. What I'm doing is eying Seth's back, the curve of his shoulders and hips. This realization makes me want to fuck and cry. While Thom was dying I looked at everything—everything—that walked by. I didn't touch; that was our rule. But, Jesus, I don't know if I'd ever been so horny in my life. We fucked some, then, almost to the end. Thom joked we were like pregnant women or little old ladies. He was afraid I wasn't attracted to him anymore; I was afraid to hurt him.

Near the end, sex took on this ritual: I would lie next to Thom, barely touching, and we would kiss. Just our lips and tongues. His lips still silver-soft from the lip balm he was addicted to. And then I would suck. As much as he was ashamed of his body at the end, he was always proud of his cock. I'm so grateful for that, that he had something to be proud of, always.

And I loved to suck him. The only part of his body that didn't lose its weight, that stayed full and heavy and alive in my mouth. I'd run my tongue up the ridges and veins, play over and over the soft curve of his head until his sighs changed from a long, slow release to a near-pant. Until he lifted his hips off the bed and put his fingers in my hair and said my name, over and over. And then, sometimes, he could fall asleep without the pain meds. Sleeping then, he looked like my Thom again. If I squinted, I could pretend I didn't see the IV poles, the hospital bed, the pill bottles, and tissues scattered around the living room. I could pretend he was just napping in the middle of the day.

And then the truth would come back and I'd go down to the laundry room and put already dry clothes in the dryer. Beneath the loud *clunk-clunk* of jeans and T-shirts, I'd masturbate, hard and fast, without lube, chafing my skin into some kind of pain. Sometimes I came. Sometimes I just cried.

But after Thom died, nothing. It was like my libido got dressed up in its best clothes, and lay down to be buried somewhere between Thom and Bella. For it to come back now, suddenly and with such force that my cock tightens in my jeans—it wrecks me.

I back away from Seth, trying to shift my legs to hide everything that's happening inside me. Seth raises his eyes to the triangle of my jeans. I turn away and grab the first thing my hand finds. One of Annie's tennis balls. When I squeeze it, the air shoots out the holes into my palm. I pick up the cans of food, put them into the cupboard, so I don't have to turn around.

"Well, I guess that's settled, then," Seth says to my back.

I'm not sure anything is settled, least of all me.

But I find myself stacking another can of food in the cupboard, saying, "I guess it is."

Even as Seth gathers his things, I keep my back turned. It isn't until he says, "I'll see you both in a week then," that everything subsides and I can turn and meet his dark eyes.

This, finally, is when I realize that somewhere between "I

can't," and "You can," I've lost the battle. Annie is staying, and this man is going to be back in my house in a week's time. And I have no idea how to feel about either.

For the next six days, Annie and I try to get acquainted with each other. She's learning to navigate the small house with her big body, and I'm learning to get used to the sound of movement in the rooms.

Every day, she chews her tennis ball at the back of my home office while I build websites and answer emails. Every night, I make up the bundle of blankets for her to sleep on in the living room and every night, she stands at the foot of my bed watching as I read or do crosswords or try not to think about Thom. She doesn't whine or even beg. If she did, I think I could turn her away, make it clear that the bedroom is not her space. But she just watches me, tongue hanging, until I sigh and pat the covers.

"C'mon then," I say. And she does. Crawls on her elbows and knees across the covers like she's trying to make herself smaller. Which is nearly impossible for a dog her size. Even the bed lilts sideways at her weight. I give her one of the holey tennis balls and she chomps on it for a while and then puts her head on Thom's pillow to sleep.

So far, we haven't needed the drugs, and I think that makes us both happy. It's a slippery slope, and slipperier at the end. And although Annie's chart says five weeks, I know that could mean anything. Bella lasted longer than she was supposed to. Thom didn't.

Every morning, before our walk, I read the quality of life checkpoints off to Annie. It's a lot of *h*'s and a few *m*'s. Hurt, hunger, hydration, hygiene, happiness, mobility, more. It's supposed to gauge how she's doing, what her quality of life is like, if she's having more good days than bad.

I don't know if we got one of these for Bella. I'm sure we did, but I don't remember it. I wish I'd paid more attention. I wish I'd had a chart like this for Thom, although he probably would have thrown it across the room. He'd voted for calling the vet to put Bella to sleep as soon as she started showing real signs of pain, when she started having more bad days than good. But for himself, he wanted to hang in until the end, no matter the cost.

On our seventh day, the day that Seth is scheduled to come by for his check-in visit, Annie seems her usual tail-whipping self. Between breakfast and her walk, she manages to knock over the vase of yellow calla lilies that I bought...well, I won't let myself think why I bought them. The vase doesn't break, but the callas aren't salvageable.

Sometimes I swear she knocks shit over just to say that she's alive. Today, I wonder if she's not doing it to spite me for running the vacuum last night. Or maybe she's as nervous as I am about Seth coming. The way my body's jumping, if I had a tail, I'd be knocking crap off every surface, too.

I tell myself that I'm just nervous because I've gotten used to having Annie in the house, and he could decide it's not working out. But the truth is I'm excited, too.

"Okay, Missy," I say as I give both of us a once-over in the bedroom mirror—the tip of her tail is soggy from its run-in with the vase and I've got a squeaky toy tucked in my shirt pocket, but otherwise we look pretty good. "We need to make a good impression today," I tell Annie, who wags her tail at me.

And then Seth's knocking, calling. Annie and I nearly trip each other up trying to get to the door. Halfway across the kitchen, I calm myself and let Annie run ahead. Even so, when I swing the door open, we're both panting like fools.

Seth's standing there with a bone the size of Texas in one hand and what looks like a hand-picked bunch of black-eyed

Susans in the other. Annie looks back at me like she's smiling. I take a big gulp of air.

"Hey," I say.

"Hi," he says. I'm not sure if I noticed his smile last time, but I do now: straight white teeth, a full bottom lip that I want to suck.

We stand there while Annie's tail goes back and forth between the two of us. Seth holds out the bone.

"For you," he says to me.

We both look down at the huge thing in his hand.

Seth realizes what he's done. "Oh, ah..." he says. The tips of his ears darken with color. I'm not sure I've ever seen anything so sexy. He tries to switch hands, to offer the flowers instead, but I take hold of his wrist. I don't mean to. If I'd thought first, if a vision of Thom had entered my head, I would not have done it. But my body moved first, took his wrist, and now I'm holding the hand that's holding the bone.

"Come in," I say. His blushing, the way he fumbles through my doorway, are things Thom would never have done. I'm so grateful for the difference, for not having to compare him to Thom, that I pull him into the kitchen and press him back against the fridge. I find his mouth, that bottom lip, and I suck it into my mouth. He tastes of peppermint and basil.

Seth says something, but I can't tell what it is. It must be good, because his arms go around my back and he pulls me against him. The knotty end of the dog bone digs into my shoulder, but I don't care because our mouths are pressed together, our chests and cocks pushing into each other. He's big and the feeling of him through his jeans makes me grow large too.

I put my hands in his hair, feeling the soft black curls, the coarse gray strands. Jesus, I want to unbutton this man right here, I want to bend him over the kitchen counter and take him.

I try to tell him these things with my hips, the curve of my cock against his. He answers with his tongue, scraping the edge of my teeth, licking the inside of my cheek.

The fridge squeaks as Seth and I press into each other, harder and harder. The sound makes Annie bark, once, sharp.

All at once, we're a tangle of flowers and dog bone and tongues and panting. I step back, away from Seth's dark eyes. A flower petal brushes my ear as I break from his arms.

"I'm sorry," I say. "I don't know…"

He smiles, and for the second time today, I am aroused by straight, white teeth. He seems to have recouped his lost confidence. His face is still flushed, but I don't think it's embarrassment this time. My own cheeks feel overly warm.

Seth goes down on his knees to give Annie the bone. She pushes the healthy side of her face against his palm before she takes it between her teeth. Still on his knees, he holds out the slightly crushed bouquet of flowers. "Would you have a vase for these?" he asks.

We do what's civilized. I refill the calla vase with water and try to rearrange the flowers in a way that makes them look less like they were in the middle of a lust crush. And then I offer him lunch and he accepts.

I slice up cheese and salami. Pull yesterday's tomato and mozzarella salad from the fridge. He takes the knife I offer and slices a loaf of bread at perfect diagonals.

"Beer?" I ask.

He seems relieved.

"I'd love one," he says.

We eat while Annie gnaws her bone in the corner of the kitchen. We don't say much. It's the lunch of two men who were too nervous to eat all day. The lunch of two men who know that dessert is going to be the best—and longest—part of the meal. I watch his hands while he dips slices of bread into olive oil. I want to suck the oil from his fingers. Better yet, suck it from his tongue. But I hold myself steady. I eat. I mention how well Annie's doing. How healthy and happy she seems.

At the end, we clear the table as though we've been doing this for years. There is no sidestepping. Seth doesn't ask where the dishes go, or how to stack things. He just does. And then there is no more to do. Annie is asleep with the bone holding her jaws apart. Her breathing is nearly silent.

Seth straightens a towel that's hanging on the fridge. "What now?" he asks, without looking at me.

I touch his back, at the curve-in place just above his ass.

His voice low, still looking at the towel, Seth says, "I want you to fuck me."

It makes my cock pulse. Oh, Jesus. I bury my face in his neck. Even here, he smells of herbs.

"I want that, too," I say against his skin. I take his hand and pull him away from the towel rack. I mean to go to the living room, something less personal, but that's where Thom is, the memories of his last months and days, and I lead Seth into the bedroom instead. I think it surprises us both, this wide, carefully made bed waiting in the middle of the room.

Seth stops in front of it. I realize that if I stop now, I'll back out. I'll send Seth on his way, and Annie and I will live out the rest of her days in the safe, lonely rooms of this house.

Instead, I push my hands against Seth's chest. Somehow, in pushing him away, I pull him closer. My fingers open the buttons one by one. I'm shaking, and I have to hold on to each button tightly. Seth kisses my neck while I work. His hands slide down the back of me, from my shoulders to my waist. I hear my belt buckle open, feel the warmth as he slides it from my jeans.

Everything's too slow for me.

"Please undress. I want to see you," I say.

Seth lets go of my jeans. He undresses quickly, dropping his clothes in piles. His body is lean but muscled. His cock swings up, long and thin, the smooth head a beautiful pinky-purple. His body is so alive, so much muscle and blood pumping, that I'm afraid to touch him.

It doesn't matter. He comes to me, undresses me as fast as he did himself. Even so, I marvel at his hands everywhere: buttons, sleeves, sliding my underwear down my thighs so my cock springs up.

"Oh," he says. And he never comes up from taking my underwear off. He stays on his knees, and I can see the lean muscle of his back, and just below that, the perfect curves of his ass. He licks his lips and presses them to the head of my cock.

It's been so long since I've felt anything other than my own hand that just the press of his lips there makes me want to grab the back of his head and fuck his mouth. I try to keep still. When he opens his lips, lets me slide inside him, against the press of tongue and teeth, it's almost too much. I grit my teeth to stem the rising pleasure. His tongue finds the sweet spot just beneath my head, laps at it.

"Ah, Jesus," I say. Through my gritted teeth, it comes out as something less awed, more primal. I pull Seth up from his knees. His lips are cherry red and wet. He licks a drop of precum from his big bottom lip.

"What are you doing to me?" I ask, even as I'm laying him down on his back on the bed. He doesn't answer. He doesn't have to. The way his cock jumps as I position myself over him, the way he puts his legs up to give me access, says it all.

I lick my finger and use it to find the swirl of his asshole. I press against it, and Seth opens for me, already pushing down on my finger.

"More," he pants. I enter with a second finger, let his body settle over it. He wraps his fingers tight around the base of his cock. The color darkens even more. My cock is jumping every time Seth's ass tightens around my fingers. It wants in. I want in.

"Seth, I want…"

"Yes," he sighs. "Yes."

I fumble in the nightstand drawer for lube and condoms, hoping there's something left over. Hoping I won't break down when my hand hits a cellophane wrapper.

Thankfully, Seth puts his other hand around my cock. He's wet his palm and his fingers slide over my skin, slick enough to take my mind off everything that came before this moment. I find a half-empty bottle of lube and one lonely condom in the bottom of the drawer.

Seth wraps his fingers around the base of my cock while I roll on the condom. He tightens his grip, a human cock ring that makes me pump my hips against his hand as I spread lube over the surface.

"It's cold," I say.

Seth's already raising his hips to me, the perfect circle of his asshole waiting.

"Don't care," he says.

I push my way inside him. Just the head at first. How much I've missed this entering is something that I feel in my whole body. This is how I try to be: Slow. Careful. But Seth is sucking me in with his low moans, with his fingers tight on my ass.

The slide inside is: *Oh, fuck.* And then I'm buried in him, his ass contracting and releasing around me. I stop.

"I don't know how long I'm going to last," I say. "I can't promise—"

Seth pulls my face down to his, offers me that big bottom lip to suck on. It shushes me.

"Just fuck me," he says against my mouth.

I do, oh, god, I do. Rising and falling inside him. Seth pushes his hips upward to meet my thrusts. We are greedy together, wanting it all.

And then I close my eyes, just for a second, and see Thom's face. For some reason, it's okay, though; he looks happy. Or at least he doesn't look unhappy.

When I open my eyes, Seth is pumping his cock at the same rhythm as I'm fucking him. His head is thrown back, and he moans low. It's visceral: the sound, the feeling of his hot skin around me. I come.

Coming is like this: Everything emptying. Everything filling. The long, slow release of something I've been holding on to for too long. It is liquid leaving and me becoming liquid and the way Seth says "Aw, god," and Annie's low whine from the other room.

When I wake up, I've got a big white paw in my face, and I realize that while we were sleeping, Annie must have crawled in bed.

Seth's already awake. His fingers are back in the fur at Annie's ear.

"I need to tell you something," he says.

My soul says: *Oh, shit.* My mind says: *Wait and listen.*

"I got assigned to you on purpose," he says.

"What?"

Seth drops his eyes, pretends to pick something out of Annie's fur. And then his words come out in a tumble.

"Thom came into the shelter in person when he signed up. He was so sweet, told us the whole story. He wanted you to have something after. It was supposed to be sooner, that's what he wanted, but there wasn't a good match. I asked to be assigned to you."

I shift Annie's paw off my shoulder, lean up a little. "Is that kind of creepy?" I ask.

The tips of Seth's ears are growing a dark red. I can't help it. I think of his cock.

"Maybe," he says. "But Thom was so nice, and I thought, 'A man who's in love with this man must be amazing, too.' I just wanted to see if it was true."

"And?"

He swallows audibly. The sure man who was in my bed minutes ago has disappeared.

"And...you were not only nice, but you were so sexy. I got sucked in."

His lip is pouting out so far I'm tempted to bite it.

Instead, I ask, "Would you like to get sucked in again?"

The tips of his ears still showing red, he nods.

I run my finger along the edges of his lips.

"Let me feed the small horse, then," I say. "And when I come back, I'll see what I can do."

It's been three months and two days, and Seth has moved in. He's brought his life with him: paperwork and photos from Pawspice, a shed full of gardening tools, his ability to grow herbs and tomatoes like he's made of fertilizer.

Annie's days are switching from mostly good to mostly bad. Something has speeded up inside her, is pushing her quickly toward the end. Five times a day, we coax her to eat by cupping Alfredo sauce in our palms and letting her lick it out.

This morning, while Seth cooks breakfast, I mix up the solution to wash Annie's coat—mostly water, a little lemon juice, and hydrogen peroxide. She lies on the rug in the kitchen, the ball between her teeth. She has it almost all the time now, and still she needs the meds.

I wring out the sponge—my skin is permeated with the scent of lemons—and I run it carefully over Annie's face. She closes her eyes when I get near her nose, and I talk low to her, tell her I'm sorry if I hurt her.

Seth chop-chops the onions on the board. The room smells of acid and tears.

"I think it's almost time," I say. I'm talking to Annie and to Seth. Somehow, they both nod.

Not today, not tomorrow, but soon, we will lose Annie and all she has brought to us. Well, not everything she has brought to us. We'll still have: Memories. Tennis balls filled with holes in every room in the house. A bed that sags on one side. Each other.

TOTAL PACKAGE

Michael Bracken

Political correctness hadn't reached my part of Texas back then and the locals still referred to me as a mailman. As a substitute letter carrier, I covered rural routes on a rotating basis, a different one each day when the regular carriers had their days off. Saturdays I ran RR#2 southwest of town, puttering along the shoulder in a right-hand drive Jeep that had seen better days, stopping every so often to fill roadside mailboxes with bills and bulk mail.

I knew more about the people on my routes than they realized. Five-foot-two, two-hundred-and-fifty-pound Ethel May Raditz told everyone she was on a diet but received a package nearly every week from Godiva. Tom Jobe seemed to be preparing for the apocalypse because he subscribed to a dozen survivalist magazines. And Vince DiMarco, at that time the newest stop on the route, had something to hide because he received more than the usual amount of mail in plain brown wrappers.

He wasn't the only one around town with something to hide.

I was so deep in the closet I wasn't sure I would ever find my way out. I'd suspected I was different in high school because I snuck glances at the other guys when we showered, and had no interest at all in the girls—even after Billy Roy Johnson found a way to sneak peeks into their locker room through a hole in the wall of the equipment room—but I'd never told anyone about my proclivity and I had certainly not done anything about it at the time. Not where I lived. Not in rural Texas.

My family didn't have the money to send me off to college, so I worked various jobs around town until I got on with the USPS. Once I had a steady income, I rented a small house three blocks from the station and proceeded to lead a double life. Derek to my family, Rick to most everyone else, I shot pool with my friends at Gully's on Saturday nights, attended the Methodist church Sunday mornings, and spent all of the holidays with my family.

Sexually frustrated because I wasn't interested in the available women my age—most of whom had been through at least one marriage and were either available to every man who bought them a drink or were seeking baby daddies—I sought release during occasional trips away from town. Dallas and Austin became my favorite travel destinations, but after a few years of casual encounters with men who had no interest in sharing phone numbers or last names, I resigned myself to the probability that I would never experience the kind of relationship that my parents—married thirty-five years and showing no signs of wear—enjoyed.

As much as I desired sexual congress with a hard-bodied young man, I wanted something more. I wanted a relationship measured in years and months, not hours and minutes. I wanted the total package. And I despaired of ever finding it.

One Saturday morning, about two months after he moved into the old Denton place, I found myself with a plain brown envelope addressed to Vince DiMarco that had been stamped with a postage due notification. I knew most of the people on my route—I'd gone to school with them or their kin, worshipped in church beside them, or was related to them in some way—so I usually left postage-due mail in their boxes. Charlie Waterson, the carrier who worked Monday through Friday, would find the appropriate amount of money waiting in the mailboxes the next delivery day. But I didn't know Vince. I'd never met him—had never even seen him—and the only things I knew about him, other than what I could discern from casual glances at his mail, was what my second cousin Sally Jo, the real estate agent who'd sold him the old Denton place, had told the family during one of our occasional Sunday afternoon cookouts. He was handsome, single, and worked out of Waco as a claims adjuster for an insurance company.

I glanced at my watch. I was ahead of schedule and nosey, so I eased the Jeep past Vince's roadside mailbox, turned up the short drive, and stopped behind a recent-model Lexus. After killing the engine, I unfolded myself from the Jeep, walked past the Lexus and up the steps to the porch, and leaned on the bell. I heard it clang somewhere deep inside the house. I waited a few minutes and then I leaned on it again.

Just as I was getting ready to leave a pink form telling Vince when he could collect his postage-due envelope from the post office in town, he opened the front door. Wet, ripped, and wearing nothing but a royal blue towel wrapped loosely around his hips, he seemed as surprised by me as I was by him.

His gaze quickly traveled from my white pith helmet down over my blue short-sleeve sport-style knit shirt with the U.S. Mail emblem above the left breast pocket, over my navy blue shorts—worn the regulation three inches above midknee—with the dark blue stripe on the outside seam, over my calf-length blue-gray socks with two navy rings at the top, on down to my polished black work shoes, and then back up to my eyes. Unlike many of my coworkers, I looked good in my regulation uniform. I groomed myself appropriately, took care of my body, bought uniforms that fit, and cared for them as well as I cared for my street clothes.

"I'm sorry," he said, apologizing for his appearance. "You caught me in the Jacuzzi."

I held up the heavy envelope. "This came postage due—"

A black-and-white Border collie shot out the door and grabbed the envelope. My free hand instinctively reached for my pepper spray before I realized the dog wasn't attacking me; it was attacking the plain brown envelope and whatever was inside. For a moment we played tug-of-war with it. Then the envelope tore open and its contents fell to the porch, revealing a familiar magazine, one that I received at my post office box two towns north of the town where I actually lived.

"No, Elroy, no!"

Vince grabbed the dog's collar and wrestled it back into the house as I bent to retrieve the magazine. As he struggled with the dog, Vince's towel dropped to the floor. He wore nothing beneath it and I found myself eye-to-thigh with his muscular legs. His thick phallus and heavy scrotum hung mere inches from my face. If he had experienced any shrinkage from his time in the Jacuzzi, it wasn't evident.

I licked my lips and slowly straightened up with the magazine in my hand, unexpected desire flooding through my entire body.

Vince, still struggling to control the Border collie, made no effort to cover himself. He asked, "How much do I owe?"

I told him.

"I'll get it. Wait here."

He pulled the dog back and closed the door, which pushed

the wet blue towel onto the porch at my feet. I nudged it with the toe of one black shoe, wondering if I should pick it up. I decided instead to step away from the door, and I waited on the edge of the porch near the steps.

When Vince reappeared, he wore chinos and a pale green polo shirt that hugged his thick chest and trim waist. He stepped onto the porch and closed the door behind him to prevent the Border collie from darting out again.

He handed me the appropriate amount of change.

I handed him the magazine.

As he took it from my outstretched hand, our fingers touched. The warmth spreading through me turned into a raging fire. I felt myself stir within my uniform shorts. I said, "I—"

"Yes?" He waited expectantly for me to continue.

My throat was dry, so I swallowed hard and tried again. "I subscribe to the same publication. I—"

Vince looked at me, his dark eyes narrowing as if seeing me for the first time. He cocked his head to one side. "Really?"

I wet my lips. "I rented a post office box a couple of towns over so no one around here would know."

"You haven't told anyone?"

"Not even my family."

"So why tell me?"

I motioned toward the magazine he now held.

"Because of this?"

I nodded. Had I made a mistake? Had I jumped to a mistaken conclusion? "I need to get back on the road," I told him. "I have lots of mail to deliver."

As I turned to go, he stopped me.

"How about dinner?" Vince suggested. "I was going to grill and it'll be no trouble to throw on another steak and couple more ears of corn."

A date? He was asking me on a date? I had planned to drink beer and shoot pool at Gully's with my friends—my clueless friends—that evening, just like I did most Saturday nights. We certainly couldn't go anywhere in town.

"Maybe you can join me in the Jacuzzi after," he continued. "You don't need a suit, and I have a towel big enough for two."

"I—" I hesitated while my mind raced in a dozen different directions at once. I had always sought companionship outside of town. Did I dare take advantage of an opportunity that came to me? Did I dare risk the possibility that someone might see my car parked in front of Vince's later that evening and question why I was spending time with an outsider? I did.

I asked, "What time?"

I returned to Vince's house that evening. I had changed from my uniform into a form-fitting polo shirt, skin-tight Wrangler jeans starched and ironed to put razor-sharp creases down the legs, and well-worn, but not worn-out ropers. Vince wore a light blue, short-sleeve seersucker shirt; tan-colored, pleated-front chino shorts, and slip-on deck shoes without socks. It couldn't have been more obvious that this was a case of country boy meets city boy.

My host led me through the house. I had not been in the place while the Dentons had owned it, but I suspected the interior had never looked so good. The white walls had been recently painted, the hardwood floors had been polished to a shine, and the furniture was sparse but tasteful. Elroy spotted me as soon as we stepped onto the back porch, but the Border collie didn't seem nearly as interested in me as he had been when I was standing on the front porch in my uniform.

"I hope you don't think I've gone overboard," Vince said, "but you're the first guest I've had since moving in."

He had gone overboard. In the center of the patio sat a glass-topped, wrought iron patio table that had been set for two, with expensive china and real silver. I said, "Maybe a little."

Vince opened a bottle of red wine and poured a glass for each of us. Then he slapped a pair of T-bones and four ears of corn still in their husks on the propane grill and closed the lid. I sipped the wine politely, adjusting my beer-trained palate to the unfamiliar taste.

We made small talk while the steaks cooked, discussing the weather more than anything else, and before I realized how much time had passed, Vince was pulling the steaks and the corn off the grill and preparing our plates.

I sat, he sat, and then we stared at each other.

After a moment of awkward silence, I blurted, "I don't know what to do. I've never done this before."

Vince's eyes widened in surprise. "Never?"

I realized he had misunderstood me so I quickly explained. "I'm not a virgin," I said. "That's not what I meant. I meant I've never done this." I indicated the dinner table with a sweep of one hand. "I've never had a date."

He smiled. "All we have to do is eat."

"I can do that," I said with a smile. "I've been doing that my entire life." Then, between bites, I told him about my trips to Dallas and Austin without providing intimate details.

"And why did you find those trips so unfulfilling?"

I explained about my parents and how I'd always wanted the kind of relationship they had and how I despaired of ever finding it in rural Texas.

"You can search the world over and not find your soul mate," Vince said, "or you can step out your front door and stumble over him."

Is that what had happened?

"What about you?" I asked. "Have you ever—?"

"I was in a relationship for about a year," Vince explained. "I thought he was the one, but I was wrong. Horribly wrong. I had to get as far away from him as I could without changing jobs, and that's why I moved here."

"Is he still in Waco?"

"As far as I know, but there's little chance our paths will cross."

Vince grilled bananas in their skins for dessert, halving them lengthwise and covering the warm fruit with brown sugar and cinnamon after removing them from the grill. We used spoons to scoop the bananas from the skins and before long we were laughing and feeding each other.

After we finished dessert, Vince tossed one of the steak bones to Elroy and then I helped him clear the table and carry the dishes into the kitchen.

I don't know how to explain it—maybe it was the wine, maybe it was the full belly—but I felt comfortable with Vince, so comfortable that we spent the better part of the evening draining a second bottle of wine and telling each other our life stories. He had been out of the closet since his sophomore year of college and I had yet to tell any of my family or friends about my secret life.

"Someday you will," Vince said, "and when you do, no matter what their reaction, it will lift a huge burden from you."

A few minutes before midnight, the second bottle of wine long emptied and the buzz mostly worn off, I excused myself, telling my host that I had church in the morning.

Vince walked me to the front door and opened it. As I hesitated in the open doorway, he told me how much he had enjoyed our evening together. Then he took my face between his hands and covered my lips with his. Surprised but not a bit hesitant, I returned his kiss with equal fervor. As we kissed, my body quivered with desire.

When the kiss ended, Vince stepped back and said, "You'd best leave now before we do something we might regret later."

As I drove away, my jeans so tight at my crotch that I thought the zipper might burst from the pressure, I realized Vince and I had not used the Jacuzzi or his towel big enough for two.

That's how our relationship began, and we spent our next several dates revealing our souls and not our scrotums. In fact, I didn't see Vince naked again until our fifth date, when we ended the evening asleep in each other's arms. By then I knew I had found someone special.

I had found my total package.

THE BELT

Kal Cobalt

The suite door snicks shut behind Tobin. David sits in the chair. Tobin starts to sweat.

"How many times?" David's words are quiet, controlled. He's fully dressed.

Tobin's gaze drops to David's waist. Shit. The leather one. David owns a woven belt, something casual and textured that reminds Tobin of tennis players and doesn't hurt much. This is the serious belt. Its buckle gleams, the same silver as David's hair. It's an extension of David's body, of his aesthetic.

This is my flesh hitting you, David had said the first time, while Tobin sniveled on his knees, uncomprehending. *This is my tongue tasting you. This is my hand caressing you. This is my cock fucking you.* A new perspective for every sharp crack of the belt. David hadn't spoken about it after that first time. He hadn't had to.

"Tobin. How many times?"

Tobin drops to his knees just inside the doorway. How many

times today? He's always aware, at the time, that he's doing it, but somehow he forgets to count. "Fourteen?"

"No. Come here."

Tobin crawls. As he nears David's feet he lowers himself further, moving forward on forearms and knees till David's scuffed black shoes are directly beneath his chin. This close, he can feel David's heat, a strange, penetrating warmth like that of a few stiff drinks. David hasn't showered yet; he's stopped smelling like cologne and started smelling like a man.

"How many times?"

"Seventeen?"

"No." Beneath Tobin's gaze, David's feet move apart. "Take it off me."

Tobin shifts up enough to unfasten David's belt buckle, keeping his eyes lowered. The leather is warm from David's body, firm but supple, reminiscent of the animal it once was. Tobin had mentioned that once, carefully. *I merged with the animal*, David had said. *I took its skin for my own and impregnated it with metal, and now it is me. It's all very primal, Tobin. It's all very evolutionary.*

"How many times?"

"Twenty-one."

"No. Give it to me."

Tobin folds the belt in half and offers it up, his head down, as if presenting a sword to a king. His king. David accepts the belt slowly, then holds it in one hand so he can stroke Tobin's cheek with the other. Tobin keeps his eyes down, hot at David's touch.

"How many, Tobin?" David's voice is soft, to match the caress.

"Twenty-five," Tobin whispers, his throat thick with shame.

"No. Hold out your hands."

Keeping his head down, Tobin holds both hands out, palms up, and waits.

Waits.

Waits.

The first strike is against Tobin's left palm; he hears it more than he feels it until the sting settles in, deep and intense. "One, Master," he gasps, straightening his posture, holding his hands out flat once more. The second slap, Tobin thinks, is harder; it always feels like David strikes his dominant hand more sharply. "Two, Master," Tobin hitches out, resisting the urge to close his hands for even a moment.

"Breathe."

Respite. Tobin lets his hands drop slightly, careful to keep them open, and takes the opportunity to pull in a full breath and moisten his lips. He can feel David's impatience as they reach the end of the breathing time—its duration has never been spelled out, but Tobin feels it all the same—and he holds his hands up again.

It could be a stronger blow, or just the illusion of it after the break; either way, Tobin holds in a cry, waiting for the sharpest of the pain to dissipate before he trusts his voice. "Three, Master." How many times? How bad has he been? The guilt hurts almost as much as the next slap of the belt. He was very bad, very disrespectful, god knows how many infractions. "Four, Master." How he could do this, to his master, day after day, how he could forget the lessons his master crafts for him, so cruel and so clear...? "Five, Master." How many times? Tobin's palms ache, burn with his shame. How many more infractions? A dozen more? Two dozen more?

The leather strikes hard, cracking sharply against Tobin's skin. He hitches in breath to count off and can't find enough air to do it. Dimly, he realizes he's crying. It doesn't matter. He has to find the breath to speak, to answer and appreciate his master's punishment. He holds his hands up higher, a silent supplication for patience, and then breath comes back to him in a single shuddering gust. "Six," he sobs out softly, "Master." He wipes his nose on the shoulder of his shirt and holds position, waiting for the next slap.

"That's all."

David's voice is calm, velvet stretched over steel. Tobin blinks away tears, raising his head, looking up past the erection tenting David's unbelted pants and into his master's eyes.

"Only six," David murmurs. His expression warms a little, crow's feet deepening as affection reaches his eyes. "You're improving. I'm pleased."

"Thank you, Master." Tobin's voice is thick through his tears. He keeps his hands out, red, swollen; his master hasn't ordered anything different.

"Are you hard?" David nudges his foot between Tobin's thighs to find out for himself.

"Yes, Master."

"Undress."

Tobin gets to his feet just long enough to divest himself of everything but his shirt. That he can remove on his knees, and once it's off, he holds out his hands.

David passes his fingertips across Tobin's right palm, then his left. "Good boy. Now suck me."

Opening his master's fly is not an easy task; Tobin's hands are swollen and burning as he forces his fingers to work the button and zipper. David's erection is wide, pale, thickly veined, and Tobin wraps one hot hand around the shaft, squeezing though the motion drives sharp pins of pain along the lines where David's belt fell. Tobin licks his lips and takes the head of David's cock into his mouth, sucking gently, nursing at the very tip till David gives that first telltale moan of approval.

Tobin closes his eyes, heated through by the sound. It's here, when that sound of satisfaction rumbles free from David's throat like the purr of a contented lion, that David transforms from his master to his lover. David's hand comes up to caress the side of Tobin's face, fingertips tracing the contours of Tobin's cheekbone as if it were some rare and delicate artifact, and Tobin opens wider, relaxing his throat, taking David in to the root.

"Enough," David breathes. "Bed."

Tobin favors David's cock with one last sucking stroke, smiling lightly as he gets to his feet. David skins off everything but his T-shirt, leaving black garments of various fabrics draped over assorted furniture as he heads to the bedroom. It's a weakness, that T-shirt. Tobin knows it, but only because David told him, and as such it's a secret, a sacred and intimate thing Tobin would never question. It's more me than I am, David had said. I am alienated from my chest.

Tobin pulls back the covers, finds the faint stain from last night's sex still present on the sand-colored sheets. It's a waste, David says, to have the bedding washed nightly, and there is a comfort to sleeping in one's own smell. That, too, Tobin has accepted without question, as he has accepted the knowledge that stretching out under the covers, on his back, legs spread, is the way David wants him every night.

There is no speaking, and after David climbs into bed and rolls on top, there is no light. David's breath is warm and affectionate at Tobin's cheek, pausing momentarily for kisses along that same cheekbone; David's scent is dark and mammalian, trapped by the sheets, as his thighs nudge Tobin's further apart. Tobin reaches, blindly, and rests a hand on David's arm, half over skin and half over T-shirt sleeve. When the lights are on, David is always directing. In the dark, David trusts Tobin enough to be himself.

A soft snap of plastic, a faintly moist, organic sound, and

David's hand is between Tobin's legs, spreading thick, viscous lube. *To ease the friction,* David had said once, on a postcoital float between drags off the joint. *Like a well-functioning piston. Like oil in a car.*

David's fingers, then, well practiced in what Tobin can take. Tobin finds David's shoulder, clings to it, squeezes hard as David presses two fingers in, scissoring mercilessly. There are times when the foreplay is lengthy, times when David starts touching Tobin just after dinner and doesn't stop till they've passed out on the bed four hours later. Not tonight. Not on a correction night. Two fingers, scissored hard, and that's all; then David's shifting up to grab the pillow, and Tobin wets his lips, releasing a breath.

Tobin knows David's cockhead as intimately as he knows the pale crescent beneath David's right thumbnail, the slightly phlegmy stuttering throat-clearing David inevitably makes in his sleep forty-five minutes after he nods off, the way David needs his toiletries arranged just so on the bathroom counter. The tip of his cock is almost flat, and Tobin breathes out again, opening up to that familiar bluntness till he feels the flare at the base of the head slide into him. He knows the way the vein that runs across the top of David's cock is bulging right now; as David resists the primal urge to drive into Tobin to the root, Tobin knows the way David's buttocks tense, knows from the glimpse he had in a suite with a mirror once. The image comes back to him brightly in the dark, David's pale ass flexing, bracketed by Tobin's tanned shins.

David exhales, warm breath washing across Tobin's chest, and presses in slow and hard. Tobin moans, arching into it, reaching down to cup his cock. On the way there his fingers clash with David's, moving to do the same. There's a soft, short grunt of laughter from above, and Tobin smiles, groping for David's wrist and then pulling it down to his cock. Better David's hand than his.

David presses in again, passing his hand over Tobin's cock in a deceptively gentle motion. Tobin hitches his legs higher on David's thighs, then shifts them up to David's hips. The angle forces him to pull in a breath as David slides in another inch without even trying. David's moist fingers—lube? saliva?—find Tobin's nipple and squeeze, eliciting another moan that just keeps going as David slides all the way in.

David always rests, here, and Tobin reaches up to cup his hand over David's nape, breathing with him, finding the rhythm. *We merge,* David had whispered the first time, when he had cradled Tobin in his arms, fucking him hard and slow and so thoroughly Tobin could not even find the words to agree. *We merge like everything else. There is no singular being. Anywhere.*

Tobin shifts slightly, aware of the way David's weight begins to move, and then David's hand is on the mattress just beneath Tobin's armpit, bracing him. Tobin grips that upper arm, again half a hand of skin and half a hand of sleeve, and waits. David only starts when he's ready.

The first thrust is slow, learning the way their bodies fit together on this particular night. Tobin tips his hips up encouragingly, and David thrusts again, his breath catching. Tobin pushes his hips up, more forward this time, impatient. He knows what's coming. He doesn't want to wait. His cock is long and full against his belly, swollen and waiting for David's hand. All of Tobin is waiting.

David finds it, that nebulous *it* that slips him into his comfort zone, and the thrusts turn rough and jarring, forcing Tobin to link his ankles in an attempt to keep their bodies joined. David's breaths are harsh, focused, and Tobin reaches up to brace himself against the headboard, gasping as David's cock rubs him just so. David's free hand goes frantic then, clutching at Tobin's hip, then his shoulder, seeking just the right way to anchor Tobin's body. Tobin works his hips up, fisting one hand in the front of David's T-shirt and yanking him closer, and that seems to do it. David cries out, a harsh, faintly startled sound, and his back arches sharply as he throws himself into Tobin for those final, crucial half-dozen thrusts. Tobin can feel David's semen jetting deep into him, and he moans; we merge, like everything else. There is no singular being. Anywhere.

David breathes, his forehead on Tobin's sweat-slicked chest. Closing his eyes, Tobin pets the back of David's T-shirt, damp and stuck to his skin with sweat. There is a transmutation that happens in these moments, Tobin has decided; there is a kind of magic that happens between when he accepts David's semen and when David coaxes his own out. The circuit is primed but not closed, and Tobin feels the whole of his being aching for completion, something far more basic and necessary than the urge to come.

David leans up and takes Tobin's cock in his hand, letting out a low murmur of pleased surprise at its state. It feels swollen in David's hand, distended like a pregnant woman's belly, as thick and filled with blood as his belt-whipped palms. David presses in again, his cock still half-hard, and Tobin sucks in a breath, waiting, again. Then David begins to stroke, long, tight passes Tobin knows intimately, as he knows the slow, languid grind David offers in counterpoint. Here, there is nothing but David; he is over and inside and all thoughts of a universe beyond him fade. David's hand tightens, working the top half of Tobin's shaft in a perfect squeeze-twist Tobin never taught him but David seemed to intuit, importing the motion from the endless lazy adolescent afternoons Tobin spent sprawled half-naked on his bed, employing the exact same technique till he'd milked himself dry.

Tobin gasps, arching his hips up into David's next press, and David quickens the pace of his hand, thumb working up the underside just below the ridge, over and over till Tobin tenses from head to toe, holding his breath till the orgasm breaks over him, forcing his cock up into David's hand again and again, semen hot on his belly as David strokes it out of him, easy at first, then with a firmer grip, seeking to squeeze it all out.

Drained, Tobin lies boneless, twitching sharply as David works the last of the semen from him. Then David's hand is on Tobin's thigh, and David gently pulls out; Tobin waits, eyes open in the dark, spent but waiting for that crucial closing of the circuit, so close now, David shifting lower and taking the sheets with him, David's breath warm against his cock.

There. David's tongue strokes Tobin's belly as he takes Tobin's semen, licking with a slow, concentrated methodology to make sure he finds it all. Tobin's skin cools where David's tongue has been, his saliva quickly chilling in the open air.

David moans, and Tobin relaxes; it's complete. David passes his hand gently over Tobin's belly as he shifts up and to the side, settling in against Tobin, and then, finally, is the kiss, thorough and quiet, David's hand at Tobin's nape, Tobin's hand at David's hip.

"I love you," David whispers in the dark, pressing his forehead to Tobin's.

Tobin had asked about that the first time, how love fit into David's mechanical, atheistic worldview. David had smiled, a coy little expression Tobin had rarely seen, and said: *I am a realist. I have experienced love, and therefore it exists.*

David takes Tobin's hand off his hip, brings it up to his lips, kisses the still-hot palm.

"I love you," Tobin whispers in return.

LONELY BOY

Doug Harrison

My pace quickened as I strode from my parents' car. I glanced back once. Dad waved from the driver's seat, a nonverbal gesture of support nurtured by his desire for me to begin the life experience he never had. He lowered his arm and flapped his hand, figuratively pushing me forward, as he had literally done many times before to urge me onto the field, any sports field. Mom also waved, sorta, a weak gesture, her hand wavering between encouragement, blowing a final kiss, or wiping a tear.

I heard the familiar sound of the engine sputtering before turning over. It was no longer a family car—I was on my own. Carless and clueless. I suppressed a chuckle. My motor mind still coughed up phrases like a nondescript character in a Gilbert and Sullivan operetta, but at least I was near Boston, home of the Lamplighters. Not that I would have time or means to wander off campus— I'd come here to study physics and math, and that was that.

I snickered. Julie was sure in for a surprise. No more dating, even though she was majoring in voice somewhere in the bowels of Boston. So she won the Best Voice in New England Contest—got a full-time scholarship. Big deal. I didn't win any Best Science Student Contest, but I had dug up a scholarship too. I wondered how she was doing during her first week in town. Probably lonely like me.

I winced at the memory of the unending stream of compliments I had shoveled into her voracious ego, and the memory of my inevitable reward—going home with lover's balls, my jockeys glued to my upper thighs with precum. I was wedded to my right hand. Well, to both hands, since I had such a big dick.

Who had the big ego now?

I rubbed my crotch, and then quickly withdrew my hand, hoping no one had noticed. My mind flashed back to the dark corner of the magazine section of my hometown's sole smoke shop, where every month I had crouched over the latest copy of *Physique Pictorial*, pressing my hard-on against the chipped wooden display case, peeking at hunks clad in posing straps. The few nude models with hard-ons didn't outrank me in endowment, but their physiques sure did. God, how I had yearned to look like them. Did that make me queer? I sure wished prissy Julie had given me the chance to find out.

I bit my lower lip. Fledgling students and their parents flowed around me as if I were an implacable boulder in a turbulent stream. No one smiled or said hello. And, of course, I didn't make any effort to engage them.

Then a guy about my height pushed his way toward me: brown hair, like mine, but close-cropped, a tailored crew cut. His freshly pressed sport shirt didn't conceal his gymnast's physique. He held out his hand.

"Hi, I'm Mark. You a new student?"

I stared at one of my suitcases, then the other. "Yeah," I mumbled. "I'm Brad Chapman."

Mark unrolled a single-sheet scroll of paper, glanced at it, and shoved it into his hip pocket. "I'm one of the brothers from Alpha Pi Omega, over there." I followed the smooth arc of his hand across a grassy field and past a cluster of tennis courts to a row of brick buildings. "We volunteered, well, it was our turn this year, to welcome the frosh and get you settled in. The guys, that is. The sorority sisters help the women." He leered. "And point them toward the frat houses."

I managed a weak smile.

"C'mon, let's get started." He turned, faced the building I had been reconnoitering, and swept his hand in a grandiose semicircle.

God, was this guy a drama student?

"You must know this is Samuels Hall," he said.

I nodded and scanned the U-shaped, ivy-covered, weathered-brick building. Its three floors rang with the creak of stubborn windows forced upward, doors slamming, and a few shouts of joy. A long banner, made of wrinkled white sheets held together by large safety pins, displayed a scrawled message: WELCOME, CLASS OF '61.

"A couple brothers from the house cobbled that together," Mark volunteered.

At least they tried, I thought. *Four years, four long years of...of what?* My mood was ironically underscored by Elvis's big hit, "Heartbreak Hotel," blasting from a corner window. I wondered if I dared tune in my favorite program, *Live from the Met*, every Saturday afternoon. I lifted my suitcases.

"I'll take those for you."

Before I could protest, he yanked them from my hands. I wasn't sure if Mark suppressed a laugh at my bargain-basement luggage, but I sure did notice the bulge of his well-tanned biceps. I followed him up two flights of stairs, past communal bathrooms, to a three-room suite, my home for the year, like it or not. We entered.

A rail-thin man several inches shorter than me introduced himself. "I'm Jim."

"And I'm Sam," grunted the second.

They both held out their hands and we shook.

"We took the room over there," Jim announced.

A third freshman meandered out of the second bedroom. "I took the lower bunk in the other room. I'm Winston." He walked back into the bedroom and resumed his unpacking. I took in the undersized living room—two small desks with matching chairs that probably creaked, and an overstuffed easy chair that needed a stitch job. I went into my room: one desk.

"I took the desk," Winston announced without looking up as he arranged pens, pencils, and a few mementos from home on the small surface. His open designer suitcases occupied most of the lower bunk. I stared at the upper bunk: no ladder. Good thing I'd hiked miles of rocky terrain and learned to hoist myself over obstacles. Mark swung my suitcases onto what was to be my nightly precarious perch, a nest with one occupant.

"Well, here you are," Mark said, and again offered his hand. "If you need anything, give me a jingle." He handed me a scrap of paper. "That's the house number." He smacked me between my shoulder blades, but his slap lingered and his hand slid a few inches down my back. He strode toward the bedroom door, quickly scanned the living room, and smiled at me, a smile that lingered like his slap as his periscope gaze traveled from my face to my feet and back to my eyes.

I blushed. He left.

I scrutinized the bedroom. The bunk beds were shoved into

an alcove. Two bureaus and Winston's desk filled the opposing wall. His monogrammed towels were neatly folded over the two towel racks screwed into the back of the door.

Shit! No goddamn privacy. I could retreat to the library to study, but where would I jerk off? In the shower? In the bushes at night? I'd managed at home with Mom and Dad downstairs. But I didn't have three roommates there, and I wasn't forced to share an upper and lower jammed into a tiny bedroom to boot. Could I manage a silent quickie under the covers? Would Winston notice? Would he smell my cum? Would he even care?

The four of us finished unpacking and found our way to the cafeteria. I filled my tray with my first nondescript college dinner; Jim, Sam and I sat together chatting about where we were from, this and that, but Winston spurned us for a group of guys wearing prep-school blazers.

After dinner I paid my respects to Jumbo, a huge stuffed elephant—P. T. Barnum's gift to the school—that was part of college lore. Jumbo was ensconced appropriately in the foyer of the biology building and was conspicuously anatomically correct. I placed a quarter in his curled trunk, as my dorm mates had told me we freshmen were supposed to do, and returned to my room to collapse onto my high-rise bed.

Winston, already in pristine underwear, had taken off his black horn-rimmed glasses and was in the act of inserting earplugs. He switched off the light as I entered. I flicked it back on and flicked him the bird at the same time, threw one set of his towels onto his desk, placed my towels on the rack above his, brushed my teeth, and hauled myself into bed. I tossed and turned while Winston snored, and I vowed to find a drugstore the next day to purchase my first set of earplugs.

No more waking up with a warm cat nestled in the crook of my legs. My coffin-sized enclosure sat over the lair of a selfish, entitled Grinch. The pleasant vibes emanating from a purring cat had been supplanted by sizzling stress, much like a high-tension wire crackling in the night.

The next morning found me seated in a large lecture hall in the physics building. At eight fifty-five, a tall man with a medium build, thin glasses and a crowlike plume of thick dark hair entered. He wore a rumpled, brown, threadbare tweed jacket, despite the early fall heat. He ambled toward the center of the long lecturer's platform, stared at his captive audience, and stepped into the wastepaper basket. None of us moved a muscle as he leaned over, grabbed the container, and yanked his shoe free. He scrutinized the room as if nothing had happened.

"I'm Professor Knapp, chairman of the physics department. I'm pleased to see so many aspiring physicists in the freshman class. More than we've ever had. I'll spare you the cliché of, 'Look to your right, and look to your left,' but the truth of the matter is, only a third of you will graduate with this major. But welcome anyway." He pointed to a pile of papers on the table. "Take one of these. It's a list of your respective advisors. Good luck." He left the room.

With the help of a map, I found my advisor's office and we worked out my courses for the first semester, the usual for a physics major, except I talked my way into a sophomore philosophy course. I again consulted the map, and headed to the gym to register, where an assemblage of tables on the basketball court, sprouting raised signs like delegates at a political convention, announced each department. I likened the maelstrom of milling students to the interior of a confused beehive. Nonetheless, I obtained signatures for all my class choices and collected the appropriate booklists, then headed for the bookstore.

My physics text was the first in a three-volume set, but I

grabbed all three hefty tomes so I could browse ahead to assuage my curiosity about upcoming topics, especially during the summer. My philosophy text was the two-volume boxed set of the complete dialogues of Plato. Would Plato even hint at Greek homosexuality, and if he did, would the instructor skedaddle around it? Math, German and English lit texts quickly followed, until all that remained to pick up was my gym uniform.

I approached the only likely counter to face a young female student, not much older than me. *Shit!*

She grinned. "You want a gym uniform, huh?"

I stammered a soft, "Yes."

She looked at my chest. "You take a medium, huh?"

An even softer, "Yep."

She reached under the glass counter—could she see my crotch through the display case?— and said, "You'll need one of these." She pushed a box containing a size-large jock toward me. I blushed and went to the register.

An older woman rang up my purchases. I used my new checkbook for the first time.

"All your books won't fit into one bag," she said. "Not even two."

"I'll just carry them," I said. "But can you put these in a bag?" I bunched my gym jersey, shorts, and jockstrap into a clump behind the books.

"Yeah, sure." She smirked. Salesmen selling bras had to control their reactions better than that.

And with that, I started across the campus, my books stacked precariously in my arms, held from the bottom at waist level, the paper bag with my gym equipment tucked between the top book and my chin. I was reminded of the giants in *Das Rheingold* sealing off the last vestige of Freia with a final golden brick.

I was staggering across the quad between bookstore and dorm when I spotted Mark walking toward me. He waved and broke into a trot.

"Here, let's put those down," he ordered as he maneuvered books and me to the grass. The tower of books toppled. I sat cross-legged amid the wreckage. Mark sat opposite me, leaned back on his elbows, and laughed. He wore black running shorts that accentuated his crotch as he spread powerful legs. His flexed biceps flowed into muscular shoulders that gripped the tops of firm pecs. His nipples and washboard stomach were outlined through a tight, sweat-soaked red singlet. A grungy white face-cloth dangled from his shorts; he yanked it out and threw it to me. I wiped sweat from my forehead and tossed it back. We caught our breaths and stared at each other.

"Quite a load," he observed.

"Yeah," I answered.

He looked into my brown paper bag and grinned. "I'd like to see you in that."

"They're just gym shorts."

"I mean the jock, man."

I blushed for the second time that day.

"You have great calves," he said. "Do lots of running? Let's back up, what sports are you into?"

"I'm no athlete. But I did develop into a good swimmer at summer camp." I took a deep breath. "So, I tried out for the swimming team freshman year. Within a week I had the worst case of athlete's feet the family doctor had ever seen. Had to soak my size elevens in purple glop twice a day for ten days. So that ended that. But, I figured, running can't be too different from swimming, just opposite body parts moving in sync. Hell, anyone can run around in circles—well, ovals, to be precise. Got to be pretty good. But the guys made fun of me, like, skinny and all that. Hell, I always thought runners were supposed to be thin. Well, it was the *sissy* part that really got to me."

Mark grimaced. I continued.

"I'd go to the track after practice to run solitary laps and I'd gaze at the hills as the setting sun cast long shadows. It was very peaceful."

"You're poetic," Mark interjected.

"Thanks. We lived in a valley, a typical New England factory town built up around a river, and I'd walk a mile home from school up steep hills. And often, weather permitting, I'd hike in the woods."

"You're quite something," Mark said.

"Well, along with being a nerd, I do like nature. Especially since trees and brooks don't poke fun at me. The gift of nature is that she returns, indeed amplifies, whatever you give her."

Mark leaned back, his hands under his head, bunching his biceps, and stared at the sky. Then he sat up.

"Like to go on a hike tomorrow?"

My mouth dropped. "Er, yes. Where? No, I mean yes, but wherever you want to go."

"Ever hear of the White Mountains?"

"Of course. I've read a lot about Mount Washington, the cog railway, the two-hundred-mile-an-hour winds at the top, fierce weather that can change in an instant. And Franconia Notch and Crawford Notch. And Lucy Crawford and her loneliness."

I paused after the last word. Silence hung between us like a sheet of glass, a transparent barrier.

Finally Mark spoke. "We'll start out easy—Mount Chocorua. Bring a jacket and be at the house at six a.m. I have a car and I'll take care of the food."

I blanched at the early hour. "Can I bring anything?"

"Just yourself." Mark stood, grabbed my hand, and hoisted me to my feet. "Back to the dorm with you." He grabbed most of my books, I took the remainder and my brown bag, and we moseyed to my room.

Winston, attired in spotless plaid Bermuda shorts and a tailored polo shirt, looked up when we entered. Mark and I deposited my books on the unclaimed desk in the living room; he said, "See you tomorrow," and left.

"*I* didn't have anyone to carry my books home," Winston snorted. He raised an eyebrow. "Where are you two going tomorrow?"

"Hiking."

"You mean walking in the woods?"

"What else, numb-nuts?"

Winston cut short a comeback, looked at my stack of books, and sneered, "Christ, you've got a lot of books. What're you majoring in? Have you even decided?"

"Of course. I knew what I wanted to study when I was in high school. Physics."

"Physics! What the hell is that good for?"

"Oh, it's led to a few things here and there, like electricity and airplanes."

"Well, I've got lots of thick books too. I'm premed. My dad's a doctor."

"And what's your specialty gonna be? Have you even thought about that?"

"Of course! Whatever makes the most bucks."

No Albert Schweitzer complex there. Better living through med school. I dashed into the bathroom to piss.

"Christ," I yelled. "There's a goddamn fish in the shower. A big one!" I dashed back into the room.

"Yeah," said Winston, hands on hips. "We each got our

specimen today for biology class. It's on ice. We're going to dissect it this semester."

"Ice or no ice, it smells," I yelled.

"You'll get used to it."

I went nose to nose with Winston. "I thought you biology creeps started with worms."

"We did that in high school. Go shower downstairs."

Jim came out of his room. "You gonna name it?"

"Goddamn!" Winston shouted and stormed out, probably to have dinner with his preppy friends. I felt like pitching his frozen fish after him.

That night I climbed into bed. Winston was already snoring. I thought about Mark. I sure would have liked to see him naked. Probably looked like the full-size reproduction of the discus thrower statue in high school. Of course, Mr. Thrower wore a fig leaf, but so what. He looked like a *Physique Pictorial* model. I retrieved an unused wad of Kleenex from under my pillow, spit on my right palm, and coaxed my boner to a hardness I seldom achieved.

"What're you doing up there?"

"What d'ya think?"

"What?" Winston must have pried out one earplug.

"I said, 'What d'ya think?'"

"Stop shaking the bed, you woke me. Go get off in the bathroom."

"And come all over your goddamn fish?"

"Fuck off!"

"That's what I'm doing, asshole!"

"Well, don't dribble on me."

"Get over it—go back to sleep. I'm almost done, anyway. To paraphrase Gilbert and Sullivan's Nanki-Poo, 'You've interrupted a private apostrophe.'"

"What the hell does an apostrophe have to do with jerking off?"

"You'd never get it, jerkoff."

The next morning my alarm went off at five-thirty, much to Winston's annoyance. I showered in our bathroom, notwithstanding the stinky fish, which I shoved to one side. Winston would be pissed when he discovered his soapy, thawing fish.

Mark met me in dawn's semidarkness at his frat house door. He turned on the porch light, aghast.

"You can't hike in your gym shorts!"

"They're all I have. Besides, they're brand new."

He waved me in. "C'mon upstairs. I'll set you straight." I followed him to his room. It was surprisingly large and had a small bathroom.

"How'd you rate your own bathroom?"

"I'm the house treasurer, and a junior," he stated matter-of-factly. "Now, get out of those shorts." I turned to go into the bathroom. "Hold on," he ordered, "I've seen it all before." So I stepped out of my shorts in front of him.

He took a hard look. "So, I finally get to see you in your new jock," he said. I blushed. "Nice. Now let me see the bottoms of your sneakers." I put my hand on the back of a leather recliner and raised my legs one at a time. He examined my soles, coming close—deliberately?—to brushing his shoulder against my crotch. "Okay, I guess they'll do. If the terrain was really rough, you'd have to get a good pair of hiking boots."

From his bureau, he retrieved a pair of long, dark brown walking shorts with deep side pockets. The material was durable, almost like corduroy.

"You can slide halfway down the mountain in these, and not tan your ass." He winked. I stepped into the shorts and ever so slowly buttoned my fly.

"Let's go!" Mark thrust his backpack into my hands and we went into the kitchen. He grabbed a small cooler and led me to his car, a red '55 Ford coupe. He opened the trunk and plunked the cooler near the front. I noticed several coils of rope, white, black, and red, and what I assumed was climbing equipment, like carabiners.

"We're not going to repel?" I squeaked.

"Not to worry. No cliff walls. Not this time, anyway."

We drove to New Hampshire, chatting along the way about our interests, hometowns, boyhood friends, and old girlfriends. His current girlfriend was also a junior. He didn't say much about her, but probed me at length about Julie until I vented my frustrations about not getting any. He nodded; he'd been there, apparently.

Finally Mount Chocorua came into view. "I'm going to take you up a fairly easy trail, but one that tourists usually don't bother with," he said as we pulled into the parking lot. Mark slung his backpack over his shoulder, and we started up the Champney Falls Trail.

The air was nippy in the early morning autumn air, but soon heated up. After a couple of hours, we stopped by the falls, rested, and drank from the water bottles clipped to our belts. Mark took his shirt off and splashed cold water over his torso. I stared at his body. I couldn't help myself.

"Well, what're you waiting for?" he asked. I slid out of my shirt. "Nice," Mark said, and splattered me with cold water. We played around like two kids for a spell, then resumed our hike, finally passing the tree line to an upward sloping field of open rock. We clambered up, Mark in the lead, occasionally turning to see how I was doing, and offering a helping hand when needed, which wasn't often. We reached the top, rewarded by a breathtaking view of forested hills, rocky ravines, and craggy summits. We were alone. Mark eased his backpack off.

It was almost noon, and the sun was directly overhead. Mark was well tanned, but he applied lotion to my shoulders, back and chest. I closed my eyes and sunk into his caresses, and we both sighed when he capped the bottle. A warm breeze embraced our half-naked bodies while we watched cumulus clouds drift among distant mountaintops, occasionally jostling for position around the peaks. Mark put his arm around my waist and pulled me close.

"There's a lot to be said for a breathtaking view when you earn it."

I murmured a husky *yes* while encircling his waist with my arm. His hand slid into my rear pocket just as we heard voices. Mark shook his head, moved away from me, and pulled a large red beach towel from his backpack. We sat cross-legged, smiling at each other while reveling in the view. He handed me a piece of cheese, I don't remember what kind, and then two wineglasses and a small bottle of wine appeared.

"Liebfraumilch," he intoned as he opened the bottle and poured. "Virgin's milk," he added through a sly smirk. "White and fruity."

A party of four had arrived, noticed us, and settled onto a far boulder. They acted like a pair of newlyweds with their kissing and fondling. I was jealous of their freedom. We finished our meal, relaxed for a few moments, cleaned up, and headed back down the trail.

The descending trek was more rapid than the ascending hike; we were about half an hour from the car when the trail forked. Mark counted a number of measured paces and stopped. He pushed his way a few feet into the dense foliage and signaled me to follow with a flick of his head. We were still shirtless. I was sure his arms and chest were getting scratched, but I was close behind him and didn't get nicked, his knapsack notwithstanding, when the bushes snapped back into place. We came to a grassy clearing, about ten feet in diameter, and Mark halted. I pictured a doe and her faun nesting for the night in this secluded spot, surrounded by an almost impenetrable thicket. Mark lowered the knapsack and again spread the large beach towel, this time with the knapsack under one end to serve as a pillow. He rested his hands on my shoulders.

"You know I'm attracted to you."

"Yes. I can sense it. I...I feel the same way about you."

"I'm going to give you your first real kiss."

I studied my shoes, hoping Mark wouldn't notice my tears.

"Don't cry," he said. "Not now. Sometime, but not now."

I nodded.

He lifted my chin with his forefinger, took me in his arms, and we kissed. Our lips formed a grotto in which two tongues lingered, searched, and caressed.

We took a breather, literally, and I began to kneel, unsure how to proceed, but willing to explore the possibilities. Mark put his strong hands on my shoulders.

"Lie down," he said, his voice a gentle command. I complied. He stood at my feet and stepped out of his shorts. I gasped.

"You've been waiting for this, haven't you?" he asked.

I couldn't speak. There he stood, clad in jock and boots, the quintessential centerfold from *Physique Pictorial*, except that the bulge in his jock was pulsing.

"It's okay, it's okay, relax," he said. He knelt and slid my shorts and jock over my sneakers. My cock *thwapped* as it bounced off my abdomen. Mark stripped off his jock and his dick, mimicking mine, sprung out and up. He lowered himself onto me and ran his fingers through my hair. I shuddered. He wiped a final tear from the corner of my eye.

"This has never happened to me," I managed to say.

"You've dreamt about it, haven't you?"

I nodded, and giggled.

"What's wrong?"

"Nothing. I'm just happy. Even though I've been taught that this is wrong. Very wrong."

"Maybe it is."

"I've tried to be with girls, but...but..."

Mark put his finger across my lips. He took me into his arms and held me. Tight. I shivered. Then he ran his index finger the length of my torso, tracing the fine line of sprouting hair from the center of my chest to my navel. "You're beautiful," he murmured.

"I'm so skinny," I countered.

"You're okay just the way you are. Besides, you're filling out. Sign up for weight lifting in gym class if you must. But I'm drawn to your innocence, your inner beauty, your purity of soul, your sincerity."

I gulped.

"You may lose your innocence, but hold on to the rest."

He pressed his lips to mine, and I melted. I again yielded my mouth to his tongue, a symbol, hopefully of a beginning, of me offering my body, my essence, my spirit.

He gently moved my arms from my sides and placed them in a crosslike position. Then he locked his hands onto my wrists. His sinuous thighs forced my legs apart and snared them in a spread-eagle position. I couldn't move. Mark ran his tongue over each of my nipples. I moaned. Then he nibbled and bit. I yelped as my dick twitched. Pleasure and pain. A new sensation. Oh, yeah, I had played with my nipples now and then. But this was different, very different. A sweaty man, a gorgeous hunk, had captured me. He was on top of me, our dicks pressed together by our firm abs.

I looked past Mark's face. It was no longer high noon, and the sun's rays filtered obliquely through pine needles, down to variegated leaves, in the first blush of fall.

I climbed the pyramid, naked and sweaty, prodded to its flat top. I was spread-eagled on a sacrificial stone, four priests in multi-colored loincloths and flaming plumed helmets stretching my limbs to their limit. The high priest approached. The obsidian blade gleamed in the sunlight. I screamed. Why? I submitted. I arched my back slightly and offered my heart to the knife. My pulsing, bleeding heart was held up to cheering crowds far below.

I knelt in church, my hands clasped in prayer. I stared at the painting of Jesus, rays of light emanating from his bleeding heart.

I couldn't give my heart to Mark—he had already taken it, and knew it. He lowered his head to my cock, and licked the tip. My imagination had never conjured such sensations. He swallowed my dick, all of it. I arched my back and pumped into his face. My body trembled. Mark raised his head, releasing me. His eyes followed the arcs of our cum, combining in a pool of ejaculate on my stomach, glistening like dewdrops in the sun.

Mark held me as our breathing slackened, then crawled next to me and put one arm under my shoulder, holding me with one hand. He ran the index finger of his other hand through the silky slickness of my belly and licked his finger clean, his tongue pausing on his lips to savor the taste. He scooped up more of our cum and offered me his finger, a silent communion.

We cleaned off, using our jocks. He stood and pulled me to my feet, offering me his jock as he stepped into mine. His wet pouch clung to my soft dick and I cupped my fist around it.

"Our own secret," he whispered through a smile.

I grinned. "Like a wedding ring."

The bushes rustled and I jumped.

Mark laughed. "Not to worry. Just a squirrel looking for nuts, not a skunk or a bear."

"Or a person," I added.

"We're safe here." He paused and lifted his finger to his chin like a mischievous kid plotting some evil. "Next time I'll bring my rope. The soft rope."

My spent dick sprung to life. Mark moved behind me, reached around my shoulders, and rubbed my chest. His hard dick in the damp jock probed my buttcrack. I moaned and clasped his hands. "It's time to start back to campus," he said.

"It's silly, but I wish we could hide in our secluded nest forever."

"You're not silly."

"Forbidden love is usually challenged, often doomed, and sometimes fatal," I whispered.

Mark spun me around. "Where did you get *that*?" His hard dick bobbed within the tented jock like a reproaching finger. "Sounds like you should be majoring in philosophy or ethics."

"*Tristan und Isolde*," I answered.

He looked perplexed.

"An old legend. My favorite opera." I paused, regrouped, and continued. "A more modern version is *Lady Chatterley's Lover*."

"Yeah, class differences."

"Yep. Class differences. Sexual preferences weren't even mentioned then. At least not openly."

"Still aren't, Kinsey notwithstanding," Mark concluded. "C'mon, let's go." He shook grass, dirt, and pine needles from our red towel. He flicked his head for the second time that day.

I latched on to the opposing corners of the makeshift blanket and we reverently folded it into a red cube, resting it in Mark's upturned palms. It was warm from the heat of our bodies. He looked into my eyes with an unblinking stare. I placed my hands on top of our portable nest and we leaned into a final kiss.

He lowered the blanket into his rumpled rucksack, brushed the creased surfaces of the bag with measured motions, and slid it over his sweaty shoulders. Unlike Tristan and Isolde, our lovers' afterglow didn't lead to round two of heightened passion. Not that day. We trudged back to the car, each lost in his own thoughts.

CHARMING PRINCES

Jamie Freeman

Our story began—as so many love stories do—with a shoe.

"Do you have this in size ten?" he asked the salesclerk. Her name tag identified her as Courtnei. A tiny heart-shaped sticker dotted the terminal letter.

Courtnei took the running shoe, turning it around in her hands, and said, "Do you want to see it in light blue too?"

"Sure." His smile was picture-perfect.

"Are you gonna buy those?" I asked.

He looked at me for the first time and my stomach lurched. He was beautiful in a way that made me look around to see if he was being filmed. A man this gorgeous could have stepped off a movie set, with his faded jeans and white Oxford shirt, perfectly manicured hands, Rolex, signet ring and expensively messy haircut. He had that fresh, sharply defined quality a man can only achieve through the consistent use of staggeringly over-priced skin-care products. Everything about him whispered: *wealth*. I looked into his pale-blue eyes, acutely aware of my tattered Levi's, stained T-shirt and army surplus jacket. I pointed to the poster I'd been clutching in front of me.

"Yes," he said.

I snorted in exasperation. Of course this child of privilege wouldn't get it.

"This woman works in a Honduran sweatshop making the shoes you're considering buying. She is paid less than twenty dollars a week despite the long hours and high productivity demands. She has no protection if she or one of her three children becomes ill. She is the sole support of her—"

"What's her name?"

"What?"

"I asked her name," he said. "Sometimes personalizing the message, say, something like, 'This is Maria Cortez. She works in a sweatshop near La Ceiba—'"

"Are you making fun of people in poverty?"

"No. I'm making fun of you." He smiled again, his lips parting in a frankly sensual manner.

"Okay, so I've got these in dark blue in ten and a half, and the light blue ones in ten." Courtnei pushed past me with a pair of shoeboxes. "He can't be here," she said to him, and then turned to me. "You can't be here."

"He's here with me," the man said.

"But he can't—"

"Thank you, Courtnei," the man said. "May I have a few minutes to talk with my friend? Then I'll try these on?"

"I'm not your friend," I said.

He shrugged. Courtnei looked dubious but drifted away.

"So you're here to keep people from buying these shoes?" he asked.

"Yes. The workers—"

"Wait." He held up his hand, the palm pink and perfect. The

gesture was strangely erotic. I shifted in place; he smiled again.

"You're still laughing at me."

"There is a difference between a smile and a laugh...and you need to tell me your name."

"I need to what?"

"Tell me your name."

I crossed me arms and considered my options.

"I'm Fletcher Alden," he said. He held out his hand. I shook it, feeling small and disoriented.

"Ashe," I said. "Ashe Stern."

He smiled again, blue eyes probing me. Sweat trickled down my back.

"You know, Ashe, in a country in which nearly forty percent of the population is unemployed or underemployed and seventy percent live in poverty, the fact that this company provides over five hundred jobs, on-site medical care, and wages that are fifty percent more than the federally mandated minimum wage could be seen as a good thing."

"Who're you supposed to be? Jeffrey Sachs?"

"No. I'm just saying this may be more complicated than it seems."

"That's a bullshit excuse."

"Most things are," he said.

"Are what?"

"More complicated than they seem."

"No," I said. I was trying unsuccessfully to work up some emotion about the Honduran workers, but all I could see was dark hair that tufted from the collar of Fletcher's bright white undershirt, the ample denim bulge between his legs and the heavily muscled runner's thighs that stretched the legs of his jeans. "This is about...this is about a definition of social justice that transcends national borders."

"As you say. You're clearly the expert."

I flushed.

"Do you believe that?" I asked.

"What? That you're an expert?"

"No. The other part, about the workers being better off."

He shook his head. "Not really. These shoes cost about seven dollars to produce, package and ship. They're on sale for a hundred and fifty. Somebody's making a bundle and I'm guessing it's not Maria Cortez, and because Courtnei works for minimum wage plus commissions, I doubt it's her either."

I hadn't really considered Courtnei's wages.

"Do you think she has health insurance?"

"Courtnei? Probably can't afford it."

"I hate this," I said.

"Then why are you here?"

"For Maria," I said.

"Don't you mean Courtnei?" he asked.

I sighed.

"Just yanking your chain," he said. "Courtnei? I'm going to pass on these."

"You're not gonna buy them?"

"No."

I blushed in confusion, unable to figure out if this was a victory. I dropped my eyes, studying my own fair-trade shoes, letting my brown hair fall down in front of my face, screening me from further scrutiny.

"So Ashe, after fighting the good fight all morning, you must be hungry."

"Are you asking me to lunch?" I asked.

"I'm pretty sure I am." Fletcher shifted his body into a cool, elegant pose. I watched the way he canted his hips and let his shoulders rise. It was a supremely natural movement, but it radiated sexiness and surety. I tried to create a quick mental note of it, wondering if I could recreate it onstage.

"Um?" I lost my train of thought somewhere between his hips and his shoulders.

"What would Maria Cortez say to the voice of the people having lunch with a prince of the merchant class?"

"You're not funny," I said, smiling slightly.

"I have my moments," he said. "And I'm getting hungry." His voice dropped into the gutter with that last word, but the inflection was so precise, so polished, that I wondered if I had heard correctly.

"So, lunch?" I said.

"Or something," he said.

He was standing closer to me suddenly, his warm body radiating the smell of clean sweat and sandalwood, the bulge in his jeans slowly becoming larger and more distinct.

He saw me glancing down at him and licked his lips. Again the gesture was subtle, could easily have been something else, but I saw the look in his eyes and knew he was toying with me. I liked it.

We left the store and cut over to Eighth Avenue, ambling uptown to the door of a little Italian bistro. The staff greeted Fletcher by name, ushering us past a crush of waiting tourists to an intimate table near the piano. The owner brought over a bottle of expensive Chianti and chatted amiably with Fletcher, asking in her throaty, sexy Italian accent about his mother and his sister; asking who I was, where we'd met and if this was a date. She clucked and laughed and winked at me, her wine-red fingernails clicking against the bottle as she poured a tasting portion for Fletcher.

When she was gone, Fletcher raised his glass. "To happy beginnings," he said. We clicked glasses and I sipped the smooth, dark wine.

Lunch was like a clever, funny romantic comedy montage scored by the tinkling ivory sounds of Arlen, Berlin and Gershwin. I'm sure we talked about all the boring things people find so fascinating when the chemistry is explosive, but I don't really remember any of it. I know we didn't talk about jobs or apartments, but Fletcher insists we traded family histories and coming out stories. I remember arguing over the check—I proposed we split it; he insisted on paying—and I remember watching him across the table throughout lunch and falling for him: for his pale, glowing skin and his perfect, lilting voice and his laugh, that perfect combination of deep, sexy rumble and high delighted peal. When we finally stood to leave, I didn't want to part from him.

After lunch, we stepped out onto the sidewalk, trying to hang on to the warm cozy feeling of the restaurant despite the honking, shoving crush of rush hour. It was a Monday after-noon; I didn't have to work that night, but I was still unsure of myself so I stood holding my backpack strap in one hand and laughing nervously.

"God, I'd like to have a go at those lips," he said finally.

"So what's stopping you?"

He grinned and blushed. He took a half step back and then, realizing what he'd done, stepped closer to me. We could almost pretend that the rush of people along the sidewalk was forcing us together. I could feel the heat of his body, smell his cologne. He laughed again and I leaned forward, planting a kiss on his beautiful, full lips, surprising us both. He leaned into the kiss, but softly, melting in my direction rather than taking a step. The kiss lasted an instant, but when I pulled back and opened my eyes I could see the heat in his.

"Oh, fuck it," he said, grabbing my elbow and yanking me into the flow of pedestrian traffic. He glanced over his shoulder and pulled me down the next street, heading back toward Times Square.

"Where are we going?"

"Someplace private." He looked over my shoulder again, pulled me across the street between a pair of tour buses, through a group of Asian tourists and into a Starbucks, then out the back door of the Starbucks and into the lobby of a hotel. We caught an elevator and he pressed the UP button, taking my hand in his and kissing my knuckles. The older straight couple with whom we shared the elevator seemed unfazed. I stepped closer to him, drawing his scent deep into my lungs. The elevator chimed and he pulled me through the door with him. I trailed along behind him through a conference center teeming with people in expesive suits.

"I take it you've been here before?" I asked.

"Yeah," he said.

"Um, where are we going?"

He looked over his shoulder with that dazzling grin of his. "Play with me, baby," he said. And he pulled me down a short corridor into a secluded restroom.

Three urinals faced three fully enclosed cubicles.

"Wait a minute." I stopped in my tracks.

"What?"

"A bathroom?" I said. "Really?"

"It's secluded."

"It's a bathroom."

"It's clean and the door goes all the way to the floor."

I stood watching him. He didn't grow impatient; he just stared at me hungrily and waited. I could see the bulge in his jeans shifting as blood rushed to his growing erection.

"C'mon," he said. "You're a rebel, Ashe."

"I'm a rebel?"

"Voice of the people, scourge of corporate America."

"You dragged me in here to make fun of me?" I laughed nervously.

"I dragged you in here to ravage you away from the prying eyes of the city."

I reached out and slid my palm along the length of his erection, feeling the heat beneath the tight denim. My own cock leapt to attention.

"So, do you come here often?" I asked.

"Ugh. You're killin' me," he said. "Get in here. C'mon, before somebody comes in. Come kiss me."

He opened the door and tugged me into the cubicle.

"What are we going to tell our grandchildren?" I asked as he closed and locked the door behind us.

"We'll tell them it started with a shoe."

"There's always a shoe," I said, turning to face him.

"And a charming prince," he said.

I blushed.

He lifted my backpack off my shoulder, hung it on the hook behind me and pulled me roughly against him. Our chests touched for the first time and I realized his body was hard and perfect beneath the flawless white cotton. I pushed closer, trying to make as much contact as possible and we kissed, not the soft, public kiss we'd shared on Eighth Avenue, but a full, insistent kiss that felt like an erotic eating contest.

His hands fumbled with my belt buckle and then my jeans and in an instant his long cool fingers were sliding along the length of my cock. He pushed my jeans down past my hips and held my cock in his hands, thumbing the slit to harvest a tiny pearl of precum. He raised his hand, looking intently at the viscous liquid and then smearing it across my lips. I shivered and he laughed that gentle, sexy laugh.

I pulled him close for another kiss, my cock sliding

insistently against the front of his jeans. I unbuttoned his Oxford and pushed his T-shirt up, revealing planes of lightly furred muscles. We were kissing and rubbing our erections against each other, laughing, breathing heavy and making a lot of noise when there was a loud knock on the cubicle door.

We froze. His face went pale.

Another knock: five loud raps and then silence.

"Occupied," I said.

Fletcher stifled a snort of laughter.

"No shit, kid. This is hotel security. Get the fuck outta here or I'm calling the police. You got thirty seconds to beat it." I held my breath and listened to his footsteps as he walked across the tile floor and stepped through the door onto the carpet beyond.

"*Shit!*" My heart was trying to pound its way through my rib cage. My whole body jumped to life, the adrenaline spike so intense I felt like the Six Million Dollar Man. I was ready to outrun anyone.

"What are you doing?" Fletcher asked.

"What?"

"You're making that sound," he said, "and moving in slow motion or whatever?"

"Bionics," I said. "*Duh-nuh-nuh-nuh-nuh.*"

He rolled his eyes. "Well, come on, Steve Austin, let's get out of here."

When we pushed through the restroom door there was nobody in sight, but when we fast-walked through the hotel lobby, a trio of guys in burgundy jackets and matching Bluetooths appeared out of nowhere and started following us. Fletcher grabbed my hand, pulling me out onto the street and hailing a cab. He shoved me inside and dove in after me. We were halfway down the block and the three security guards were still standing in the street watching us.

"Where do you live?" he asked.

I hesitated. I lived in a tiny one-bedroom apartment with a roommate. I looked down at his perfect hands jutting from perfectly ironed, spotless white cuffs, and I froze, embarrassed and undecided about what to do next.

"What's the matter?" he asked. He touched my cheek. "It's okay."

I shook my head, changing the subject. "That was intense."

"Yeah, I guess so. Sorry. I never thought..." His voice trailed off.

He slid close to me and kissed me gently on the lips, his fingers gliding along my thigh and gently kneading the life back into my cock.

I gave the driver the cross streets.

My roommate, Bayani, was gone when we got to the apartment, so I dragged Fletcher into the tiny bedroom and locked the door behind us. He looked around, reading the titles of the books lined up on the shelves, scanning the posters and flyers that cluttered the walls on my half of the room.

"Street theater, political causes, boycotts, 'Fight Corporate Domination,' and this..." He pointed to a poster for the Disney production of *Cinderella* at the New Amsterdam.

"It's Rogers and Hammerstein," I said.

"Big Broadway is big business," he said.

"I should boycott art because it's corporately produced?"

He pointed to a bumper sticker tacked up over my desk. "You're boycotting NBC because it's owned by a defense contractor."

"Disney isn't a defense contractor."

There was an awkward moment of silence. He looked at me and winked. "It's okay. I'm just learning about you," he said. "And playing with you a little."

"Come play over here," I whispered.

"I'm almost done here," he said.

I dropped my backpack on the floor, kicked off my shoes and sat on my bed watching him.

"I love that you're so passionate about what you believe," he said. "These political causes and the incident in the shoe store; I like that a lot."

"Thanks?"

He turned around to face me. "I've never really been very politically active. I leave that to my father, or the family attorneys, you know; I never get too involved in anything."

"Not in anything at all?"

He smiled again. "Well, some things warrant involvement."

"So come get involved," I said. "*Now!*"

He chuckled, kicked off his shoes and stood at the edge of the bed looking at me.

"Sorry about the hotel thing," he said. "That was stupid."

"Nah. It's okay, I—"

"C'mere." He didn't wait for me to respond, he just pulled me over to the edge of the bed and started yanking my shirt up over my head. He stripped me out of my clothes and then slowly, his eyes never leaving mine, took off his own clothes. He was gym-toned and perfect, his chest and legs covered in dark, closely manicured fur. His body tapered from broad, muscular shoulders to ribs and rippling abs in a perfect V-shape.

I pulled him on top of me and we rolled around for a while, kissing and exploring each other. His cock was long and straight with an intimidatingly large head that left streaks of shimmery precum on my legs, my stomach and my cheeks. The heady saltiness of his skin made me want to take a bite out of him.

He rolled on top of me, spreading my arms above my head and pinning me to the mattress. "Don't move," he whispered, sliding his tongue inside my ear and sending a shiver down the length of my body. A dimpled landscape of goose bumps appeared across my arms and legs.

He kissed and licked his way down the side of my face and neck, and then wandered toward my left armpit. When his tongue touched the delicate skin under my arm, my body jerked involuntarily.

"Jerking away will send me away for a while, but I always come back for what I want," he said.

"I'll remember that," I said, gasping as his teeth clamped down on my nipple.

"Please do," he murmured.

He traced the contours of my body like an intimate cartographer while I shifted and quaked beneath his lips.

When I could stand it no longer, I told him to get condoms and lube out of the desk drawer. He pulled the pale-green condom down over my cock, lubed us both up and straddled me. I watched his face crinkle and relax as he worked my cock inside him; sweat beaded on his forehead. He let out a long, breathy sigh as he finally settled onto me, sliding down to the root and reaching forward to kiss me again. He took charge from the top, moving until he found a rhythm that suited him and then looking down into my eyes and coaxing me forward with him. His six-pack abs rippled beneath the taut skin; his breath was heavy, rising sometimes into moans that shook his body and tightened all of his internal muscles. I was sweating beneath him, coaxed into a delirium of sensation, and just when I thought I might pass out from the strain, I felt hot blasts of cum splashing onto my chest, neck and face. I tilted my head, letting the cum fall onto my lips and tongue. The taste of him sent me over the edge. I leaned forward, pulling him against me and pumping everything I had into his body. I groaned and felt tears mingling with the sweat on my cheeks.

* * *

Later, when I opened my eyes, he was still lying on top of me, his face inches from my own. I lifted myself on one elbow, shifting our bodies and looking down at him. His eyes opened, slowly gaining focus. There was a moment of stillness and then he kissed me so passionately I collapsed back on the bed, his body still glued to mine. My cock slid out of him. He reached down to drop the condom on the floor beside the bed without breaking the kiss.

We kissed for a long time, through the heat and exhaustion, his body melding itself to mine. I reached to pull a blanket over the two of us as his lips fluttered against my neck. I didn't ask him at the time, but later Fletcher told me he kept saying, "This is the one, this is the one" over and over until he drifted off to sleep.

We were awakened by Bayani banging on the bedroom door.

"Occupied," Fletcher said.

I laughed and then covered my mouth with my fingers.

"What the fuck? Ashe, let me in."

We scrambled into our clothes; Fletcher disposed of the condom and I opened the door.

"Oh, Jesus, Ashe, it smells like a sex club in here." Bayani stormed into the room wearing lace-up Daisy Dukes, knee-high Doc Martens and glitter. He pushed past me without seeming to notice Fletcher. He dropped to his knees and started pulling wads of clothing from under his bed.

"This is Fletcher."

"Hey, Fletch." He didn't turn around. "What are you still doing here? We've got, like ten minutes to get to the theater."

I glanced at Fletcher.

"Dude, today's Monday," I said.

"Seriously?" Bayani looked genuinely startled.

"You're in a play?" Fletcher asked.

Bayani laughed. "Are you kidding me? He's—"

I hit him in the face with a pillow.

"What? Is it some kind of embarrassing guerrilla theater? Anticorporate flash mobs or something? Hassling the shoppers in the Disney Store?"

I'm sure Fletcher was being sincere, but this sent Bayani to the floor, laughing and rolling back and forth, then beating his heels on the floor, tears seeping from the corners of his eyes. He was only a moderately talented actor, so I was pretty sure the tears were real.

"What?" Fletcher said again.

"Disney!" Bayani hooted and collapsed again, laughing and on the verge of hysteria.

"What?" Fletcher turned to me.

I didn't say anything, but Bayani rolled onto his back, panting. "He's fucking Prince Charming," he said. "You know? In *Cinderella*? At the New Amsterdam," Bayani said, hooting with laughter. "It's a Disney show. Flash mobs! Fuckin' guerrilla theater."

Fletcher's eyes widened perceptibly but he didn't say anything.

Bayani was staggering to his knees, saying something about *Tarzan* being the only Disney show he'd ever heard of with gorillas.

"Come on, man. It's not that funny," I said.

This resulted in another round of panting and giggling.

"Can you give us a minute, B?"

Bayani pulled on a purple rain slicker and stalked into the other room.

"Disney isn't a defense contractor," Fletcher said, his tone gentle but mocking.

I couldn't read his face, but it didn't really matter; I was so embarrassed I wanted to die.

"You protest people buying those shoes when you work across the street in a show that charges five hundred dollars for front-row tickets?"

"It's not the same thing," I said.

"Isn't it?" I still couldn't read his face. There was something there that wasn't there before, something that looked dark, maybe angry. "Disney is not a defense contractor, but they own ABC and they use the media to shape American public policy; they fight American unions tooth and nail; they rely on underpaid foreign labor for their production base.... I could go on."

"Please don't."

We stared at each other for a moment in silence.

"I thought this meant something to you," he said, pointing to the protest posters on the wall.

I heard my father's voice in his words. Old wounds reopened and tears welled in my eyes.

"Maybe this was a bad idea," I said.

"What?" He seemed genuinely surprised.

"Maybe I'm not what you think I am."

"Don't say that. It doesn't—"

"I think you should go," I said.

"Ashe, no—"

"Just go, Fletcher."

"You're a fucking idiot," Bayani said, when Fletcher was gone.

"Can you just shut the fuck up? Quit your giggling and laughing and stay the fuck out of my life just this once?" I screamed, grabbing my jacket and storming out the door. I took the service elevator and went out through the back alley, heading uptown toward the park.

I was so full of angry energy that I broke into a run, sprinting as far as Columbus Circle, letting sweat and heat loosen my joints and clear my head. I crossed into the park and plotted a rambling course toward the Bethesda Fountain.

Embarrassment was thick inside me, viscous and hot and acidic.

An actor? A lousy fuckin' actor? Jesus, Ashe, I thought your political beliefs meant something to you. My father's disapproval echoed in Fletcher's words; they both thought I was a complete sellout. And wasn't I?

I stormed through the darkening park, sometimes walking, sometimes running, always trying to keep a few paces ahead of the choking shame. I was running when I passed the reservoir and staggering by the time I reached Central Park North. I collapsed on a bench, breathless and exhausted, a wreck of wounded pride. I hated myself so much I considered throwing myself in front of the Number Three bus. I imagined the scrape of asphalt on my face and the crunching progress of the tires across my back and legs. It took me an hour to calm down, but as my anger and embarrassment ebbed, a rising tide of despair washed over me.

What the fuck had I done? Had I just sent a gorgeous, funny, smart, rich man packing because of my wounded pride?

I called Bayani on my cell.

"I don't know what to do," I said.

"Have you considered throwing yourself in the river?"

"I was thinking of a launching myself under the tires of a crosstown bus."

"Right. And then I'll be stuck pushing your crippled ass around in a wheelchair—*But ya are, Blanche! Ya are in that chair!*" He broke into peals of laughter.

"Not funny," I said.

"You know I'm funny, bitch," he said.

"I'm sorry about before," I said.

He sighed loudly, and then said: "You white boys are so dramatic. Just call him."

I smiled.

Until I realized I had absolutely no way of contacting Fletcher.

My grandmother used to say, "Pride goeth before a fall."

I always hated the crazy old bat.

I went back to work the next day, stumbling through the week in a half-dazed stupor that would have gotten me fired if it weren't for the persistent and skillful intervention of the company's Equity steward, Bambi. But even she was getting tired of my lackluster performances by the end of the week. She pulled me aside before the Sunday evening show and whispered in my ear: "You quit fucking up or I'm letting you tank. You got your week; now get your shit together."

I caked on makeup to cover the bags under my eyes and tried not to cry during the love songs. The Sunday evening performance was a significant improvement. Bambi stopped me in the hall after curtain, grabbed my arms and said, "Better. Now go home, sleep until Tuesday afternoon, and come back in here reborn. You got it, Ashe?" I nodded and slinked away.

Bayani was waiting for me in the hallway in his street clothes.

"There's a package back there for you." He jerked his head in the direction of my dressing room.

"My walking papers?" I asked.

"I'm thinking, no," he said.

There was a rectangular package wrapped in royal purple with an extravagant blue ribbon. There was a card tucked under the bow. I pulled out the envelope with trembling fingers and read the note.

Best show all week. If the shoe doesn't fit, the shop's
open 'til midnight—Fletcher.

I pulled the top off the box, revealing a pair of the blue running shoes Fletcher had not bought at the shoe store on the day we met.

I arrived at the store at ten minutes to midnight. The place was packed with tourists scooping up last-minute deals to take home to Scranton or Cleveland or Baltimore.

I had the box tucked under one arm and I was looking for Fletcher. Courtnei approached me and said, "Can I help you?"

"Yes, I'd like to return these," I said.

"Oh, it's *you*. Where's your protest sign?"

"I retired the sign."

"Change of heart?"

"You could say that."

"Did you steal these?"

"No."

"Do you have the receipt?"

"I've got it," a voice said from behind me.

I turned around. Fletcher was wearing jeans and a tight white T-shirt. In the very center of his chest, nestled in the gentle slope between his pecs, was a cartoon frog wearing a jeweled crown.

I handed the box to Courtnei without looking at her. Fletcher handed her the receipt, took me in his arms and kissed me.

We came up for air when Courtnei nudged Fletcher with a clipboard. He scrawled his signature on the return slip and handed her his American Express Black card.

"Should I expect drama every time I uncover an inconsistency in your character?" he asked.

"Probably," I said. "Does that scare you?"

"I guess not. How many can there possibly be?"

"There are a lot of them, I'm afraid."

"So it could take years to work through them all."

"Decades, maybe."

"It sounds exhausting."

"Oh, I'll definitely exhaust you."

"I don't doubt that for a minute." He said. "And the drama?"

"I *am* an actor," I said. "A master thespian, you might say."

"Oh, I wouldn't say that. Not *this* week anyway," he said, laughing.

I dug my knuckles into his rib cage.

"You came to the show?"

"Seven times."

"You missed one?"

"It was a matinee."

"Still..."

"I have a life," he said.

"Got any pointers for me?" I asked.

"Yeah, try reining it in a little when you do that thing you do with your left hand. You know, the thing with the flick and the bow and the kiss." He demonstrated, exaggerating my flourish, making it look outrageously effeminate. "I mean, you're kissing Cinderella, not Lady Gaga."

"I worked hard on that move," I said, but I was laughing.

"Right."

"You didn't like it?"

"Kinda gay."

"Ya think?" I slid my hand across his chest, tweaking his right nipple through the tight cotton.

"Oh, yeah," he said. "Way gay."

"Any other notes?" I asked.

"Don't run away from me." He put his hands on my arms,

suddenly serious.

"Never again."

"Never again," he said. "Because I'll just follow you."

"There's no escaping a happy ending," I said.

The overhead lights flashed and the manager made an announcement that the store would be closing in three minutes.

Fletcher wrapped his arm around my waist and pulled me close, kissing me hard on the mouth, recreating in exact detail the final kiss from the show.

"And curtain," he whispered, his lips warm against my cheek.

SANDWICH ARTIST

Shane Allison

I stole the keys out of Ma's purse. It was a damn shame that I was still living at home. My sister got out early at the sweet age of eighteen. She couldn't take the curfews and the beatings that came if she was a minute late. I never could get it right. I should have left for New York as soon as I finished junior college. Yet, had I done that, I never would have met Armando. I waited until they'd gone to bed, fighting off fears in their nightmares. The road I live on was slick with mud, the holes overrun with rainwater from last night's storm. I hate the house with its leaky roof, its cobwebbed corners and bad childhood memories. I've cried in my plate of chicken and rice, bled in the sweet ice tea. They try to keep me away from Armando with barred windows. But nothing's gonna keep me away from my baby. I put the car in NEUTRAL and pushed it with my weight out of the carport, up that slick road, through the barking of vicious pit bulls and puddles of muddy water. I'll do anything to get to him. Streetlights of white light my way through this ravenous night up Woodville Highway. I'd made it; I'd escaped the bear claws of my folks. I'd rather have run the streets like a Frenchtown whore than live with them another day. I was invisible anyway, a ghost caught in limbo between the heavens of freedom and the hell of slavery. I followed the yellow dashes that led me closer to Armando. Chris Isaac's "Wicked Game" was playing on 98.9, Armando's favorite song. I was hoarse from all the hollering. Ma had given me that *As long as you're in this house* speech. "You ain't go'n stop 'til you don' run me outta here," I yelled. "Well, go…go'n then," she screamed. So I'd be going, hauling ass and never darkening the door of Charlie Ash Lane again. They'd be sorry, those venomous bullies. Why couldn't we have been the Bradys? Why couldn't they have been Claire and Cliff Huxtable? I felt like some C-list child star. Armando and I were so close. One more paycheck and we'd have enough money to get our own place. I'd already picked out some sofas and end tables. We had our eye on this posh apartment in Verandas Villas; pricey, but nice. We'd be graduating college in three months. We were already looking for full-time jobs. We had to get away from my bible-beating parents, and his drill sergeant dad who's a staunch supporter of Don't Ask, Don't Tell.

I screeched into the lot of Jimmy John's Sandwich Shop. Armando was stocking chairs on the tables, smearing a wet mop across a linoleum floor. The moon was full and orange. Cars whooshed down the streets of South Magnolia. Armando was alone. The bell that hung above the door tolled as I walked in. The shop was redolent of sharp spices and baked breads.

"Hey, babe," I said. He stopped cleaning and walked over to give me a hug, cute in his uniform of green and black. Tufts of black hair escaped the brim of his cap. Elvis Presley sideburns ran along the sides of his face. He's a lean Italian with a skate border waistline, a body decorated with tats.

"What's wrong?" he asked.

"Nothin'," I said.

"You look mad about something." I lifted my glasses to wipe my face. "Is it your folks again?" Armando asked. "What the fuck did they do to you?" I didn't want him to worry. Armando goes off the deep end when he knows I'm upset about something. "I jus' got into anotha knock down, drag out with my mom again."

"Goddamn them," he said.

"It's no big deal," I said, taking his hand in mine.

"No, fuck that. Look, I know you love them, but your folks are assholes." My white knight and Prince Charming all rolled into one.

"Forget it. Jus' leave it alone."

"Are you hungry? Have you eaten?" Armando asked.

"Jus' a chicken biscuit from Chic-Fil-A this mornin'."

"Let me make you something. What do you want to eat?"

"I been wontuh try that new chicken Parmesan ya'll got." Armando's shirt was stained with who the hell knew what. SANDWICH ARTIST was embroidered in yellow on the top lefthand corner of his shirt. He wiped his wet hands dry on his pants.

"We gotta get you outta that house," Armando said as he yanked a pair of plastic, transparent gloves from a box next to the register. I looked at the name tag pinned to his chest.

I remembered the first time I laid eyes on Armando. It was right here at J.J.'s. I was sick of burgers and greasy Chinese food, and it was the only place open. My weight was another thing me and Ma fought about; I got sick of Ma preaching to me: "You need tuh cut back, boy." Armando had been the only one working that night when I walked in. I ordered the corned beef on wheat. I don't remember how the conversation started, but Armando and I started talking about comic books and horror movies in film history. We both agreed that *An American Were-wolf in London* kicks ass. He had a beard at the time, but still looked boyish. I watched as he sprinkled my sandwich with lettuce, pickles, banana peppers. I glimpsed the sliver of a tattoo on his furred chest through the open top buttons of his uniform. I paid for my food with a twenty.

"Keep the change," I told him.

"Are you sure, man?" he asked.

"Consider it a tip." I watched him watch me, the two of us reflected in the glass door with the store's hours plastered across it. I couldn't stop thinking about him on the way home that night, with that movie-star smile, those eyes that could melt glaciers. I became a loyal customer. I tried every sandwich on the menu: from veggie to tuna and I hate fucking tuna. I would come in some nights just to see if Armando was working. Usually there was some girl with a bad dye job working, so I'd only buy lemonade or a cookie. I heard later she told him about this black dude with glasses who kept coming in and asking about him.

"All he ever bought was a cookie."

I ate a shit load of corn beef subs before I grew the balls to ask him out. After a while, I didn't want to have nothing to do with anything that ended in *sandwich*. But Armando and I grew to know each other very well.

My parents found out about Armando when Ma overheard me talking to him late one night. Life had been hell since I came out to them when I was nineteen.

"I would rather be dead than for you to be gay," she had said. I thought telling her that I was bisexual would soften the emotional blow, but she didn't care. I was going to hell either way. Daddy didn't speak to me for weeks and often referred to me as a *sissy* when he thought I couldn't hear. "Freaks," he had said. He was pissed that the family name would stop with me, his freaky, sissy son. Ma tried to get me to go to church.

"I want you to get saved like your sister." She started crying when I refused. Her preacher said that I was just running from Jesus. She stormed into my room after she so rudely eavesdropped on my conversation with Armando.

"Get off th' phone, an' come in me an' yuh daddy room." If looks could kill, hers would have skinned me alive.

"Hey, lemme call you back," I told Armando. Pearls of sweat dripped from my pits. Daddy just lay in bed with his back turned, disappointed that I was not a pussy-loving high school quarterback like he was in his heyday.

"As long azhoo in this house, I 'on' wan'choo talkin' tuh that boy."

We fussed and fought for months. I wanted to tell her to go fuck herself, but lost the nerve. Still, nothing was going to keep me away from Armando. Nothing and nobody. They put me on ten o' clock curfews, but I would always sneak out. That house was like a jail cell, a dungeon in an evil castle. If I had a dime for every scrape and scratch I'd endured to meet my Armando, I'd have enough to pay the rent on our villa apartment for the rest of the year.

I watched Armando slice the Italian herb-flavored bread.

"Did you deposit your check yet?" he asked.

"Yeah," I replied. "Did it yesterday."

"I'll be getting paid this Friday, and that oughta be enough for the security deposit and first and last months' rent." He put four pieces of breaded chicken on a sheet of wax paper and placed them in the microwave.

"We're almost there. Think I should start packing my stuff?" I asked.

"Yeah. We gotta get you from under your parents' roof. Enough's enough. If they put their hands on you again..." I'd told Armando the cuts and scratches were from my bedroom window, but I didn't think he believed me. I studied Armando's fingers as he covered one side of the bread with slices of provolone. The microwave sounded. He pulled the chicken out and onto the bread. He didn't need to ask what I wanted on the sandwich. Armando squeezed out mayo and a little mustard. Too much can ruin a sandwich. He finished it off with a decoration of green peppers, pickles and my favorite, jalapeno peppers. Armando grabbed the Parmesan, always the final ingredient, but the shaker was empty.

"I got some in back, babe," he said. My dick began to twitch in my shorts to the image of pants riding between the crack of his ass. Armando came back with the powdered cheese and a canister of fresh black olives. He knew I liked extra. He took a handful and dressed my sandwich.

"Baby, can you do me a favor?" he asked. "Could you turn the sign on the door?"

I locked the door and switched the sign to CLOSED.

"I gotta take a piss," I said, making my way to the crapper.

"I'm cleaning that one right now," he said. "Use the employee bathroom in back."

I sauntered past the big bread ovens and empty cardboard boxes. I didn't really need to go. My dick was at full salute but it wasn't because of a full bladder.

As I forked it out of my cutoff sweats, I began to think just how lucky I was to have someone as great as Armando. He's my prince. And believe me—I've had to kiss a shitload of frogs to get to him.

"Your sandwich is on the table, babe," he said, as he started to break down the boxes. I stood in the doorway watching him work while I caressed my dick, fingered my balls.

I admired him from behind as he bent and pulled cardboard.

He had a black boy's ass. I cleared my throat to get his attention. I turned toward the toilet and stood in front of the mirror, fondling myself while watching a reflection of Armando's every move.

Armando moved closer to see what I was up to. He pressed the door open to get an eyeful of me working my dick.

"What are you doing?" Armando asked, grinning.

"What does it look like?" With my shorts down around my ass, and my dick thick and curved outward, I roped a hand around the back of his neck and pulled him in, giving him a warm kiss of the French persuasion. Armando's tongue tasted like pink lemonade. His lips were supple against my own. He ran his hand beneath my T-shirt, fingers traipsing through chest hair. I released a hot sigh between our bodies, as he started to jerk me off.

He paused. "Hold on," he said. "Follow me."

I tailed him around the sandwich shop, erect and anxious. Armando closed the venetians then took a chair down from one of the tables.

"Have a seat." He ran his fingers along his crotch. I couldn't wait to release that *thing* from his pants. What he doesn't have in girth, he makes up for in length. I heard Italian boys were big, and with Armando, I'll be damned if it don't ring true. He unzipped his pants and reached in to pull out his dick. The head was pink, with a shaft of muscle, veins and tender foreskin. People could see through verticals, but I was hoping the closed sign would keep voyeurs away. I took Armando's dick and tilted it up to my mouth and began to lick along the slit. I have no gag reflex, so I was able to take as much of him as I wanted down my throat.

"Look up at me," he ordered. He likes to look into my eyes while I'm sucking.

His groin was ripe with all-day crotch sweat, mixed with the scent of onions and bell peppers. I worked the head, lapping at Italian flesh.

"You know what to do," he said. I turned my attentions reluctantly from devouring his dick to sucking his balls.

"Yeah, that's it, right there." He ran his hands over my head, toying with my ears. He shaves down there, so there's no hair to get in the way. Armando lifted up his shirt, exposing that chest I adore so.

"Do it," he said. I tweaked his nipples, so sensitive under my fingers when I pull at them. My own dick was throbbing like a heart. He took off his shirt and tossed it. We didn't care where. I moved back to his dick to give him proper thanks. I was a bruised boy and he was my savior.

His legs quivered. I kneaded his flesh like dough, running my hands over his beauty-marked hips. Spit rolled along his dick as I feasted. The sandwich, wrapped tightly in paper, was within reach as well as the meat, mustard and mayo. I was hungry, but not for any sandwich.

"I got an idea." Armando looked down at me. He was annoyed I'd stopped worshipping at his altar of dick.

"Come behind here," I said, leading him by the arm, his dick wet and full. I slid my sandwich off to the side.

"Hop up," I told him, tapping the table.

"What? Why?"

"Come on, trust me," I said. The table was sturdy enough to hold Armando. He stretched his body across the cutting board easy like a cat. His socked feet stuck off one end.

"Relax." I ran one hand along a firm, hairy thigh. Armando has an awesome body, but you wouldn't know it, the way he covers up in big tees and baggy jeans, and shadows his gorgeous mug under baseball caps and hoodies. I compliment him on his body all the time, but he says he's too skinny. Armando's the only guy I know who can eat shit like pizza and burgers and never gain an ounce. Says he wants a wrestler build. He even thought of steroids at one point, but I talked him out of it.

I studied the canisters filled with lettuce, tomatoes, tufts of onions and other veggies.

"Let's see what kind of sandwich I want." I looked to the menu on the wall.

"A Cold Cut Combo." I plucked a pair of gloves out of the box and worked them over my hands. I peeled paper off slices of bologna. I spread Armando wide, and packed the cold cuts delicately between the cheeks of his tanned booty.

"Oh, it's cold," he said.

"What's next?"

"How about some pepperoni?" I patted several slices between his half moons.

"Now ham. The other white meat."

"Yeah, that'll do it," he said with growing excitement. I couldn't wait to devour this homemade man sandwich of mine. I stood back to admire my handiwork. The best part was yet to come. It was time to add color to the gustatory canvas my boyfriend had become. I thought of the dressing and was sure I wanted lettuce. I grabbed a handful and sprinkled the greenery along Armando's stuffed crevice, then added slices of juicy, vine-ripened tomatoes.

"That's cold."

"Complain, complain," I said. A sandwich ain't a sandwich without olives. Or green peppers. Next something spicy. When I mentioned jalapenos, he just about jumped from the table.

"Fuck that!" he yelled.

"All right, all right. Nothing hot." I added a dash of salt. No pepper. "Eat your fuckin' heart out, Picasso."

"Are you done?" he asked, "'cause my legs are starting to fall asleep."

I pulled off the gloves and shoved them in the metal trough beneath the cutting board.

I was tempted to just ram my face into his scrumptious butt, piggish and messy. Armando shifted anxiously. My dick was dripping in anticipation of the feast to come. He had never looked more delicious. His ass was so pretty I didn't want to touch it. But I couldn't hold back. I pulled at his thighs, opening him up as I began to chew. He heaved and sighed as I ate. I was a mess, but I didn't give a shit. I pressed him into the table, occasionally nipping his ass with bites of love. My appetite was insatiable. He was an all-you-can-eat buffet of manliness. When I was done, his ass was littered with bits of olives, pieces of tomato, scraps of meat and streaks of mustard. Armando was a nasty, naked beautiful sight.

"I can't eat another bite."

Armando eased his legs off the cutting board. He sat up and stretched happily, still hard but hardly satisfied. I went back to sucking him off. Armando ran his dickhead over my lips, across the rug of my tongue.

"Ready for some dessert?" he asked. He cocked his legs on my shoulders as I uncorked his dick out of my mouth. The left-over mayonnaise was slick on my dick. I slid myself into his ass. I hugged Armando's thighs as I pressed and pushed. Tears of sweat beaded his taut stomach. He whacked off as I thrust into him. He spoke dirty to me in Italian. Armando's face was flushed. I couldn't hold back. I slid out of my baby and came across his stomach. Armando came seconds after me. I rubbed my cum into his chest and tongued the last few droplets into my mouth.

We sat, flesh touching flesh and sweat mixing with sweat, hearts still pounding.

I'd be so glad when we got our own crib, when we didn't have to meet behind closed blinds and locked doors.

"I'll help yuh clean up," I said, exhausted. I grabbed a wet cloth from the kitchen sink and wiped off Armando and myself the best I could. Every muscle ached as we pulled on our pants, worked our arms through the sleeves of our shirts. Armando finished stacking the chairs and mopping, while I cleaned the food area of the store and the kitchen.

"Anything else I can do?"

"Just go home and pack," he said, kissing me good night. I didn't want to let go. I wanted to hold him, breathe in his sandwich shop scent of pepperoni and mustard.

I was worried about getting caught when I got home, but I was excited because I would soon be leaving the evil castle on Charlie Ash Lane. I killed the headlights and the engine in the road, put the car in NEUTRAL and pushed it quietly the rest of the way into the driveway. I climbed carefully back through the window, but just as I climbed into bed, lights blazed on. There she was: Ma, with anger in her eyes.

"Boy, where you been?" she asked.

"Jus' up th' street."

"You a lie!" she hollered. "You went to go see that boy didn't you?"

I thought of Armando and what he would do if he were here. He'd stand up to her. I took my beating in stride, with pride and strength, because with Armando in my heart, I could feel no pain.

HENRY AND JIM

J. M. Snyder

His folded hands are pale and fragile in the early morning light, the faint veins beneath translucent skin like faded ink on forgotten love letters written long ago. His fingers lace through mine; his body curves along my back, still asleep despite the sun that spills between the shades. I lie awake for long minutes, clasped tight against him, unable or unwilling to move and bring the day crashing in. Only in sleep am I sure that he fully remembers me. When he wakes, the sun will burn that memory away and I'll have to watch him struggle to recall my name. After a moment or two he'll get it without my prompting but one day I know it will be gone, lost like the dozen other little things he no longer remembers, and no matter how long I stare into his weathered blue eyes, he won't be able to get it back.

Cradled in his arms, I squeeze his hands in my arthritic fists and pray this isn't that day.

After some time he stirs, his even breath breaking with a shuddery sigh that tells me he's up. There's a scary moment when he freezes against me, unsure of where he is or who I am. I hold my breath and wait for the moment it all falls into place. His thumb smoothes along my wrist, and an eternity passes before he kisses behind my ear, my name a whisper on his lips. "Henry."

I sigh, relieved. Today he still remembers, and that gives me the strength to get out of bed. "Morning, Jim." I stretch like an old cat, first one arm then the other, feeling the blush of energy as my blood stirs and familiar aches settle into place. Over my shoulder I see Jim watching, a half smile on his face that tells me he still likes what he sees. As I reach for my robe, I ask him, "How about some eggs this morning? That sound good?"

"You know how I like them," he says, voice still graveled from sleep. His reply wearies me—I don't know if he's forgotten how he prefers his eggs or if he simply trusts me to get them right. I want to believe in his trust, so I don't push it. After fifty years of living with Jim, of loving him, I choose my battles carefully, and this isn't one either of us would win.

Leaning across the bed, I plant a quick kiss on the corner of his mouth. "Be down in ten minutes," I murmur.

His gnarled fingers catch the knot in the belt of my robe and keep me close. My lower back groans in protest, but I brush the wisps of white hair from his forehead and smile through the discomfort as he tells me, "I have to shower."

"Jim," I sigh. When I close my eyes he's eighteen again, the fingers at my waist long and graceful and firm, his gaunt cheeks smooth and unwrinkled, his lips a wet smile below dark eyes and darker hair. It pains me to have to remind him, "We showered last night."

He runs a hand through his thinning hair, then laughs. "Ten minutes then," he says with a playful poke at my stomach. I catch his hand in mine and lean against it heavily to help myself up.

We met in the late spring, 1956, when I graduated from State. It seems so long ago now—it's hard to imagine we were ever anything but the old men we've become. My youngest sister Betty had a boy she wanted me to meet, someone I thought she was courting at the time, and she arranged an afternoon date. I thought she wanted my approval before she married the guy; that's the way things were done back in the day. But when I drove up to Jim's parents' house and saw those long legs unfold as he pushed himself up off the front steps of the porch, I thought I'd spend the rest of my life aching for him. I could just imagine the jealousy that would eat me alive, knowing my sister slept in those gangly arms every night; family gatherings would become unbearable as I watched the two of them kiss and canoodle together. By the time he reached my car, I decided to tell Betty she had to find someone else. That nice Italian kid on the corner perhaps, or the McKeever's son around the block. Anyone but this tall, gawkish man-boy with the thin face and unruly mop of dark hair, whose mouth curved into a shy smile when those stormy eyes met mine. "You must be Henry," he said, before I could introduce myself. He offered me a hand I never wanted to let go. "Betty's told me all about you."

Betty. My sister. Who thought I should spend the day with her current beau, checking up on him instead of checking him out. My voice croaked, each word a sentence as final as death. "Jim. Yes. Hello."

I vowed to keep a distance between us but somehow Jim worked through my defenses. He had a quick laugh, a quicker grin, and an unnerving way of touching my arm or leg or bumping into me at odd moments that caught me off guard. He skirted a fine line, too nice to be just my sister's boyfriend but not overtly flirting with me. Once or twice I thought I had his measure, thought I knew for sure which side of the coin he'd call, but then he would be up in the air again, turning heads over tails as I held my breath to see how he would land. That first afternoon was excruciating—lunch, ice cream afterward, a walk along the boulevard as I tried to pin him down with questions he laughed off or refused to answer. I played it safe, stuck to topics I thought he'd favor, like how he met my sister and what he planned to do now that he was out of high school. But his maddening grin kept me at bay. "Oh, leave Betty out of this," he told me at one point, exasperated. "I know her already. Tell me more about you."

I didn't want to talk about myself. There was nothing I could say that would make him fall for me instead of Betty, and I just wanted the day to be over. I didn't want to see him again, didn't want to *think* about him if I could help it, and in my mind I was already running through a list of excuses as to why I couldn't attend my sister's wedding if she married him, when Jim noticed a matinee sign outside the local theater. "You like these kind of movies?" he wanted to know. Some creature flick, not my style at all, but before I could tell him we should be heading back, Jim grabbed my elbow and dragged me to the ticket window.

Two seats, a dime apiece, and he chose one of the last rows in the back of the theater, away from the shrieking kids that threw popcorn and candy at the screen. He waited until I sat down, then plopped into the seat beside mine, his arm draped casually over the armrest and half in my lap. "Do you bring Betty here?" I asked, shifting away from him. Better to bring my sister up like a shield between us, in the drowsy heat and close darkness of the theater, to remind me why I was there. Betty trusted me, even if I didn't trust myself.

Jim shrugged, uninterested. As the lights dimmed and the film began, he crossed his legs, then slid down a bit in the seat, let his legs spread apart until the ankle rested on his knee. His leg shook with nervous energy, jostling the seat in front of him and moving at the edges of my vision, an annoying habit, distracting, and when I couldn't stand it any longer, I put my hand on his knee to stop it. As if he had been waiting for me to make the first move, Jim snatched my hand in both of his, threaded his fingers through mine, and pulled my arm into his lap. "Jim," I whispered with a slight tug, but he didn't seem to hear me and didn't release my hand. I tried again—he just held on tighter, refused to acknowledge that I wanted him to let go. Leaning closer so I wouldn't have to raise my voice, I tried again. "Jim—"

He turned and mashed his lips against mine in a damp, feverish kiss. *I shouldn't*, my mind started, then *I can't*, then *Betty*. Then his tongue licked into me, softer than I had imagined and so much sweeter than a man had the right to be, and I stopped thinking altogether. I was a whirl of sensation and every touch, every breath, every part of my world was replaced with Jim. *Betty isn't getting him back*; that was my last coherent thought before I stopped fighting him and gave in.

Later that evening, my sister was waiting when I finally got home. "Well?" she wanted to know.

I shrugged to avoid meeting her steady gaze and mumbled, "Do you really think he's right for you?"

"Me?" she asked with a laugh. "Not at all. But Henry, isn't he just perfect for *you?*"

From the kitchen, I hear Jim come down the stairs. He opens the front door and I force myself to stay at the stove, fighting the urge to check on him. I wait, head cocked for the slightest sound—somewhere outside, an early bird twitters in the morning air and further away, a lawn mower roars to life. Only when I hear a shuffled step do I call out. "Jim?"

No reply. Dropping the spatula into the pan of scrambled

eggs, I wipe my hands on a nearby towel and move toward the doorway as I try to keep the panic from my voice. "Jim, that you?"

Before I reach the hall, the door shuts quietly. When the lock latches, I let out a shaky breath and pray, *Thank you*. Then I see him at the foot of the stairs, thumbing through a small pile of mail I left stacked beside the phone. The way he lifts each envelope makes me sad, and I force a smile to combat the frown that furrows his wrinkled brow. "Bills," I tell him. "Breakfast's almost done. Did you get the paper?"

He glances up at me with blank eyes and my heart lurches in my chest. Then recognition settles in and he smiles. "Henry," he says, as if to remind himself who I am. I nod, encouraging. "The paper? No. Did you want me to?"

"Didn't you go out to get it?" I ask gently. At the confusion on his harried face, I shake my head. "Never mind. Go sit down, I'll get it for you."

"I can—" he starts.

I pat his shoulder as I move around him toward the door. "I've got it. Have a seat."

It's only when I'm on the stoop, digging the paper out of the roses, that I remember the stove is on. "Jim?" I holler as I shut the door behind me. I hate that I'm like this—I know I should trust him but I can't. If anything happens to him, it'll be my fault because I know I need to be more careful, he needs me to watch out for him. I imagine him by the stove, the sleeve of his robe brushing across the heating element, unnoticed flames eating along his side... "Jim, where—"

The kitchen is empty. The eggs sizzle in the pan where I left them and I turn the burner off before they get too hard. In the dining room, a chair scrapes across the floor: Jim sitting down. Without comment, I gather up the plates and silverware I had set out in the breakfast nook and carry them into the other room.

Jim sits at the head of the long, polished table where we rarely eat, but he gives me a smile when I hand over the newspaper, and as I place a plate in front of him, he catches me in a quick hug. He sighs my name into my belly, his arms tight around my waist, then rests his head against my stomach and wants to know, "What's for breakfast?"

I don't have the energy to tell him again. "It's almost ready," I promise, extracting myself from his embrace.

My parents always called Jim *Betty's friend*, right up until the day she got married to someone else. By then the two of us had an apartment together, and at the reception my mother introduced us as simply, "Henry and Jim." Not *friend* or *roommate*, just Jim—in those days, no one felt compelled to define us further. My mother treated him like one of the family when we visited, and that was all I wanted. Let her believe we slept in separate bedrooms, if that's what she needed to think to welcome him into her home.

We bought this house in '64; the market was good and the realtor didn't question both our names on the mortgage. Jim was in college at the time, working nights at the packing plant just to pay his half of the bills. We had plans for the house—I wanted a large garden and Jim loved to swim, but we didn't have the extra money to sink into landscaping yet; we couldn't afford the house most months, let alone flowers and an inground pool. I had a job in marketing and spent most of that first year in the house waiting for Jim to come home. Sometime after midnight he'd stagger through the door, weary from standing on his feet all evening, clothes and hands and face black with grime and soot. I hovered in the doorway of the bathroom, watching the dirt and soap swirl away down the drain as he washed up. Some nights he sat on the closed lid of the toilet seat, pressed the palms of his freshly scrubbed hands against his eyes, and struggled not to cry from mere exhaustion. "I can't do this much longer, Henry," he sobbed, my man reduced to a child by the weight of his world. I knelt on the floor and gathered him into my arms, ignoring the stench of sweat and oil that rose from his soiled clothing. He slid off the toilet and into my lap as he hugged me close. Hot tears burned my neck where he buried his face against me. "I can't," he whispered, hands fisting in my clean shirt. "I just can't."

I helped when I could, but times were hard for us. Many nights we sat together on the floor of the bathroom, me smoothing my hand along his back as he railed against it all. It was college that held him back, Jim believed—if he could just drop the few classes he took, he could work full-time at the plant and make more money, but I wouldn't let him. In those days a degree guaranteed a good paying job, no matter what the field of study, and I knew Jim wanted to be more than a line worker the rest of his life. I wanted him to be something more—I wanted him at a day job and home in the evenings, in the bed beside me at night. He wanted it too, so he would cry himself out as I held him, but eventually he kissed my neck and whispered my name. "How are you feeling?" I'd want to know.

With a shaky sigh, he would admit, "Better."

One evening I was in the kitchen, washing the dishes, when I heard him come in the front. "Jim?" I called out, raising my voice above the running tap. The slam of the bathroom door was his only reply. Shutting off the water, I dried my hands and glanced at the time—barely eight o'clock. My first thought was that he had managed to get off early somehow, but the slammed door made me worry. In the hallway, I knocked on the bathroom door. "Jim? You in there?"

"Be right out," he promised.

Absently my hand strayed to the doorknob but when I tried

to turn it, I found it locked. That bothered me more than I cared to admit—there were no locked doors between us. "Jim?" I asked again, twisting the knob in a futile gesture. I wanted to watch him get cleaned up, to see the man emerge from beneath the sooty worker, to watch his strong hands smooth over one another to wash dirty suds away. It had become a nightly tradition of sorts, and I saw so little of him as it was. With my ear pressed against the door, I could hear water and Jim's low humming. "Open the door," I told him and then, because that sounded too harsh, I added, "Are you all right?"

He hollered back, "Fine, Henry. I'll be right there."

I couldn't shake the feeling that something was off, so I stood outside the bathroom door and ran through a dozen scenarios in my mind, reasons why Jim would refuse to let me see him before he got cleaned up, but none of them made any sense. I couldn't imagine what he might be hiding from me, why he needed to wash up alone; there was no reason for the impromptu shower I heard running on the other side of this locked door. Never one for waiting, I wedged myself against the doorjamb, knob gripped tight in my sweaty palm. As soon as the shower cut off, I started rattling the knob again. "Jim—" I started, but then the lock disengaged and the knob turned in my hand. "What's all this about?"

He wasn't standing on the other side of the door, so I eased it open and peered behind it. Jim leaned back against the counter by the sink, a bath towel around his shoulders that barely covered his crotch. His legs, damp and swirled with dark curlicues of wet hair, stretched out for miles beneath the towel. One corner of the towel was caught between his teeth, and he stared at me with wide eyes full of an anticipation that excited me. "Well?" I wanted to know. I tried hard to hang on to my sour mood but the sight of water beaded on so much bare skin made it hard to remember what it was I might be angry about. "What's going on?"

Without replying, Jim scooted over. On the counter behind him sat a potted bush in full bloom. Salmon colored rosebuds peeked through thick green leaves, one or two in full bloom like bubblegum bubbles, their petals opening to a deep, gorgeous color that reminded me of hidden flesh. "Jim," I started, but I couldn't think of anything else to say. I had done enough window-shopping at the local nursery to know the plant must've cost a pretty penny. I wanted to ask how he could afford it, with tuition on the rise and the bills we had piling up, but I tamped that down and took a tentative step toward the counter. "It's beautiful."

"It's for you," Jim said. His eyes flashed above an eager grin he hid behind the towel. Before I could thank him, he added, "You know why?"

I brushed my fingers across one velvet petal and shook my head. "I can't begin to imagine," I murmured. My birthday was months away. Burying my nose into an open rose, I breathed deep the flower's heady perfume and sighed. "Did you get a raise? Did you graduate?" With a sidelong glance, I teased, "We didn't have a fight this morning, did we? Am I forgetting something?"

Jim laughed. "It's sort of our anniversary," he said, watching me, waiting for it to click.

It didn't. "Which one?" I ticked them off on my hand, one finger for each occasion. "We got the apartment in August, bought the house in February, first had sex in June, first kissed in..." A slow smile spread across my face. "In May. This is the day we met, isn't it? God, how long as it been?"

"Ten years today," Jim admitted. To the roses, he said, "They say red means love but these were the prettiest ones they had. I thought you'd like them—"

"I love them," I said simply, then gave him a smoldering look and added, "I love you. Come here."

He stepped toward me, away from the counter, and my hand brushed his arm before slipping beneath the towel to smooth over warm, tight skin. The towel fell away; Jim fumbled with the zipper of my pants, his hands undressing me as my mouth closed over his. We held on to each other as we met in a heated clash of lust and desire—against the wall, on the counter, sprawled across the lid of the toilet seat before we fell to the floor, aching and hard and seeking release. "I love you," I told him, again and again. I kissed the words into the hollow of his throat, the small of his back. I whispered them in his ear, then licked after them as he gave in to me.

Time has banked the fire that once burned so brightly between us. It still simmers just below the surface of our lives and occasionally flares at a word, a touch, a smile, but we are no longer the hot lovers we were before. When we make love now it's a gentle affair, languid and slow, the movements careful like turning the crumbling pages of an ancient book. Most evenings we settle for lying close together, Jim's arms around me, my body clutched tight against his. There will come a time when one or the other of us finally lies alone, maybe sooner than we care to think, and the thought of going on without him terrifies me. I've lived with him for so long now that I can't imagine anything else. So I smooth over his forgetfulness, these little spells that seem to come more frequently now, and I tell myself I can take care of us both. If ever the day comes when he wakes beside me and my name doesn't come to his lips, when that bewildered look in his eyes doesn't fade away, I'll remember for us both. I won't let him forget the life we built together. I won't let him go.

In the kitchen, I scrape the congealed eggs into a large bowl and stir them up to keep them fresh. If we were eating in the breakfast nook like I had planned, I wouldn't have to make several trips to deposit everything onto the table, but Jim chose the dining room and I give him an encouraging smile when I set the bowl of eggs down in front of him. "Help yourself," I say over my shoulder as I head back into the kitchen for coffee that's just beginning to perk. I busy myself with buttering toast, then rescue two overcooked sausages from the stove where I left them. When I bring the bread and meat out, I notice that Jim hasn't touched the eggs yet. "Everything okay?" I ask him.

He takes the plate of toast from me with one hand—the other is under the table, out of sight. I wonder if he's burned himself on the stove earlier while I retrieved the paper or maybe on the bowl of eggs; that ceramic gets pretty hot. But he gives me a quick grin and a flash of the boy I fell for peeks out through the face of the old man I love. "Everything's fine, Henry. You worry too much. You always have. Do I smell coffee?"

"Coming right up." I hurry back to the kitchen to pour two steaming mugs, with a dash of milk and a spoonful of sugar in Jim's because that's the way he likes it. I take mine black. As I blow across his mug to cool it off, I wonder what the rest of the day will bring. Will it turn out all right in the end? Or will this be one of those bad days, with Jim locked in the past, unable to follow my conversations because he can't remember one moment to the next? Some days he's a different man, aged by forgetfulness that borders on something I'm afraid to admit, much older than me despite the fact that I'm five years his senior. Since the scare at the front door, I'm on guard, suspicious and cautious and hating myself for not being able to trust him.

Back in the dining room, Jim holds the newspaper open in front of him, hiding from me. I'm about to ask him to lower it when I see the single rose on my plate. The flower isn't in full bloom yet, but all the thorns have been broken off and the long stem is ragged at the end, as if plucked in haste. Already the soft petals that peek through the green have that deep pink of young, forbidden skin. One of my roses...

My hands begin to tremble and I have to set the mugs down before I spill the coffee. It's May already, I should have remembered—when I close my eyes, we're both young again, awkward with sudden desire, each desperately waiting for the other to make the first move. In the darkness of my memory I recall that first fumbling kiss and the hot hands that held mine in his lap. The years between us peel away like the petals of a rose and the day we met is laid bare, the core around which we have built this life together. My vision blurs and I have to blink back an old man's tears as I finger the barely budding rose. "Jim," I sigh.

The paper rattles and I know he's trying to hide that grin of his from me. When I push down the top of the newspaper, he smiles as he says, "Of all the anniversaries we celebrate, you always forget this one."

"You always remind me," I point out. I can tell by the laughter dancing in his pale blue eyes and the promise in his smile that today is going to turn out to be a good day after all.

ABOUT THE AUTHORS

FYN ALEXANDER grew up in Liverpool, England, with a great love of books and the English language. As an adult Fyn moved to Canada, but returns to England to visit every few years to reconnect with his roots. Fyn is also the author of the *Angel and the Assassin* series.

SHANE ALLISON is the proud editor of *Hot Cops, Backdraft, College Boys,* and *Hard Working Men.* His stories have appeared in *Best Black Gay Erotica,* five editions of *Best Gay Erotica, Bears, Biker Boys, Leathermen, Surfer Boys, Country Boys,* and over a dozen other lusty anthologies. His first book of poems, *Slut Machine* is out from Rebel Satori Press. Shane currently lives in Tallahassee, Florida.

MICHAEL BRACKEN's short stories have appeared in *Country Boys, Ellery Queen's Mystery Magazine, Espionage Magazine, Flesh & Blood: Guilty as Sin, Freshmen, Hot Blood: Strange Bedfellows, The Mammoth Book of Best New Erotica 4, Men,*

Mike Shayne Mystery Magazine, Ultimate Gay Erotica 2006, and many other anthologies and periodicals.

KAL COBALT (kalcobalt.com) is a native Oregonian who recently relocated to Portland. Read more of Kal's work in *Country Boys, Hot Gay Erotica, Velvet Mafia, Distant Horizons,* edited by Greg Herren, and *Best Fantastic Erotica,* edited by Cecilia Tan.

JAMESON CURRIER is the author of two novels, *Where the Rainbow Ends* and *The Wolf at the Door,* and four collections of short stories, *Dancing on the Moon; Desire, Lust, Passion, Sex; Still Dancing;* and *The Haunted Heart and Other Tales.* "July 2002" is an excerpt from his new novel, *The Third Buddha.*

MARTIN DELACROIX's (martindelacroix.com) stories appear in over twenty erotic anthologies. He has published four novels: *Adrian's Scar, Maui, Love Quest,* and *De Narvaez.* He lives with his partner, Greg, on Florida's Gulf Coast.

JAMIE FREEMAN (jamiefreeman.net) lives in a small Florida town. He has published the romantic novella *The Marriage of True Minds* and his stories can be found in *Best Gay Romance 2010, Necking, Sindustry,* and elsewhere. He writes in a variety of genres including erotica, romance, science fiction and horror.

SHANNA GERMAIN's (shannagermain.com) work has appeared in places like *Absinthe Literary Review, Best American Erotica 2007, Best Gay Bondage 2008, Best Gay Romance 2008, Best Lesbian Erotica 2008, The Mammoth Book of Best American Erotica Volume 7,* and *Salon.*

DOUG HARRISON's (pumadoug@gmail.com) erotic ruminations have appeared in zines, twenty anthologies, and a spiritual memoir, *In Pursuit of Ecstasy*. He was active in San Francisco's leather scene, is a father and grandfather, and has a firm but gregarious leather partner with whom he experiments in Hawaii.

T. HITMAN is the pen name of a full-time professional writer who lives with his two husbands—the human one and his mysterious, otherworldy muse—in a small cottage somewhere in the wilds of New England. In their home, much romance is made, both on the page and in the bedroom.

GEORGINA LI says that when she's not writing, she likes to paint—bright colors on small canvases, torn pages, odd bits pulled from the recycling bin. Her first published story, "Like They Always Been Free," appears in the science fiction anthology *Federations*, edited by John Joseph Adams, alongside stories by Anne McCaffrey and Robert Silverberg.

EDWARD MORENO has finally settled down in Melbourne after years of wandering aimlessly in search of pleasure. A native of New Mexico and a one-time San Franciscan, he now calls Australia home. He studies writing and Spanish at the University of Melbourne. His work has been published in *Best Gay Erotica* and at blithe.com.

MAX PIERCE's (maxpierce.com) debut novel is the gothic mystery *The Master of Seacliff*. His musings on gay culture and Hollywood history have appeared online for *The Advocate* and other national publications. He previously contributed to the vampire anthology *Blood Lust*. He lives in Los Angeles.

NEIL PLAKCY is the author of *Mahu, Mahu Surfer,* and *Mahu Fire,* mysteries set in Hawaii. He is coeditor of *Paws & Reflect: A Special Bond Between Man and Dog* and editor of *Hard Hats.* A journalist, book reviewer, and college professor, he is also a frequent contributor to gay anthologies.

J. M. SNYDER (jmsnyder.net) writes gay erotic/romantic fiction. Originally self-published, Snyder now works with the e-publishers Amber Heat Press and Aspen Mountain Press. Snyder's highly erotic short gay fiction has been published online at Ruthie's Club, Tit-Elation, and Amazon Shorts, as well as in anthologies published by Cleis Press, Haworth Press, and Alyson Books.

NATTY SOLTESZ (bacteriaburger.com) has had stories published in *Best Gay Erotica 2009, Second Person Queer,* and *Best Gay Romance 2009,* regularly publishes fiction in *Freshmen, Mandate,* and *Handjobs,* is a faithful contributor to the Nifty Erotic Stories Archive, and is writing his first novel, *Backwoods.* He lives in Pittsburgh with his lover.

C. C. WILLIAMS (ccwilliamsonline.net), after moving several times about the country and through Europe, is now settled in the Southwestern United States with his partner, JT. When not critiquing cooking or dance show contestants, he is at work on several writing projects.

ABOUT THE EDITOR

RICHARD LABONTÉ (tattyhill@gmail.com), when he's not skimming dozens of anthology submissions a month, or reviewing one hundred or so books a year for Q Syndicate, or turning turgid bureaucratic prose into comprehensible English for the Inter-American Development Bank or the Reeves of Renfrew County, Ontario, or coordinating the judging of the Lambda Literary Awards, or crafting the best croutons ever at his weekend work in a Bowen Island recovery center kitchen, likes to startle deer as he walks terrier/schnauzer Zak, accompanied by husband Asa, through the island's temperate rainforest. In season, he fills pails with salmonberries, blackberries and huckleberries. Yum. Since 1997, he has edited almost forty erotic anthologies, though "pornographer" was not an original career goal.

PERMISSIONS